THE WATER TOWER CLUB

THE WATER TOWER CLUB

a novel

B K Mayo

FIR VALLEY PRESS

Copyright © 2019 B K Mayo

All rights reserved.

No part of this book may be reproduced by any mechanical, photographic, or electronic process, or in the form of a phonographic recording; nor may it be stored in a retrieval system, transmitted, or otherwise be copied for public or private use—other than for "fair use" as brief quotations embodied in articles and reviews—without prior written permission of the publisher.

This is a work of fiction. All the characters and events portrayed in this book are either products of the author's imagination or are used fictitiously.

Library of Congress Control Number: 2018901499

ISBN 978-0-9815884-4-5

Book design by Linda Parke

Printed in the United States of America

Published by Fir Valley Press
P.O. Box 1114
Roseburg, Oregon 97470

For Karen

1

YOU SEE IT all the time on the news. The shaking heads. The startled looks. The stammered declaration: "I just can't believe it." What they can't believe is that their next-door neighbor, the unassuming Mr. Wouldn't-Hurt-a-Fly, is a serial killer. Or their boss at the electronics factory is a spy for the Chinese government. Or their minister, who refuses to preside at gay weddings, is sleeping with a male prostitute. We are stricken with incredulity when someone we know acts in a way that is outside our understanding of who they are.

I was one of those dumbstruck disbelievers when I got word via a late-night phone call from my hysterical mother that my little sister had been arrested on suspicion of attempted murder. "They're gonna hang her!" Mom said. She sobbed in my ear with Wailing Wall fervor. "Darryl, you've got to come home."

My mind lurched with the news, and I might even have muttered, "I just can't believe it." But all I could think of to say was, "Mom, they don't hang people in Kansas anymore."

Mom screamed into the phone. "You know what I mean!"

I did and I didn't. When I was growing up, my mother said things to me all the time that I didn't understand. That's because she always spoke in hyperbole. Life was never good or bad on a sliding scale. Everything was life or death. If I made a mistake, like forgetting to haul the garbage out to the curb before seven o'clock on a Thursday morning, it wasn't simply a disappointment to her; it was another nail in her coffin. "You're killing me," she'd say. And I would wait, trembling, for her to keel over dead. When she didn't, I'd gaze at her with wide-eyed wonder, as if witnessing a miracle. She'd wag a finger at me and say, "Don't pretend you don't understand."

Some things change, but one thing that doesn't is that mothers will always be mothers and sons will always be sons. So, at the age of twenty-eight, ten years removed from her loving domination, I said to my mother the same thing I'd always said to her when confronted with her gaudy insistence. "Yes, ma'am."

As I hung up the phone, my hand was shaking and I was breathing hard. Precious Libby in jail? It was a jolting thought. But more troubling to me was my mother's plea for me to come home.

It was the overarching theme of all our telephone conversations—conversations that had become less frequent and more strained over the years of my absence from my hometown. "Mom, I *am* home," I would tell her. To which she would respond with an invective that expressed what I took to be a latent desire to wash my mouth out with soap.

But, for once, her entreaty had a real-world rationale I couldn't easily dismiss: *Libby arrested on suspicion of attempted murder? Attempted murder of whom?* When I'd put the question to my mother, she'd responded with another classic Motherism—"What does it matter!"—before flogging me with a reprise of "You've got to come home!"

I paced around my apartment barefoot and in my underwear, feeling stripped of more than just my clothing as I reflected on that dreadful possibility. If it had been anyone but Libby in trouble, I wouldn't have exercised a single brain cell contemplating going back to Grotin. I hadn't set foot in my hometown since boarding a Greyhound bus the day after my high school graduation. Desperate to escape the cycle of misfortune that plagued me there, I did the only thing I could think of doing: I sold my most valuable possession, a collection of Avengers comic books, and bought a one-way bus ticket to the farthest destination south my funds allowed, which turned out to be San Antonio, Texas. I hadn't ventured north of the Red River since.

My only regret during the intervening decade was that I hadn't taken my little sister with me. I'd left her behind in the care of a mother whose reaction to life's disappointments was to withdraw to a place of emotional isolation that made it nearly impossible for her children to reach out to her. The concoction of professed love and demonstrated detachment my mother doled out, especially after my father's tragic death when Libby was six years old, was a bad prescription for my little sister's welfare. I knew this even as I enacted my hasty retreat from my hometown.

But how could I have rescued her? Libby was only nine years old at the time of my departure. And, at eighteen, I was just a kid myself—a screwed-up kid at that. The best thing about childhood is that you only have to go through it once. I had survived the rock tumbler of my youth and had the emotional scars to prove it. What I didn't have was the slightest inkling as to the working of the cosmos. If experience truly is the best teacher, what I had learned during my minority was to forego trying to make sense of things.

Even so, it hadn't taken the wisdom of age for me to realize that if I were to have any shot at a normal life—whatever that entailed—I had to put Grotin and the twisted wreckage of my past behind me. I had only a shadowy conception of what existence was like outside the communal dome of my hometown. But as I stood upon the promontory of a failed childhood, peering through the telescope of time, I glimpsed my future, and what I saw was that if I stayed in Grotin my life was destined for deposit on the scrapheap of personal destruction.

So I made my escape via Greyhound Bus Lines. I landed in San Antonio as if by shipwreck, disgorged onto the big-city streets with nothing but a scuffed Samsonite suitcase I'd bought at a garage sale for two dollars and the determination to divorce myself from my past and wed myself to the future. And that's exactly what I did. I got a job and an apartment, put myself through college, became an accountant, and when the time was right, found myself a steady girlfriend. It wasn't easy, but I did it. I altered the trajectory of my life. I put the pieces of my shattered self-esteem back together. I worked my way up the ladder of respectability. I forged a new existence for myself.

And I did one other thing: I bottled up the memories of my childhood and kept the bottle stoppered. I relegated my life in Grotin to a time and place as remote and recessed as the Roman catacombs. The last thing I wanted to do was to return to my hometown and roam those ancient burial grounds.

But now my beloved little sister was in trouble, and I could do nothing to help her from seven hundred miles away. My mother was right—I had to go home.

2

"HOME WHERE?" Charlotte said, her face a tapestry of question marks.

We were at her courtyard apartment in Alamo Heights, a step up from the southside efficiency she'd lived in when we began dating nearly three years ago after a cat-and-mouse pursuit at the accounting firm where we both worked. I had stopped by her place on my way out of town, which seemed preferable to jangling her nerves with a midnight phone call. Before I'd had a chance to explain the lateness of my visit, I found myself in bed with her. It was where we were most comfortable with each other. Some relationships are that way.

"Kansas," I said in answer to her question.

Charlotte still looked puzzled.

It was no wonder. She knew little about my personal history. During our time together, I'd made only passing references to my Midwestern upbringing. She knew I had a younger sister whom I adored and kept in regular contact with: she'd seen the photos of Libby prominently displayed in my apartment. She knew my mother was still alive and my father was not. But I'd shared with her little else about my past. I'd never spoken at length about the small Kansas town where I'd grown up, or recounted any of the sad tales of my youth. We all live with battle scars from our childhood, painful memories we'd prefer to blot out of our consciousness. I had hoped that by not talking about my own youthful misadventures I could forget they ever happened.

My early life was forgettable, I had informed Charlotte at the outset of our relationship, and she seemed satisfied with that explanation in a way no other woman I'd been with had. This was, I suspected, because her journey to adulthood had been no joyride either. In her teens, she had become estranged from her family, she told me once. "They live on the West Coast, or did, last I knew," she said. That was the extent of her openness. The remainder of her past she glossed over the way women hide ugly toenails with bright-red nail polish. "I was a foolish girl with foolish dreams," she declared, without bothering to explain. And I respected her desire to leave it at that, because I had no right to ask questions I didn't want to answer myself.

So we accepted not knowing certain things about each other's past. But over time, an element of unease about the not knowing engendered a mutual lack of sure-footedness in our relationship that had kept it from progressing beyond its current state—this bedroom connection we had.

"Kansas?" Charlotte said. She looked at me with hooded eyes, as if her vision had turned inward. "Ahh—*home*—a place far off but never far away."

I sensed a personal revelation teetering on the brink of her remark but had neither time nor inclination to divine it.

"I don't know how long I'll be gone," I said.

She responded by rolling her lithe nude frame on top of me, straddling my midsection. In the sparse light that seeped into the room through the window sheers, the delicate features of her face, the hollows at her neckline, the swell of her breasts were cast in shadow. But her intent was not. When she leaned down to kiss me, strands of her raven hair cascaded over her bare shoulders and brushed across my nipples. An inner light flashed in her coffee-colored eyes.

"Then take this moment with you as remembrance," she said.

And the lovemaking was easy because it was something we knew about each other.

I LEFT SAN ANTONIO in the dead of night, intending to drive straight through to Grotin. Bleary-eyed even before I'd exited The Lone Star State, I pulled into a truck stop off the interstate just north of Fort Worth in search of a caffeine fix. I took a seat at the counter in the truck stop's diner, where a buxom waitress wearing a red bandanna and a heart-shaped nose stud poured me coffee that tasted more like burnt motor oil. I stayed there the better part of an hour, hunched over my coffee cup, my butt planted on a round swivel stool, trying to work up the courage to spin the stool around and leave.

By the time I got back on the road, a reddish smear of light was calling attention to the eastern horizon. Traffic was flowing freely on the interstate between Fort Worth and Denton—the lull before the commuter storm. I had filled up with gas at the truck stop. I'd also bought two bottles of water and placed them in the cup holders built into the console of my Explorer. This would be my sustenance for the balance of my journey home.

Home? Was I truly going home? *Home is where the heart is. There's no place like home. A house is made of walls and beams; a home is built with love and dreams.*

No, I wasn't going home any more than a soldier does when, years later, he visits a battlefield he'd warred in and survived.

Libby. I had left Libby on the battlefield of our childhood in Grotin. Was she about to become its next casualty?

I drove on in a mindless stupor. The eager August sun showed its face, its radiant beams bathing the landscape in the golden glow of a newborn day. Before long a halo of blue ceilinged the heartland of America. The monotonous horizontal countryside of north Texas eventually gave way to the monotonous horizontal countryside of southern Oklahoma. I hit Oklahoma City post-morning rush hour and gave thanks for that small favor.

I opened a bottle of water, sipped from it, splashed some of its contents on my face, and motored on. The genial undulations of northern Oklahoma whizzed past me in a blur of torpid non-cognition. Before long I was being welcomed to Kansas by amber waves of grain. I didn't feel patriotic.

I stopped for fuel in Wichita and, while I was at it, called my employer. Late morning on a Tuesday, and my absence would have been noticed.

Leaning against my car at the gas station, feeling heady from the fumes wafting from the pumps, I took out my cell phone and dialed the number for the accounting firm of Campbell and Associates. Ruth, the receptionist, answered in a voice with just the right amount of honey in it. "Oh, Mr. Coombs, there you are," she said. "I have messages for you."

I took mental note of my messages, then told her to cancel all my appointments for the next several days. I wouldn't be able to make it in to the office. A family emergency. I wasn't sure how long I'd be gone. But she could reach me on my cell phone.

"I hope everything will be all right," she said.

"So do I," I told her.

I got back in my car, and that's when my resolve stalled. I knew I had to go on to my intended destination. About some things in life you have a choice; about others you don't. But there's always a part of you that tries to rationalize its way out of facing up to a difficult situation. It's that inner voice that says,

"It's a lost cause" or "You'll only make things worse" or "What good can you do? You are powerless and inept."

I sat there and listened to that voice tell me that my sister didn't need me so much right now as she needed a good attorney. And doubtless there was some truth in that. But that wasn't why I was balking at returning to Grotin. The real reason was that I was terrified of the reawakening of my dormant memories. Already the corpses of my dead-and-buried past had begun their zombie journey back into my consciousness, and I knew that I was defenseless against them.

3

GROTIN IS A small farming town set on a windswept plain in north-central Kansas. The surrounding countryside, open and oceanic, is a monument to flatness. Grasslands and crop fields—planted mostly in wheat, corn, and soybeans—dominate the landscape, along with a scattering of farmhouses, each a testament to humankind's (often miscalculated) desire to partner with the land.

I approached Grotin from the south on a rural, two-lane highway, the interstate on which I'd traveled for most of my journey north having wisely veered off in the direction of more populated and more promising communities.

A mile or so short of my destination, my progress was slowed by a John Deere harvester whose bulk unavoidably hogged the roadway as it rumbled along the pavement in front of me. I did not resent the delay. The harvester driver hugged the shoulder of the road for a quarter mile or so, kicking up swirling plumes of chaff and dust, before turning off the highway into a farmyard that provided a snapshot of grange life in Harbin County: surrounded by sweeping fields of hay and grain, a homestead—a tree-sheltered wood frame house with wraparound porch, a red barn, dual metal silos, a Quonset-style shop building, and a menagerie of bladed and tined farm implements awaiting their season of use.

With the roadway ahead of me clear now, I was presented with a panoramic view of the horizon. Visible against a backdrop of azure sky was the imprint of my hometown, looking like an artist's rendering of small-town America, Midwest style.

I could see it with my eyes open or closed: the clapboard houses lining streets laid out in perfect north-south and east-west grids, as if on a giant game board; the weather-worn commercial buildings clustered like a bull's eye at the town's center; the cooperative grain elevator rising missile-like into the air; and the most conspicuous sight of all, the city water tower—that pot-bellied, iron-legged colossus mounted on its lofty perch as a symbol of humanity's needs and aspirations.

I tore my gaze away from the hulking water tower, but not before the pull of memory forced me to acknowledge the shape of all my fears. *If you never look down, you might as well be two feet off the ground.* And for a few woozy moments I could hear in my head the raw-egg-tossing voices of scorn, taunting me during one of the beat-down moments of my youth.

> WELCOME TO GROTIN
> POPULATION 3,273

When I came upon the city limits sign, my heart sank. Without thinking or checking my rearview mirror, I took my foot off the accelerator. There was an immediate explosion of sound behind me as the driver of a semi, who did not appreciate the roadblock my Explorer had become, laid on his horn.

Shaken, I veered onto the shoulder of the road. The truck whizzed past me, the blare of its horn tearing a hole in the air. I wanted to hit the gas and follow the truck on up the highway. Forget Grotin, forget my childhood, forget the frantic phone call from my mother the night before. The truck had Nebraska plates. I could stay on the highway behind it—follow those plates north to some good-karma town in Cornhusker country. I'd know it when I got there. I'd feel it deep inside me, the way a woman knows she's just conceived.

But I had no such option. Had it been anyone but my little sister, I could journey on despite my mother's pleas, keeping my eyes straight ahead as one does when passing a beggar on the street. But it wasn't anyone else. It was the one person in the world I cared about the most.

I rolled my window down and swigged some hay-scented air before steering my Explorer back onto the roadway.

It was three-thirty in the afternoon when I entered Grotin. It was an odd feeling being back, the kind of feeling you get when you fly to an exotic locale, a place you've always known existed but that seems more mythical than real to you until that moment you step off the plane and come face to face with its physicality. Over the last ten years, I'd done my best to trick myself into believing Grotin didn't exist. That was no longer possible. Once again, I was a prisoner of time and place.

Glancing about as I cruised up Main Street, I was not surprised to see that the town had changed little in my absence. A bit more frayed around the edges, perhaps—no hint of urban renewal here. Like most small Midwestern towns, Grotin is most easily characterized by what it does not have: shopping malls, chain restaurants, multiple traffic lights, high-rise buildings, and curbs and sidewalks along streets outside the business district.

But while many such towns are thought to be charming, Grotin is not. It is as humdrum and utilitarian as the vintage wind-powered gristmill that stands as its preeminent historical landmark. It is inhabited for the most part by people who've worked hard all their lives but have little to show for it. They are farmhands and fry cooks, truck drivers and mechanics, warehousemen and waitstaff, store clerks and custodians, none of whom earn enough each week to unburden themselves of the yoke of debt. Or they own one of the small businesses in town—the gas station, the hole-in-the-wall café, the butcher shop, the secondhand store, the budget motel, or the drugstore that also houses the post office—and are able to stay financially afloat only because every member of the family works there for little recompense.

Truth is, the town would have declined into nonexistence long ago had it not been for its designation as the seat of rural Harbin County. It was the infusion of county government jobs that provided the financial grist to keep the wheels of the local economy turning, however slowly.

Downtown Grotin is a whole two blocks long, with brick-faced, common-walled storefronts lining both sides of Main Street, giving it an Old West feel. On this Tuesday afternoon in early August, few of the diagonal parking spaces downtown were occupied. Judging by those that were, the biggest draw at this hour was the Farm Bureau. Coming in second in popularity, the Hardly Used Shop, followed by Fat Chance Bar and Grill, Fealty Realty and Auction Services, and Bill's Barber Shop. As always, a number of the storefronts were shuttered, with FOR LEASE signs being their only offer of exchange.

School being out for the summer, I would have expected to see cutoff-clad teenagers clogging the entrance to Waldrop's Drugs, which boasts the town's lone soda fountain. A sandwich reader board stationed on the sidewalk outside the drugstore thwarted that expectation: AIR CONDITIONER BROKEN. Across the street, the digital sign at People's Bank was flashing a current temperature of ninety-six degrees.

Grotin's two-block downtown strip is bisected by Center Street. In the middle of this intersection hangs the only traffic signal in town, which blinks yellow for north- and southbound traffic on Main, and red for the east- and westbound traffic on Center.

I turned right onto Center Street and, at the next intersection, took another right onto Court Street. The courthouse square was on my left now. Its wide lawn, well past heatstroke, resembled a brown latch-hook rug come undone. A row of ancient oaks shaded the benches stationed along the walkway leading to the main entrance to the courthouse. On one of the benches, a booted person of unidentifiable gender lay supine, an unfolded newspaper tenting the upper body. Not far away, a man with a small dog on an extendable leash looked the other way as his pooch urinated on the base of the courthouse flagpole.

Two women wearing capris and crop tops emerged from the courthouse and quick-stepped away from the building as if eager to distance themselves from any trappings of the law. Behind them loomed the imposing Romanesque façade of the Harbin County Courthouse. Built of massive stone blocks faced with soaring engaged columns, the three-story structure had served as the centerpiece of justice in the county for nearly a hundred years and looked as if it was determined to serve for hundreds more.

Moving past the courthouse, I turned left onto the lane that would take me to the Harbin County Jail, where, according to my mother, Libby was being held. "They have her caged up like an animal," she had blubbered into the phone the night before. "She's not an animal!"

"I know, Mom. I'll get there as soon as I can."

Since Grotin has no police force or lockup facility of its own, the sheriff's department—consisting of the sheriff, an undersheriff, and a small band of not-so-merry deputies—staff the jail and see to the safety of all the souls in Harbin County.

It isn't a monumental task even for such a modest workforce. The entire population of the county is just over four thousand.

Most of these folks are God-fearing people. They go to church and at least pretend to abide by the Ten Commandments, and the ones who don't are looked down on. No doubt as much sinning goes on in the dark as anywhere else, as well as petty crimes like thievery and criminal mischief. And no community in America is without a drug problem. But Harbin County's violent crime rate is historically low, unless you count the slaughter of hogs and cattle. Whenever someone does resort to physical violence, he or she is generally dealt with harshly by the justice system and in the court of public opinion. After all, as the Bible says, "an eye for an eye."

The Harbin County Jail occupies one wing of the Harbin County Sheriff's Office, a nondescript single-story brick building tucked in behind the courthouse. The jail wing houses three holding cells, a twelve-bed cellblock for male prisoners, and a six-bed cellblock for female prisoners.

For once my mother was not hyperbolizing when she'd decried the conditions under which my sister was being held. I knew this because, during one of the more bizarre episodes of my hapless youth, I'd been forced to attend a *scared straight* tour of the Harbin County Jail—along with a half-dozen other *troubled* kids—in lieu of being shipped off to an out-of-county juvenile facility. I was sixteen years old at the time and guilty of felony gullibility.

The jail guard giving us the tour, insistent on making his point—*You do not want to come here as an inmate!*—gave us verbal lashings every chance he got: "Look at me when I talk to you! . . . You think this is funny? No? Then wipe that smirk off your face. . . . You're a momma's boy. I can see that. Momma's boys don't do well in here."

When we got to the holding cells, the guard had me, another boy, and the lone girl in the tour step inside one of them. It was an eight-foot-square, block-wall vault containing only a stainless steel toilet and sink and a bed that was nothing more than a narrow ledge topped with a thin mattress. Upon the guard's radio command, the cell's thick metal door slid closed with such electromagnetic violence as to evoke the image of the gates of hell slamming shut in our faces. The girl in the cell with us began to cry. I choked back an upwelling of antipathy.

I can't speak to the girl's state of mind following our tour of the jail that day, but I resented every minute of the two-hour emotional bashing we'd endured. I hadn't needed to be scared straight then, and I didn't need my mother's histrionic declaration now to know that my little sister, having been lodged in the Harbin County Jail, was being served a full plate of misery.

4

I PULLED INTO the sheriff's office parking lot and filled a space next to a dusty green and white sheriff's cruiser. I'd been on the road for almost fourteen hours with few breaks. My neck muscles ached, my back was threatening to seize up on me, and my eyes blurred from seven hundred miles of road-reading. I slumped in my seat and closed my eyes, but dared not leave them shut for long for fear of falling asleep.

The sheriff's office is the point of entry for all visitors to the jail. Squinting at the arrows of sunlight glinting off the hood of my car, I got out and trudged up the sidewalk toward the entrance. Recessed off to my right was the jail exercise yard, a basketball court-sized plot of ground bordered by slatted, razor wire-topped cyclone fencing. A few of the slats were missing, and through the opening I observed two men wearing orange jumpsuits standing in a shaded corner of the yard smoking, their hand-to-mouth movements jerky. One of the men coughed several times and then spat on the ground. When he saw me looking his way, he gave me the finger.

Welcome back to Harbin County.

"I'm Darryl Coombs," I told the deputy standing behind the counter in the sheriff's office, hunched over an open drawer.

His brown short-sleeved uniform reminded me of that of a UPS driver, except he wasn't wearing shorts and his duty belt bristled with instruments of enforcement. "I'm here to see—"

"I know who you're here to see," the man said. He banged the drawer shut and straightened to his considerable height—a head taller than my five-foot-ten-inch frame.

I took a more prolonged look at the fellow. He had brush-cut hair, a Nixon nose, and a Dick Tracy jawline. His eyes were close together and his shaggy eyebrows came within a pencil lead's width of meeting in the middle. "Do I know you, Deputy"—I scanned his nametag—"Rawlins?"

"Not likely," he said, pinning me with his eyes. "But I know who you are."

A surge of uneasiness tightened my throat. I'd detected a note of disdain in the deputy's voice, and awareness in his gaze that went beyond mere recognition. He knew more about me than just who I was. But why? And why the open hostility? Had our paths crossed before today? I had no recollection of this fellow or what connection he had with my past that would have remained intact for a decade or more.

"Do we have a mutual acquaintance?" I asked.

Something flickered at the back of his eyes, a hint of affirmation, but the question went unanswered. He moved behind an outmoded desktop computer on the counter and pounded out some keystrokes. "Your sister is in holding," he said as he viewed the information displayed on the monitor. "No visitation of detainees in holding except for their attorneys or their minister." He flashed a mocking smile. "I take it you're not a man of the cloth."

"Why is she still in holding?" I said, ignoring his last remark.

The deputy shrugged. "All's I know is what it says here." He aimed an index finger at the computer screen and shot each word as he recited it. "Libby—Coombs—Assignment—Holding."

A shudder of frustration rippled through my body. I muzzled an inclination to swear and was about to stomp out of the place, when I realized that this might be good news.

"Does this mean she hasn't officially been charged with a crime?" I seemed to recall from my scared straight experience (maybe it hadn't been a total waste after all) that in Kansas the law requires a person to be charged with a crime within forty-eight hours of being arrested. If no charges are brought within that time, then the person must be released from custody. If Libby was still in holding, it could mean that charges against her were still pending, and *pending* could become *dropped*. Maybe her situation wasn't so dire after all.

"That'd be a question for her attorney," the deputy said.

So Libby had legal representation. That was good news too. Had that been Mom's doing? She hadn't mentioned it. "Who is the attorney?"

Rawlins peered at me out of the corners of his eyes as if assessing just how cooperative he wanted to be. After several silent measures of hesitation, he once again consulted his computer screen. "One Harvey Broward," he announced, as if ordering a specialty plate at a diner.

I didn't recognize the name. "Thank you," I told the deputy as I left, not out of gratitude for the man but as acknowledgment that, in this present scenario, I was the monkey and he was the organ-grinder. At least he had thrown me a peanut.

FIFTEEN MINUTES LATER, intent on perpetrating an act of role reversal, I was back inside the sheriff's office, once again facing off with Deputy Rawlins. During the interlude, standing outside in the hammering heat, I had used my cell phone to make a series of calls that eventually put me in contact with Harvey Broward. I had introduced myself and explained my situation.

"I can't talk at length right now," the attorney said. "I'm on a break from a deposition meeting. But I'm glad to know you're in town, because I could use your help, and it looks like you could use mine. I'll let my assistant know what you need, and she'll take care of it for you. Hold on a sec." I could hear him talking to someone but couldn't make out the words. "Okay," the attorney said into the phone, "I'm turning you over to Kate. She'll explain things to you. I'll join you at the jail as soon as I can. Shouldn't be long. I don't expect this deposition to run much longer. I'll bring you up to speed on Libby's case when I get there."

"Did I not make myself clear?" Deputy Rawlins said as I reappeared at the front counter in the sheriff's office. He was seated behind a desk now and did not get up.

"I could use the air conditioning," I said, feeling prickles of perspiration at the roots of my hair. I gladly filled my lungs with refrigerated air. "By the way, you're going to get a phone call."

"Oh yeah?"

I nodded.

The deputy retrieved some paperwork from a tray on his desk and began sorting through it.

I waited.

He found what he was looking for, put the rest of the paperwork back in the tray, and began making some markings on a form.

I waited some more.

When the telephone on his desk rang, the deputy stared at it for a moment before answering. "Duty desk." He listened to the person on the other end of the line. "Yes, sir," he said. "I'll take care of it." He hung up the phone and went back to his paperwork.

I waited some more.

When enough ticks of the clock had elapsed to drive home his point (*I'm still in charge here*), Deputy Rawlins put down his pen, rose from his desk, and plodded over to the counter.

"Not one to take no for an answer, eh?" he said, giving me a look that held the promise of return fire. He handed me a clipboard with a form on it and a container about the size and shape of a cigar box but without a lid. "Sign in," he said, "and I'll need to see some I.D."

I signed the form and handed him my Texas driver's license. He examined it, examined me, and handed it back.

"Remove everything from your pockets and attached to your person," he said. "Watch, wallet, phone, keys, comb, belt—*everything*—and put it in the box. Leave the box on the counter. Then walk through the metal detector over there." He thumbed toward an archway off to the side. "I'll have your sister brought to an interview room."

"You could have told me," I said as I began emptying my pockets.

"Yeah, and you could've stayed in Texas."

5

I PASSED THROUGH the metal detector undetected, except by Deputy Rawlins, who met me on the other side and led me to a green door inset in an alcove at the back of the room. He punched a sequence of numbers on a keypad mounted on the wall. The door buzzed and clunked.

"After you," he said, pushing it open.

We entered a brightly lit hallway and continued down it to the first doorway on the right. The door was open. Beyond the threshold was a room hardly more accommodating than a public restroom stall. The room contained a small table with four straight-back chairs tucked in around it, and little consideration for foot traffic. Cozy.

"Wait in here. Someone will bring your sister," Rawlins said, like a man used to giving orders.

It was an order I could live with, especially since I was sure it had galled the deputy to have to yield to an order himself, one from his superior that he hadn't seen coming.

What he'd neglected to tell me upon my arrival at the jail was that visitation of detainees in holding—except for their attorneys and ministers, who had unlimited access—was at the discretion of the jail commander. I had learned that from

Kate, Harvey Broward's assistant, who, following her boss's instructions, had called the lieutenant in charge of the jail and successfully lobbied for me to be allowed to visit my sister. I had thanked her profusely. "No problem," she said. "The jail commander is my brother-in-law."

"How long will it take?" I asked the deputy, wearing on my sleeve my eagerness to see my sister.

"As long as it takes," Rawlins said. "Believe it or not, we got procedures to follow. When you're done, push the button on the wall by the door and someone will come and collect your sister." He gave me a high-caliber stare. "Don't overstay your welcome."

What welcome? I thought, but kept the thought to myself. I took a seat at the little table as the *clomp, clomp, clomp* of the deputy's unhappy footsteps echoed down the hallway. In the fog of my fatigue, the moment felt surreal. Was this really happening? Libby arrested and thrown in jail? It seemed so . . . not possible.

Every thirty seconds I checked my watch, which only magnified each passing minute. Five minutes. Ten. I jumped to my feet when I heard more footsteps in the hallway—this time an intermingling of shuffling and clomping. My heart pounded with the anticipation of getting my first non-digital look at my sister since she was nine years old.

Her escort, another brown-clad officer, appeared first. He filled the doorway as he peered into the room, presumably to ensure that I had not somehow managed to smuggle in a jackhammer or dynamite, or otherwise posed a threat to him or his domain. Duly satisfied, he stepped back and allowed Libby passage before closing the door.

When Libby entered the room, she pulled up short, her eyes widening as she gawped at me. They'd obviously not told her *who* had come to visit her. Was she expecting Mother? Her attorney?

My little sister had not grown up to be a classically beautiful woman. She was too bony and boyish-looking for that appraisal. Hers was an unaffected allure accentuated by her crop-cut hairstyle, unplucked eyebrows, and want of makeup. She was nonetheless lovely to my sight—no matter that the baggy orange jumpsuit and floppy sandals she wore at the moment were the antithesis of haute couture.

"Libby!" I said, opening my arms.

She flung herself at me. She buried her face in my chest, and I clung to her with an arm cinched around her waist and a hand clutching a fistful of her auburn hair as I pressed her cheek against my palpitating heart.

We held each other for the longest time.

Despite the miles that separated us, Libby and I had remained close during the years of my estrangement from my hometown. I called her nearly every week. We texted frequently and chatted on occasion via FaceTime. I had fled Grotin to save myself, but I wanted her to know that my leaving had nothing to do with her. I loved her and missed her, and I told her so every chance I got. But now, as I held her in my arms, I was sorely mindful of my physical absence during the watershed moments of her life. Was it too late to make amends?

"What are you doing here?" she said.

"Mom called me."

She drew back from me, her face a portrait of pique. "I told her not to do that."

"She's been in to see you?"

Libby frowned. "Not a chance. You know Mother. Her delicate disposition couldn't handle a jail visit. But I talked to her on the phone—my one allowed call after being mug-shot and fingerprinted." Her eyes sparked with alarm. "You shouldn't have come."

"Of course I should have come. You're in trouble."

"No," she said, wagging her head, "you shouldn't allow yourself to get dragged into this."

By *this*, I knew she meant more than just her legal difficulties. This was Grotin after all, a place I had referred to in the past as *the heart of darkness*. But for Libby's sake, I had to push all such thinking aside.

I glanced toward the door to the room, noticing only then its pocket-book-sized peephole of a window. So much for privacy. Was the room otherwise being surveilled? I didn't know. The walls were windowless and bare. I didn't see any glowing camera eyes. But were there hidden listening devices? Bugs stuck to the underside of the table? In the air vent? In the fluorescent light fixture? I decided not to care.

I sat Libby down in a chair and pulled up another one facing it so that we sat knee to knee, holding hands. "Libby, what happened? Mom said you've been arrested for attempted murder. Is that true?"

She rolled her eyes. "It's so stupid."

"What is?"

"I wasn't trying to kill him."

"Kill who?"

"Bobby Hobson."

"Bobby Hobson?" I felt a g-force-like jolt to my senses that left me dazed as my mind snapped back in time. Since escaping Grotin, I had deliberately not kept up with the goings-on in my hometown or the personal lives of its citizens. This willful inattentiveness was part of my out-of-sight, out-of-mind strategy for moving on with my life. Libby understood and respected my desire to exist behind a wall of selective amnesia. In my conversations with her, she rarely made reference to any person or happening outside her own circle of friends. And she never said, "Remember when . . ."

But it took only the mention of his name to trigger a torrent of memories involving Bobby Hobson, none of them pleasant. Bobby was my age, and since there was only one elementary school in Grotin and one high school, we'd been classmates throughout our school years. But we were never friends—*antagonists* was closer to the truth, though not in a competitive sense, just in the way our lives seemed destined to collide.

Bobby didn't need my friendship. He had plenty of admirers growing up. He was Tom Cruise handsome, athletic, and self-assured, while I was none of those things. And it didn't hurt his popularity that his family, who owned the local farm supply store, was more prosperous than most.

But what I remembered most about Bobby was that he almost always got what he wanted, including all the cute girls at school. And whenever he got into trouble, which like most boys he occasionally did, all he had to do was flash that golden grin of his and all would be forgiven, swept under the rug, or atoned for with punishment so lenient as to seem like a reward. I hadn't recalled Libby ever mentioning Bobby by name and couldn't imagine what connection existed between him and my little sister.

"What happened between you and Bobby?" I said.

Libby hung her head. "I stabbed him."

I winced. "Why would you have—?" A thought intruded like a brick through a window. "Were you and he—?" Had I been that out of touch with what was going on in my sister's life?

"No way," Libby said. "He's not my type. Besides, Bobby's married. Not that that—"

"Not that that *what*?"

Her face darkened, but she said no more.

"*Why* then? Why did you stab him?"

Her upper body stiffened. "You should ask him."

"I will, you can be sure of that. But right now I'm asking you."

"I don't want to talk about it," she said. It was a pose that didn't surprise me. Libby had a generous spirit, but she was also stubborn. In temperament, she was a human version of a cross between a golden retriever and a pit bull—an indomitable combination. "Let's talk about you," she said, her eyes brightening. "How's Charlotte? How's life in the big city?"

I gently clasped my hands on her shoulders and gazed into her sparkling violet eyes. "Libby," I said, "I'm not here to talk about me, not now anyway. I'm here because you're in jail, facing a serious charge. You might think it's stupid, but others obviously do not or you wouldn't be here. Now, please, tell me why you stabbed Bobby. Did he do something to you? Did he . . . make unwanted advances toward you?" I had no reason to believe that Bobby was a leopard who had changed his spots.

She shook her head but said nothing.

"Libby, talk to me."

She looked away, her face taking on that sullen cast of intransigence I knew to be as unbreakable as a blood oath.

I tried again anyway because I could think of no other recourse. "Sis," I said, infusing my words with all the love and concern welling up inside me, "I'm here to help you. I'm here because I care about you more than anything else in the world. But I can't help you unless I know what happened between you and Bobby. Was there some sort of struggle and you grabbed a knife and stabbed him?"

Her chest rose and fell as she took an extended breath and let it out. "I didn't stab him with a knife."

"With what then?"

Her lips curled up in a rueful smile. "The only sharp object I had in my purse at the time—a metal fingernail file."

"A fingernail file?" I laughed in spite of the weight of my concern. "That's what this is all about? They arrested you and hauled you off to jail because you stuck Bobby Hobson with a fingernail file?"

Libby responded with a timid bob of her head.

Only in Grotin, I thought.

But in that very instant the lightness of the moment dissipated like a lighted match extinguished in the deepest, darkest cavern on earth. After all, this was Grotin, a place where innocence comes to die.

6

FROM THE HALLWAY outside the interview room came a murmur of voices. Glancing toward the door, I spied Deputy Rawlins's shaggy-browed eyes framed by its little window. A quick knock, more of a warning than a courtesy, and the door opened.

Rawlins straddled the doorway. Behind him stood another man mostly hidden from view. "Reunion's over, Coombs," the deputy said. "Say your goodbyes."

"Actually," said the other man, shouldering his way into the room, "I'd like Darryl to stay." He was a lanky fellow with a pockmarked face embellished by tortoise shell eyeglasses. He wore a rumpled suit and had a dense crop of mousy brown hair parted slightly off center. He looked to be in his forties. The battered leather briefcase he carried looked older.

Rawlins grumbled while his right hand slapped a drumbeat of annoyance against the gun side of his hip. "Whatever you say, counsellor," he said, and withdrew.

"I'm Harvey Broward," the man with the briefcase said as he extended a hand toward me. He nodded at Libby. "Hello, Miss Coombs."

Libby did not return the greeting.

I rose and shook the man's hand. "Glad to meet you. Thanks for getting me through the door."

I rearranged the chairs so that Libby and I sat together on one side of the table opposite the attorney. I felt a chest-swelling sense of relief having him there. The cavalry had arrived, the battle was about to be engaged, and the forces of good would prevail—although it was obvious that Libby, for some reason, didn't share my feelings. She sat there with her arms folded across her chest and her face set in hard lines of resistance.

"Miss Coombs," Broward said, "I know you don't want to talk to me, but believe me, it's in your best interest to do so."

"Says you," Libby snapped.

I looked back and forth between the two of them. "What's going on here?" I said, confused by my sister's antagonistic tone.

"She hasn't filled you in?" the attorney said.

I shook my head.

"Then, if you'll allow me to do so . . ."

"I wish someone would."

The attorney exhaled heavily. "Your sister was taken into custody on a probable cause warrant at ten-thirty last night at your mother's house. She was booked into the county jail and put in a holding cell. At nine o'clock this morning, she appeared via video link between the jail and the courthouse at an initial hearing for a reading of the charge against her: attempted murder. Having been assigned her case as a public defender, I appeared with her at the hearing." The attorney's countenance turned grave. "Darryl, I'm an experienced attorney with a successful practice in criminal law. We have no public defender's office here. A judge merely designates local attorneys as public defenders as needed. Today it's me. I approach every case with the same care and determination however it comes across my desk, so I'm committed to defending your sister to the best of my ability. But I can't do that if she won't talk to me, which up to this point she has refused to do. I was hoping, with your being here, she would change her mind."

Suddenly I found the simple act of breathing difficult. The charge against my sister—attempted murder—was real and official. My balloon of optimism was punctured, its only remaining lift stemming from the question of whether such a severe charge was warranted. But what could not be questioned was her attorney's concern about her unwillingness to help with her defense. This obviously needed to be addressed.

"Libby," I said, "you should talk to him. You need legal representation."

Her head drooped toward the tabletop. "I have nothing to say."

"Then will you at least listen to what I have to say?" the attorney said.

"Please, Libby," I said. "What can it hurt?"

Her head jerked up. "Fine," she said in a petulant tone I was not used to hearing from her. "I'll listen. But only because Darryl asked me to."

Broward opened his briefcase, pulled out a file folder, and laid it on the table. "The first thing we need to do, Libby, is to get you out of lockup. Unfortunately, that won't happen until tomorrow at the earliest."

I expected my sister to protest, but she sat there silently staring at a tabletop marred with scratches resembling Egyptian hieroglyphics.

"Why not today?" I said, protesting on her behalf. "And if she's already been charged, why is she still in holding?"

The attorney gave me a look of appraisal that he promptly airbrushed with a polite smile. "Libby remains in holding because there is currently no bed available for her in the women's cellblock. But I'm hoping that becomes a moot point. Let me explain," he said, tapping the tabletop with his fingertips.

"Earlier today, I conferred with the county attorney, who will be prosecuting Libby's case himself. He informed me that she's scheduled to be arraigned in Courtroom B tomorrow morning at ten o'clock. The charge, as it now stands, will be attempted murder, to which we will plead not guilty. The question of bail will be addressed, at which time Libby will either be allowed the opportunity to post bail or will be transitioned into the general population here at the jail to await trial—that is, as soon as a bed opens up. Of course, we're hoping for her release on bail. But for that to happen—"

"Hold on," I said, startled at the breakneck pace of Libby's prescribed descent into the jaws of the criminal justice system. "Is there something I'm missing here? Libby stabbed Bobby Hobson with a fingernail file. How badly can he be hurt?"

"He's been hospitalized," the attorney said, "but fortunately it appears that his wound is not life threatening."

"Then why the heavy charge? Attempted murder? That's"—I was about to say *overkill* but caught myself—"excessive, don't you think?"

Broward removed his glasses long enough to rub his eyes. "Normally I would say yes, the county attorney is overreaching. But considering the aggravating circumstances, I'm not surprised at the severity of the charge."

"Aggravating circumstances?" I said, becoming more confounded by the second.

"Yes, anytime a public official is assaulted—"

I about fell out of my chair. "Bobby is a public official?"

The attorney regarded me with a bemused expression.

I gaped at Libby, begging with my eyes for an explanation. She hunched her shoulders and ducked her head as if seeking to withdraw, turtle-like, into the shell of her body. "Bobby is a county commissioner," she said in a small voice that trailed off into a hollow silence.

I maintained the silence as I dealt with the mind-jarring effects of this revelation. I don't know whether I was more shocked to learn of the *aggravating circumstances* or that Bobby had somehow attained a position of public trust. Although I shouldn't have been surprised at his becoming a politician. He'd always been a good BSer.

"As I was saying," Broward said, "my first priority is to get Libby out of jail as soon as possible. To that end, between now and tomorrow morning's arraignment, I will continue my dialogue with the county attorney with the goal of convincing him to reduce the charge against her, thus enhancing the likelihood of bail. But for that to happen, Libby needs to talk to me." He glanced in her direction as if to say, *Are you hearing this?*

"In particular, she needs to explain the motivation for her actions. If we can show there was no malice aforethought on her part when she stabbed Bobby, then we stand a chance of getting the charge knocked down to felony assault. Then Libby can plead no contest to the lesser charge and throw herself on the mercy of the court. Under the circumstances, I think that's the best course of action to take. Going to trial on the attempted murder charge would be pointless given the preponderance—"

"Wait a minute," I said, regaining my voice if not my composure. "I'm no attorney, but it seems to me you're throwing in the towel prematurely here. A plea of no contest to felony assault sounds like a roll-over-and-play-dead strategy to me. Why not fight these charges?" I rested a hand on Libby's forearm. "I know my sister. There had to be a good reason for her to stab Bobby. Who is to say it wasn't a justifiable act? An act of self-defense. How could the prosecutor prove otherwise?" I was grasping at legal straws here, but I couldn't help myself. "It would be a case of *he said, she said*. It seems to me that a jury would be sympathetic to Libby's side of the story even though Bobby is a public official. Or, perhaps, expressly because he *is* a public official—using his position of power to . . . do whatever he did to provoke Libby."

Broward sat back in his chair and waited for me to run out of steam. When I finally did, he addressed me with benign indulgence, the way one might respond to the nonsensical jabbering of a child. "Darryl," he said, "just how much do you know about what happened here?"

"Very little," I confessed. I told him about the frantic call from my mother and my all-night drive from San Antonio. "All I know is that Libby stabbed Bobby with a fingernail file and that, evidently, he's not critically injured. And now you're telling her she should, just like that"—I snapped my fingers—"cop to a charge of felony assault without mounting any kind of defense. That just doesn't seem right to me."

The attorney eyed Libby with a raised brow. "You haven't told him?"

Libby gave a little head waggle while keeping her eyes averted from me.

"Would you like to tell him now?"

"Tell me what?" I said, feeling an unpleasant needling between my shoulder blades.

Libby pinched her lips together and said nothing.

The attorney opened the file folder and pulled out a disc in a plastic case. "Do you have access to a DVD player?"

"I brought my laptop. It has a DVD drive."

"Good," he said, handing me the disc. "Watch this. It will explain everything."

I glanced at the DVD then at Libby. "What is he talking about?"

Tears formed in the corners of her eyes, but still no words came out of her mouth.

"Darryl," the attorney said, "forty-three people witnessed

your sister stab Commissioner Hobson. And if you watch the DVD, you can witness the stabbing too. If we go to trial, this video will be Exhibit A, and there won't be a need for Exhibit B." He shook his head. "There is no *he said, she said* here. There is only *she did*." He slid the file folder back into his briefcase and snapped it closed. "By the way," he added, "you'd be surprised at the piercing capability of a metal fingernail file wielded with force—especially one with a pearl handle. Your sister missed puncturing Bobby Hobson's carotid artery by half a centimeter. Otherwise, we'd be looking at a murder charge here."

I HELD UP the DVD. "What's on the disc?"

The attorney was gone and I knew my visit with Libby was about to come to an abrupt end. Deputy Rawlins would see to that.

"I don't know," Libby said. "I haven't seen it."

"Guess," I said, irritated by her continued evasiveness.

Her eyes darted about the room as if looking for a way out of answering the question. She didn't find one. "It's probably a video of last night's board of commissioners' meeting. The meetings are videotaped for viewing on the local public access television channel."

I stared at her gape-mouthed.

"You stabbed Bobby during a board of commissioners' meeting?" One apparently attended by forty-three people.

She screwed up her face, nodded.

"For God's sake, Libby, why did you do that?"

Her hands came together in front of her as fists, and she juddered in agitation. "I just did," she said, "and that's all there is to it."

I sat there struggling to take in everything I'd just heard, but my mind was unable to process it in a way that made sense.

Everything felt off to my inner vision, as if my personal world had suddenly tilted sharply on its axis. The only thing that remained upright was an emerging catalog of questions.

I slipped an arm around Libby's waist. Her trunk was statue stiff. I waited for it to soften. When it finally did, I pulled her toward me. She rested her head on my shoulder.

"I'm sorry," I said. "I don't mean to upset you. It's just that I don't understand."

"I know," she said, but offered nothing more by way of explanation.

"I wish you would talk to me about what happened."

She sighed. "It wouldn't matter. It wouldn't change anything."

"You don't know that. You heard the attorney. It's possible he can get the charge reduced if you explain why you stabbed Bobby. What do the lawyers call it—mitigating circumstances?"

Her head came off my shoulder. "Here is your mitigating circumstance," she said, hissing her words. "I stabbed Bobby because he deserved it."

"But why did he deserve it?"

"He just did."

I experienced a lockjawed moment of exasperation. I wanted to say something more to her—something penetrating and persuasive, something Solomonesque—that would convince her to open up to me about why she had attacked Bobby. I was her big brother. I was supposed to protect her, to shelter her from life's adversity. I had rushed to her side in her time of need and, with vigilante zeal, stood ready to act. All I needed was information to act upon. Had she not confided in me other times about her personal affairs? Her ups and downs with friendships and infatuations. Her doubts about her own sanity. She was the sanest person I knew. So why now was I being cut off from her confidence? What was there about her interaction with Bobby Hobson that was so appalling she couldn't share it with me of all people?

I wanted to press her on this matter for her own good. The attorney had said that a viable defense required her cooperation, and he was apparently relying on me to obtain it. "Libby—" I said, but was unable to continue. The will was there, but my faculties had abandoned me. My mind had wandered off into parts unknown. My body, from lack of sleep and nourishment, had gone into shutdown mode.

"I have to go now," I told her. "But I'll come back this evening."

"Can't you stay a little longer?" she said, clinging to me as if I were a security blanket.

Deputy Rawlins's rabid-knuckled knock at the door answered the question for me.

7

THE PRAIRIE INN, the only motel in Grotin, is on Main Street a few blocks north of downtown. It's a typical small-town motel—a single-story courtyard affair with a tired demeanor, noisy air conditioners, and beds with mattresses as lumpy as a corncrib. Like most businesses in town, it is locally owned and operated. Three successive generations of the Dolman family have made it their life's work to provide out-of-towners with clean rooms at a reasonable rate, the only hindrance to their success being the scarcity of out-of-towners who wish to overnight in Grotin.

This day was no exception, and so I had no problem renting a room. I could have stayed with my mother while in town, but that wouldn't have been pleasant for either of us.

"How long will you be with us?" the desk clerk inquired as he entered data from my driver's license into his computer. He looked about seventeen, had the prominent forehead and underbite typical of a Dolman, and undoubtedly had been helping out around the motel since he was old enough to make a bed.

"Can we leave that open?"

"Sure thing," young Dolman said. He handed me a key to Room 6 and a form to sign. "Park anywhere you like."

That wasn't going to be a problem, since the motel parking lot was as congested as the tarmac of an abandoned airstrip.

Upon entering the motel room, I was confronted by air that felt like the blowback from opening a pizza oven. I turned the air conditioner on to high and shed my shirt. I shoved my suitcase into an uninhabited corner of the room, set my laptop on a small table in the opposite corner, and stood there staring at the bed, which occupied three quarters of the room. I knew there were things I needed to do: view the DVD the attorney had given me, go see my mother, talk to Bobby Hobson, return to the jail to spend more time with Libby. All those things, I decided as I belly-flopped onto the bed, would have to wait their turn.

I slept two hours, and got up feeling drugged. I took a cold shower, shaved, and dressed in the most lightweight clothes I'd brought—tan Dockers and a polo shirt. Not exactly an incognito outfit in these parts.

The Silver Platter Diner is directly across the street from the Prairie Inn. I grabbed my laptop, along with the DVD, and trekked across to the diner.

I was well acquainted with The Silver Platter Diner. I'd been there numerous times with my parents, before my dad's accidental death. It had been Dad's eatery of choice, not because the food was anything to shout about but because the owners, John and Lori Hoffman, were clients of his. My dad sold insurance for Midwest Mutual: home, auto, life, business. He had sold the Hoffmans one of each kind of policy and returned the favor of their business by patronizing their diner.

"Loyalty is a two-way street," my dad used to say. He was full of sayings like that, clichés mostly, but to a young boy they were nuggets of wisdom to be treasured. My mother harped at him for repeating the same sayings time and again. My father, who steered clear of conflict as if it were a cliff without a guardrail, declined to respond to her. But quietly to me he would say,

"Truth thrice spoken is no less true." Then he'd wink and add, "Say that quickly five times." I tried but was never able to keep my tongue wrapped around those words.

As I walked into the diner, I was greeted with the smell of hot grease and some furtive stares from its current occupants. There are two classes of people in a small town—locals and strangers—and judging by the angle-eyed scrutiny I received upon making my entrance to the diner, it was obvious I'd been pegged as the latter. It was a comforting feeling.

A sign near the register read SEAT YOURSELF, so I did, in a booth toward the back. A waitress bustled over to the table carrying a sweating glass of water and a menu. "Hello, Darryl," she said, as if greeting a regular customer. "I'm surprised to see you back in town. But I guess I shouldn't be, what with Libby in trouble."

So much for my being a stranger in this town.

I smiled politely at the waitress as I googled the memory bank in my head for a name or connection. She looked familiar, but I couldn't hit upon the desired information. I glanced at her nametag. "Oh, hi, Debbie."

She set the water glass down and handed me the menu. "It's okay if you don't remember me. You haven't changed much in ten years, but I have." She patted her ample waistline and laughed. "Marriage and three kids will do that to you. You always think, after each pregnancy, that you'll work off the extra pounds, but then it's just easier to buy bigger clothes."

It clicked for me then who Debbie was. She'd been a year behind me in school. She was sweet and funny, and not so pretty as to be intimidating. I liked her and if I'd had the courage then to ask a girl out, it would have been her. To say I was no Bobby Hobson in the romance department was an understatement.

"Well," I said, "you look nice in your bigger clothes. You were too skinny in high school anyway."

"That's sweet of you to lie like that, Darryl. I'll be back shortly to take your order. Can I start you off with some coffee?"

"Bring the pot."

"Cream?"

"Please."

She paused. "Sorry to hear about Libby. She's a good kid."

"Yes, she is."

I set my laptop on the table, pressed the power button, and waited for it to boot up. When it did, I inserted the DVD Libby's attorney had given me.

Debbie brought my coffee, a steaming cupful and a backup carafe, and creamer in a little stainless steel decanter. I ordered a cheeseburger and fries.

"Coming right up."

I started the DVD of the board of commissioners' meeting. The camera that recorded the meeting had captured the action from a fixed position at the back of a room that appeared to have a seating capacity of sixty or so. A little more than half the seats were filled. The camera was aimed at a dais at the front of the room flanked by two flag stands. Old Glory hung limply from a stanchion on the left. The state flag of Kansas, its sunflower and state seal hidden in furls of dark-blue silk, drooped from a stand on the right.

On the dais was a skirted table behind which two men and two women sat in high-back padded office chairs. They each wore a white or pastel dress shirt—short-sleeved—sans tie. These, I assumed, were the county commissioners, although it soon became apparent that the woman seated on the far left was a clerical assistant. Her chair was spaced slightly apart from the other three, and she occasionally handed packets of paperwork to the commissioner nearest her—the other female on the dais—who passed them along to the other two commissioners.

Bobby Hobson was seated camera right. He didn't look much different than I remembered. He'd put on a few pounds and had a trimmer haircut, but he looked as handsome and self-possessed as ever. The other two commissioners looked older, in their fifties or early sixties, I reckoned. On the table in front of each commissioner were a nameplate (indecipherable from camera distance), microphone, notepad, and bottle of water. Also up front, at audience level, facing the commissioners' table, was a lectern with a gooseneck microphone.

Given the camera angle, the foreground of the scene was populated by the backs of the heads of the citizens in attendance at the meeting. The attendees were seated in rows on either side of an aisle that ran down the middle of the room to the commissioners' dais and the lectern with the gooseneck microphone. I searched for the back of Libby's head but didn't see it. She was either seated out of camera range or had yet to arrive at the meeting.

Shortly after the recording began, the commissioner seated in the center position—the older male commissioner—whom I assumed to be the chairman, called the meeting to order. I plugged in my earbuds so as not to disturb the other diners in the restaurant and listened as the chairman issued a perfunctory greeting to the audience. Following these remarks, a motion was made and seconded and a vote taken to dispense with the reading of the minutes of the prior board meeting. Then the clerk read aloud the agenda for the current proceedings. I sipped my coffee and waited for something unbusinesslike to happen.

The first item up for discussion was a proposal to allow overnight camping in a select number of county parks currently designated as day-use only. After brief remarks by each commissioner, the floor was opened for comment by members of the audience. A man with a pirate's beard got up and made his way down to the lectern up front. He spoke in a subdued voice with his face angled away from the microphone, rendering his words mostly inaudible. I caught only enough of what he said to know that he favored allowing overnight camping. When he was finished, an elf-like woman stood on her tiptoes behind the lectern and spoke against the proposal. A couple of other citizens offered their opinions. Eventually, the item was tabled pending further *study*, which I took to mean that the commissioners needed time to determine how a *yea* or *nay* vote would impact their chances of reelection.

I skipped forward in the video, stopping at intermittent points to listen in on the meeting. So far, there had been no appearance by my sister.

When Debbie showed up with a plate of food in hand, I paused the recording and pushed the laptop aside.

"Enjoy," she said.

I did. I ate half the burger in three bites. I stuffed my mouth with as many fries as it would hold and chewed only enough to allow me to swallow. I was fortunate not to have choked to death.

When I was done eating, I poured myself another cup of coffee and continued watching the video. The meeting progressed at the anesthetizing pace and manner of most civic meetings. An agenda item was introduced and briefly discussed by the panel of commissioners. Then public comment was invited. Some items prompted public comment. Others did not. Audience members who wished to speak rose from their seats and proceeded to the lectern up front. After discussion was closed on a particular agenda item, the item was either tabled in favor of future discussion or a vote was taken.

I continued alternately fast-forwarding and playing the video at normal speed. I poured myself a third cup of coffee. It seemed as if the meeting was a circular drama without a closing act.

I zipped through a long stretch of discussion and public comment before picking up the proceedings again. At this point no one was speaking, but a conspicuous murmuring permeated the room, the kind of vocal buzz that follows the reading of a verdict in a controversial trial. Up front, the commissioners busied themselves as they waited for the buzzing to subside. The woman commissioner sipped from her water bottle. Bobby scribbled on his notepad. The chairman riffled through some paperwork. "Shall we move on to new business?" he finally said.

Then it happened.

The camera picked up Libby's backside as she sidled between two rows of seats to reach the center aisle. Lodged in the crook of her left arm was a small brown purse. She ambled down the aisle, bypassed the public-comment lectern, and moved to a position in front of Bobby Hobson.

Bobby looked up at her with an inquisitive expression. For a brief moment they seemed to lock eyes. Bobby opened his mouth as if to speak. Libby leaned forward. Her right hand flew up, out, and down, landing firmly on the left side of Bobby's neck where it merged with his shoulder.

I don't know if it was the abruptness of my sister's action that was more shocking or the measure of its violence. My whole body clenched as I heard Bobby scream and watched his right hand grope toward the left side of his neck.

Members of the audience gasped. The other two board members lurched back in their seats as if in fear of being the next one attacked. In the commotion, a water bottle toppled and rolled off the table.

Libby turned and walked back up the aisle as calmly as she had gone down it. She stared straight ahead, face immobile, eyes vacant.

Behind her, Bobby hunched forward over the table with the fingers of his right hand curled around the fingernail file that jutted from his neck, its pearl handle shimmering from the overhead lighting. Blood trickled from between his fingers and trailed down the front of his shirt like an excess of red paint splashed on an otherwise bare canvas. His face was nearly as white as his shirt. His eyes were wide and unblinking.

The board chairman, having sufficiently collected himself, jumped to his feet and pointed at Libby. "Stop her!"

No one made a move to do so. Meeting attendees, some standing and some remaining seated, turned and watched her leave.

"Stop her!" the chairman repeated. But by then, Libby was gone.

For the next few minutes the scene was one of general confusion. The female commissioner, assisted by two members of the audience, helped Bobby out of his chair and off to the side, where they assisted him in lying down. A voice in the crowd said, "I've called 911. They're sending an ambulance and the police." Audience members milled about now, craning their necks to see.

Then the video ended. I couldn't tell if someone had turned off the camera at that point or if what remained of the aftermath of the meeting had been edited out.

I glanced up to find Debbie standing beside my table with a cash register receipt in hand. "Can I get you anything else?" she said, her voice muffled.

I withdrew my earbuds. "No, thank you," I said. "I've had all I can handle for now."

THE HOUSE I grew up in, and where my mother still lives, is on Plover Lane, on the western edge of town within smelling distance of a dairy farm. It's a modest cottage-style home amid a cluster of modest cottage-style homes built in haste following World War II. My grandfather bought the house on the G.I. Bill in 1952 and passed it on to my father a few months before my birth, when my grandparents moved to Florida to get away from the prairie wind and the cold.

The house had seen better days even in my youth. My dad kept it up as best he could, but he was no handyman and most of his time and energy was devoted to peddling insurance, a commodity he called *peace of mind*. So the house received little TLC from his hands and as a result fell into disrepair.

After my father died in an auto accident while on his way home from a meeting at his company's regional office in Omaha—I was fifteen at the time—our house, now the object of overt neglect, lost its battle with decay. The roof developed a swaybacked sag at its peak. Its composition shingles cracked and crinkled. The red-brick chimney settled into a sideways list that, from the front, gave the house a skewed look. The once vibrant bumblebee-yellow exterior paint, already sun-bleached to the color of soured milk, curled and flaked like building dandruff. The front yard took on the scab-ground look of a vacant lot.

My mother kept threatening to sell the place and move to "a more welcoming community," but she never followed through on the threat. To the contrary, I think she became comfortably ensconced in her dilapidated surroundings because they accommodated her emotional poverty.

It is said that reality exists only in the present, that the future is an illusion, and the past is occupied by nothing more than shadows. As I pulled into the driveway of my mother's home, I struggled to keep myself planted in the present, to keep my vision focused squarely on the task at hand, like a carriage horse fitted with blinders. But as I had known from the very outset of my journey back to Grotin, that was not possible. Like the town itself, this derelict structure in front of me enshrined my past. One look at it, one whiff of dairy air, was all it took. Memory, as it always will, tunneled its way back through time, and I tumbled through the hole it made and came out on the other side.

WHEN I WAS barely four years old, a man knocked on the door of our house. I was home with my mother, just the two of us. It was summertime and I had been playing outside in the backyard, in my favorite element—dirt. As the sun rose higher in the sky, taking direct aim with its UV rays, my mother made me come inside. I was sweaty and soiled from head to toe, and my clothes looked as if they'd been tie-dyed with turd-colored handprints. Mother gave me a bath and dressed me in a fresh T-shirt and a clean pair of shorts. I was sitting at the kitchen table eating apple slices when the man knocked on the door.

When my mother answered the door, the man, who looked to be in his twenties, introduced himself as Jack Forrester. He said he was a medical intern at a hospital in Topeka. He was wearing scrubs, although that didn't mean anything to me at the time, and he had a stethoscope dangling from around his neck. He was carrying a black leather bag.

His medical internship had an *outreach* component, he told my mom. To satisfy this component he was traveling around to small towns in the state and offering free medical checkups to young boys who were under school age.

"Are there any boys under school age living in the house?" he asked.

My mother told him there was—one.

"Would you like your boy to receive a free medical checkup?"

When my mother hesitated, the man smiled at her. He had curly blond hair and was handsome in a boyish way. He had an aura of innocence about him, as if he'd only recently exchanged his Boy Scout uniform for medical garb. "It's for your son's benefit," he said. "It won't take long, and it will help me in my internship."

"I . . . guess . . . that would be all right," my mother said.

Jack Forrester came into the house and my mother called for me to come into the living room.

"This is Darryl," my mother said. "He's four years old." And to me she said, "This is Dr. Jack and he's going to give you a checkup for free. Isn't that nice of him." I must have looked scared, because my mother said, "It'll be okay, Dare." (She called me Dare back then.) She placed her hands on my shoulders and marched me over to the doctor.

Dr. Jack kneeled down, opened his black bag, and took out a Tootsie Pop. It had an orange-colored wrapper. He held it out to me. "Would you like this?"

When I reached for it, he pulled it back. "First," he said, "we need to have a look inside your mouth to make sure there are no bad germs in there." He winked at my mother, who had sat down on the sofa to watch me get my checkup.

Dr. Jack took a flat stick out of his bag. "Open wide," he said.

I looked at my mother.

"Do as the doctor says," she told me.

I opened my mouth. Dr. Jack pressed down on my tongue with the stick and peered down my throat. "I see he still has his tonsils," he said.

"Yes," my mother said.

"I don't see any inflammation."

My mother smiled.

Dr. Jack handed me the Tootsie Pop. I tore off its wrapper and stuck it in my mouth. The Tootsie Pop was too big for my mouth and I nearly choked on it, but I persisted in sucking on it because it tasted so good.

Dr. Jack took the stethoscope from around his neck and showed it to me. "This is called a stethoscope," he said. "It will allow me to listen to your heart. Is it okay if I listen to your heart?"

I looked at my mother again. She bobbed her head and grinned as if pleased at how well my checkup was going. I was just happy to be sucking on my Tootsie Pop.

"I'll need to pull up your T-shirt," Dr. Jack said. Which he did. "It would be better if we got your arms out of it." I took my arms out of it so that it was left hanging around my neck. "Good," Dr. Jack said.

He put the listening ends of the stethoscope to his ears and held out the other end. "I'm going to touch this little disk to your chest above your heart. Do you know where your heart is? Show me." I put a finger to my chest where I thought my heart was. "That's right," he said. "Smart boy." He touched the disk to my chest close to where I had put my finger. It was cool against my skin. I stopped sucking on my Tootsie Pop and listened. I wondered what he was hearing.

"Very good," Dr. Jack said. "Now let's listen to your lungs." He turned me around. A moment later, I felt the contact of the disk against my back. "Now take a big breath," he said, "and then let it out." I did as I was told. "That's it." He pressed the disk to the other side of my back. "One more big breath and let it out. Very good." He brought me back around to face him.

"His lungs sound clear," Dr. Jack told my mom. He put his stethoscope away. "Almost done." And again addressing my mother: "With your permission, ma'am, I'm going to check him for head lice. I'm told there's been an outbreak of head lice among young children in the area. Have you heard about that?"

"Oh . . . no, I haven't," my mother said, looking concerned. I didn't know what head lice was, but I imagined it must be something very bad.

Dr. Jack retrieved a long black comb from his bag. He tipped my head forward and to the side. "Let's see if we find any of those nasty nits," he said, and began raking the comb through my hair, one small section at a time. "This will take a few minutes," he told my mom. "You have to be thorough or you can miss those little buggers. By the way, could I trouble you for a glass of water?"

"Certainly," my mother said, pushing herself up off the sofa. "Better yet, how about some sun tea?"

"Wonderful," said Dr. Jack.

"Sugar and lemon?"

"Yes, please."

As soon as my mother was out of the room, Dr. Jack put away his comb. He brought his face close to mine. His breath was hot against my cheek. It smelled like root beer or licorice or cherry cough drops; I couldn't decide.

"Stand still," he said in a hushed voice, "and be very quiet. Do you understand?"

I nodded, my child-mind's sense of understanding carrying with it no foreknowledge of events to come.

"Good boy," he said.

I stood still and silent as he pulled down my shorts and underwear and cupped his hand under my private parts. His face flushed and he breathed heavily as he caressed my genitals. Beads of sweat broke out on his forehead and upper lip. My legs trembled and I did my best not to move. Candy juice leaked from the corners of my mouth and trickled down my chin.

From the kitchen came the sound of the refrigerator door slamming shut. Dr. Jack reached into his bag and brought out a camera. I heard the camera's shutter clicking in rapid succession as he took pictures of me. Moments before my mother returned with his glass of sun tea, Dr. Jack put away his camera and pulled up my underwear and shorts.

"Thank you," he told my mom as he rose to his feet and took the glass from her. "All clear of head lice," he said. "No worries there." He wiped his brow with a handkerchief from his pocket. "You have a very healthy boy, I'm happy to say."

I went over and huddled against my mother's legs. She stroked the back of my neck. "He's my pride and joy," she said. "Thank the nice doctor for the checkup," she told me.

"Thank you," I said, but kept my face pressed against her thigh.

"He's a little shy," my mother said.

Dr. Jack drank his tea, thanked my mother, and left. A few days later, he was arrested outside a town about forty miles from Grotin. During one of his *free checkups*, he had been observed fondling the genitals of another young boy, whose mother immediately called the police and then smartly got the license plate number of his car as he drove away.

He, of course, turned out to be a fraud. But the most shocking thing was who he really was. His real name was Avery Collins. He was thirty-two years old, and he was an elementary school teacher in Wichita.

After Avery Collins's arrest, the police searched his black bag and found his camera, along with several exposed rolls of film. When the film was developed, it was found to contain photos of dozens of young boys in various states of nakedness. It took the investigating officers a couple of months to track down the parents of all the boys in the photos.

When two detectives came to our house to talk to my parents about the case, my mother at first denied that the man who'd called himself Jack Forrester had ever come to our house. The detectives showed her photos of me wearing only a T-shirt around my neck. "Mrs. Coombs, is this your boy? Is this Darryl?" one of the detectives asked.

My mother broke down and told them everything. "I thought he was a real doctor," she said through her tears.

"So did a lot of other mothers," the detective said.

The newspapers and TV news shows had a field day with the story, but state law kept them from publishing the names of any of the boys who had been molested. Word got out nevertheless, and it wasn't long before the people of Grotin knew I had been one of the victims. So my mother suffered both the public humiliation and private shame of having been duped by Jack Forrester, a.k.a. Avery Collins, into allowing him to molest her son.

As for me, I was too young at the time of the incident to know what had really happened. It was only later, as I was growing up in Grotin, that I was made to wear the mantle of indignity that came with being widely known as *one of those poor boys molested by that school teacher from Wichita.*

9

OUR PAST IS the skin we can never shed even as we stretch and grow and morph into an unrecognizably different person. I knew that by coming back to Grotin I had put myself in jeopardy. The bubble of privacy that protected me in the big city had burst the moment I set foot back in this place. And as I walked up the front steps of the house on Plover Lane, I sensed an erosion of the self-respect I had worked so hard to build up since escaping this town. In Grotin, I was like a child running naked in the streets, an outlandish sight for all to see, to point at laughingly: "There goes the luckless son of Bud and Meryl Coombs."

My inclination was to turn away, to flee as quickly as I could back to the sanctuary of my new life in Texas. But it was too late for that. You can't run far enough or fast enough to outdistance your past. My only choice at this point was to meet it head on.

The darkening shades on the mullioned front windows of my mother's house were drawn when I arrived, which did not surprise me. Mother was known to sit in a blinded house for hours with neither the TV nor radio on. I always wondered what she was thinking during these times. Ultimately, I came to believe that she was doing her best to unplug herself from reality, that she wished to achieve a Zen-like state of nullity absent life's disappointments. For my mother, life was never simply *what is*; it was always *what might have been*.

Looking back, it wasn't hard to see that I was one of her greatest disappointments. She'd given up her job as a cosmetologist when she'd become pregnant with me. Raising me and celebrating my achievements became the focal point of her existence. But I turned out to be a middling achiever. I excelled in mediocrity—as a son, as a student, and as a resident of the universe. Without realizing it at the time, I was determined not to stand out. I did not want to be thrust into the spotlight of my accomplishments, so I set about being average in every way I could. In time, my mother's hopes for me waned like day fading into night. She believed that my failures were her failures. But more than that, she blamed herself for not protecting me from life's vicissitudes.

It didn't dawn on me until I was older and away from the crucible of life in Grotin how much my behavior growing up was a result of my ill-fated encounter with Jack Forrester/Avery Collins. I didn't consciously blame my mother for what had happened. But I think, subconsciously, I decided that I no longer wanted to be the epicenter of her affection, and the way I chose to make that happen was to disappoint her at every turn. I know now that this skewed thinking was the result of my feeling vulnerable in my mother's care—because, *in* her loving care, a very bad thing had happened to me.

And I believe that, in my mother's own slanted thinking, she at least partially blamed me for what had happened. A mother's first job is to keep her children safe. That she failed in that regard horrified her. But the guilt she heaped on herself was too much for her to absorb, and so she poured some of it back on me in the form of reproach. I went from *the child who could do no wrong* to the butt of the question "what's *wrong* with you, child?" As a result, a wedge was driven between me and my mother that we were never able to overcome.

Eventually, she set her sights on having other children who could fulfill the role originally intended for me. But she had one miscarriage after another, which only heightened her disappointment with life. With each misstep on my part and each unfinished pregnancy on hers, her spirit took another hit, as did her devotion to me—and to her marriage.

It was Libby's unexpected birth when I was nine years old that gave Mother a new lease on life—that rehydrated her joyless existence, at least for a time.

From the moment she was born, Libby was the ideal child. As an infant she hardly ever cried, and when she did—out of hunger or need of diaper changing—her complaints were more akin to the melancholy warble of a dove. Mother responded with feather-soft tenderness. As Libby grew, she achieved at an accelerated rate. She walked at eight months; began talking in sentences before her second birthday. When she was three, she crawled up on the bench of Mother's battered upright piano and, after a few minutes of plinking keys, proceeded to play the melody to the theme song from *Sesame Street*.

Mother was overjoyed with her wunderkind. Her hopes for a brighter future were renewed. She now had a child through whom she could live vicariously.

And as Libby continued to perform beyond her years—in preschool, reading Dr. Seuss books to the other children; shunning finger painting for, albeit crude, watercolor renderings of the landscape outside the classroom window—Mother became protective of her little treasure. Libby was a gift she did not wish to share with the rest of the world, or the rest of her family.

But little girls love their fathers, and Libby was no exception. Each evening when my father came home from work, she would run into his arms and demand that he tell her about his day. "Did you sell lots of *insurance*?" She said the word with reverence, as if it were a thing with magical properties, because my father had always spoken of it that way. To him, insurance was an elixir for which everyone had a need. My dad would beam and sit in his easy chair with Libby on his knee. But before he could get out more than a few words, my mother would swoop in and relieve him of his daughter with some excuse: she needed a bath, her hair needed brushing, she had a runny nose and he shouldn't catch her cold.

This closed relationship my mother cultivated with Libby left me even more on the outside, along with my father, who by way of comparison had been nearly as big a disappointment to Mom as I had been. As hard as he worked, he had not provided for her in the manner she felt deserving of. Following his death, my mother seemed hardly to notice his absence. And she failed to give him his due for leaving her with a lifetime annuity that allowed her to provide for her basic needs and those of her children.

She also failed to comprehend the profound impact my father's death had on Libby and me, but especially on my sister, who was six years old at the time. In her intractable grief, Libby turned inward, became a sullen, silent, and often unmanageable child. And to my mother's dismay, in attempting to close the door to her sadness, Libby underwent a kind of self-inflicted dumbing down. Equating thinking with feeling, she became inarticulate, emotionally remote, and indifferent to pursuits that had previously excited her.

When finally she did reach out to someone for solace, it was not to our mother but to me. "Hold me, Darryl," she said to me one day, "and never let me go. Because if you do, I will surely die." And I held her until we both went numb from the lack of blood flowing to our limbs.

For her part, Mother interpreted this emotional bonding that took place between her children as an alliance against her, which it was never meant to be. Libby and I had merely joined forces in our time of sorrow the way two people lost at sea climb into the same lifeboat. But mother responded to our presumed violation of her maternal priority by being overly demonstrative in her affection toward us, and demanding payment in kind. And when she didn't get it, she became harsh and resentful in her behavior toward us.

Such is the tyranny of love.

"Mom," I hollered into the darkened house, "I'm going to raise the shades."

Crosshatched bands of sunlight burst into the house through dust-encrusted windowpanes. It took a few seconds for my eyes to adjust to the increased volume of light.

I found Mom sitting in an overstuffed chair in a corner of the living room. I was startled by the sight of her. Either the chair had swollen in proportion or Mom had shrunk. It was as if she were a child who had climbed up into her daddy's big chair.

I went over and kissed her on the cheek. Her facial skin was leathery and drawn. Her prairie-dog brown hair had turned mostly gray. Her eyes had sunk deep in their sockets.

"How are you, Mom?"

"Have you seen Libby?" she said in a flat, dry voice.

I sat down on the end of the sofa nearest her. "I went to see her as soon as I got into town, and I plan on going back this evening."

"Are they feeding her? Does she have a bed to sleep in?"

"Yes, Mom. It's not the Grand Hotel, but she's okay. The attorney assigned to her case is hoping to get her released on bail tomorrow."

Mom looked at me, her too-deep eyes harboring ancient grievances. "You should have been here for her. She wouldn't have gotten into this mess if you'd been here."

I wasn't about to argue that point, because Mom was right. I was Libby's big brother and I should have been around to protect her. But playing the blame game now was not going to help Libby's cause.

"What mess are you talking about, Mom? Do you know anything about why Libby assaulted Bobby Hobson?"

"What mess? *Jail*—that's what I mean." She took a backhanded swipe at the air in front of her. "And how the hell would I know anything about it? Your sister don't tell me about the goin's on in her life any more than you do."

When I didn't respond to my mother's outburst, a brittle silence filled the space between us that I was reluctant to break.

Mother blinked hard several times. "I've been thinking," she said.

I waited.

"I've been thinking about where I went wrong with you kids."

"Mom," I said, "you didn't go wrong. Things just happen. Good things. Bad things. It's a myth that life is what you make it. Life is what makes you."

"It's made me sad."

"I know, Mom. And I'm sorry." Truly, I was.

Minutes passed before she spoke again, this time in a more conciliatory tone. "You can stay in your old room. I put fresh sheets on the bed."

A shiver slid, like an ice flow, down my spine. Even after all this time, I could feel the ill winds of my childhood blowing through this house.

"Thanks, Mom," I said, "but I've taken a room at the Prairie Inn. It's nearer the jail. I thought it would be better for Libby if I stayed there."

"Oh," Mom said, her brow pinching and then relaxing, as if she'd realized after a moment of pique that this arrangement was best for all concerned. She lowered her head and stared numbly at her hands folded in her lap.

Thinking our conversation had come to an end, I got up to leave.

Mom reached out and clutched my wrist with vise-grip firmness. "You have to help her," she said, her voice charged with urgency, as if she were speaking to a 911 operator.

"I'll do my best, Mom. I'm just not sure I know how."

"You've got to find a way."

"I know, Mom. I know."

10

TO SAY THAT Bobby Hobson and I had a history does not tell the story. Although we were never friends, neither were we sworn enemies. Growing up, we were like two boys jogging side by side along the same rugged path, each doing his best to maintain a sure footing. It was inevitable that we bumped into each other on occasion as we jostled for position. The difference was, Bobby charged down life's path with the determination and confidence of a bull, while I scampered along warily, like a deer expecting any moment to be pounced upon by a mountain lion. Too often, my fears became reality. And too often, Bobby was there to witness the carnage—sometimes as spectator, sometimes as participant.

It was half past eight when I walked up the sidewalk toward the main entrance to Harbin County Community Hospital. The broad canopy of sky was masked now by a veil of deepening twilight that cast the townscape in nothing more than a rumor of color. The remaining heat of the day radiated up from the ground and mixed with air that had cooled enough to allow breathing that did not penalize the lungs.

I had slept some and eaten some, but the rest and food hadn't improved my mood any, and neither had my visit with my mother. I was jittery and out of sorts. As much as I desired to avoid this very thing, here I was being pulled back into a drama from which I had willingly withdrawn. And now I was about to cross swords with another player from my past.

Although I was all but certain it would be an exercise in futility, I wanted to have a chat with Bobby Hobson before heading back to the jail to see Libby. I was convinced he had committed some indecency that had provoked my sister's wrath. It was the only explanation that made sense to me. But I also knew that Bobby was not one to admit responsibility for anything that cast him in an unfavorable light.

Harbin County Community Hospital looks more like an industrial building than a medical facility. It is a long, low, shed-roof structure that occupies the entire block between 1st and 2nd Streets, west of south Main. Its buff-colored brick façade was popular in the early fifties when the first phase of the hospital was built. A succession of additions has since been LEGO'ed to either end of the building, stretching it to its current size. A towering flagpole invites visitors to the hospital's main portal. This evening, as usual, a steady breeze was keeping the flags atop the flagpole—The Star-Spangled Banner and, beneath it, the Kansas state flag—unfurled to their fullest dimensions.

This wasn't my first visit to the county hospital. I was born here, although my memories of the place don't extend that far back. I do recall, however, being brought here by my parents when I was four years old, not long after my *checkup* with Dr. Jack. That memory has stayed with me because of the odd fact that a policeman waited outside a ring of curtains while a doctor examined me for reasons known at the time to everyone involved but me. When I asked my mother if I was sick, she responded angrily, "No, but someone else is."

I was brought here again when I was seven, to the emergency

room, after falling out of the cottonwood tree in our backyard. My best friend, Gilbert, and I were vying to see who could climb the highest. I won—my prize, a fractured forearm. Years later, not long before my exodus from Grotin, I visited Gilbert in a hospital room here. We were no longer friends by then, and I don't think he ever knew I came to see him.

At the information desk in the lobby of the hospital's main entrance, I encountered a wizened, white-haired lady wearing a purple smock with the word VOLUNTEER stitched in red thread above her left breast. She looked to be in her eighties, but when she smiled and said "What can I do for you, hon?" her face radiated a youthfulness in counterpoint to her veteran frame. I inquired as to Bobby's location and was relieved—for Libby's sake—to be informed that he was not in ICU but in a private room in the General Care Unit. I was also heartened when, minutes later, the attendant at the nurse's station in General Care didn't seem to recognize me as I passed by.

I don't know anyone who is fond of hospital visitation. To non-medicos, hospitals are alien places, and as I strode down the corridor past a succession of sick rooms, my senses were assaulted by the sights, sounds, and smells native to the setting: the vacant-eyed stares of the infirm, the *blip-blip-blip* of heart monitors, the invasive odor of bleach, the ubiquitous wall-mounted hand sanitizers, and personnel in pastel smocks spouting the clipped jargon of the medical class.

I was not moved to sympathy: this was not a mission of mercy. And if I felt anything as I approached Bobby's room, it was the tautening of my nerve-strings as I came closer to reentering the rabbit hole of my past.

The door to Bobby's room was open. He was propped up in bed, holding a *Sports Illustrated* magazine. Other magazines were piled on a mobile service cart next to his bed, along with a box of tissues, a plastic water pitcher, and a drinking glass with a flexible straw inserted. A square bandage covered the left side of his neck at its junction with his shoulder. A tube attached to an IV in his right forearm ran up to a drip bag hanging from a pedestal at the head of his bed. Another line swagged down from a stanchioned vital-signs monitor to a blood-pressure cuff wrapped around his left bicep.

Despite his surroundings, Bobby didn't appear to be a man in medical peril. His wavy brown hair was tousled and he needed a shave, but he looked quite comfortable lying there, as if, rather than being confined to a hospital bed, he was lounging under an umbrella at some beach resort.

I thought, seeing him up close and personal, that he must have done lots of lounging over the last ten years. His hospital gown had a noticeable bulge where it once would have covered rippled abs. His face was fleshier than in his youth; his shoulders rounder, softer-looking. Bobby had been the starting halfback on the Grotin High football team three years running. He wasn't big—I remember him being listed as 5'9", 160 lbs. in the team stat sheet—but he lifted weights religiously and strutted his ripped body on and off the field as proudly as a Victoria's Secret model flaunts the latest look in lingerie. But by the looks of him now, it appeared he spent more time these days hoisting a beer growler than barbells.

He didn't seem surprised to see me, even though it had been a decade since our last encounter. "So, the prodigal son has returned," he said. "How long has it been?"

"Not long enough."

Bobby laughed, but he wasn't smiling. "Well, I don't need to ask you what brings you back to Grotin."

"No."

An awkward silence filled the room to overflowing as we exchanged wary stares. Then Bobby said, "I heard you were in San Antonio. An accountant. You were always good with numbers."

"And you were always good at convincing people you knew what you were talking about."

"Look where it's gotten me."

"Apparently, it's gotten you a job with a title. I'm impressed."

"Don't be," he said. "The pay is lousy and there's always someone carping at you about something."

"Then why do it?" But I knew the answer. Bobby always liked the limelight.

"I ask myself that every day."

My eyes revisited the bandage on his neck. It had a blot of dried blood at its center. "So what are the doctors saying about your injury?"

"They say I'm gonna live."

My thoughts darted back to what Harvey Broward had said about the stabbing. Libby had missed puncturing Bobby's carotid artery by half a centimeter. Otherwise, we'd be looking at a murder charge here. "Congratulations," I said.

Bobby closed the magazine he'd been reading and tossed it on top of the others. "Now, if they'd just unhook me from these lines and send me home, I'd be happy as a horned toad." He settled back in bed with a self-satisfied smile on his face.

His cheerfulness did not sit well with me. "So what's going on, Bobby?" I said, feeling my pulse quicken in anticipation of the confrontation about to take place.

"What do you mean?"

I stepped to the edge of the bed and leaned over its railing so that I was standing almost directly over him. "I mean, we both know that Libby didn't stick you with a fingernail file for sport. She must have had a reason."

He brandished open palms. "If she did, then it's news to me."

I peered into his hazel eyes. They had flecks of gold in them. But it was fool's gold. "You never were a good liar," I said.

"And you never let well enough alone."

I felt like punching him in the face, something I had done before. But that was a long time ago. I hadn't regretted it then, but I knew I'd regret it now.

"Listen, Mr. Commissioner," I said. "It isn't *well enough* for my little sister to be tossed in jail on account of a dustup she had with the likes of you. So I will not be letting well enough alone. And when I find out what's behind all this, you can be sure we'll be having another chat."

"Can't wait," Bobby said.

We locked eyes, and it was as if we were boys again, facing off in a decades-old struggle for survival, except this time I was determined not to let Bobby get the best of me.

"Get well soon," I said, and turned to leave. Only then did I realize there were no flowers in the room.

11

I GOT BACK to the sheriff's office a little after 9 p.m. There was no sneaking up on this place at night. The entire compound—office section, jail wing, exercise yard, parking lot—was illuminated by multiple security lights aimed at angles and directions so as to dispel the darkness as effectively as the midday sun. The only gloom on site was my increasingly dusky disposition.

When I entered the front office, a different deputy sat behind the duty desk, although Deputy Rawlins was there also, still in uniform. He stood tilted back against a filing cabinet with his thumbs hooked on his duty belt, engaged in conversation with his fellow deputy—conversation that ended abruptly with my appearance at the counter.

"I'd like to visit Libby Coombs," I told the duty officer, a long-faced fellow with a five o'clock shadow that looked impervious to a razor. "I'm her brother."

He looked me up and down as if doing a visual threat assessment. "She's in holding. No visitors allowed for inmates in holding except for—"

"I'm aware of the visitation restrictions on those in holding," I said, "but I've been given special permission by the jail commander to visit my sister."

"Is that right?"

I dipped my head toward Rawlins. "Deputy Rawlins can verify that."

"Deputy Rawlins is off duty," Deputy Longface said.

"He's also standing less than ten feet from you."

Longface glanced over at Rawlins. "So he is."

Rawlins didn't say anything. I waited in case he changed his mind. He didn't. He was obviously having too much fun watching me jump through all the procedural hoops to get to Libby again.

"You keep a visitor's log," I said. "I know because I signed it earlier today. If you will kindly refer to it, you'll see that I visited my sister at approximately three forty-five this afternoon."

"By permission of the jail commander, you say?"

"That's right. If you doubt my veracity, please give him a call."

Deputy Longface displayed a lopsided smile. "I don't doubt your *ver-a-ci-ty*, but your timing's not too good. It's late. Your sister's probably asleep."

"I don't think so," I said. "I told Libby when I visited her this afternoon that I'd come back and see her this evening. I'm sure she's expecting me."

"Oh, you are?" Longface said.

I took a deep breath and stifled an impulse to lash out at this insensitive lout. "I know it's late," I said, "and I'm sorry for the inconvenience. But I would greatly appreciate it if—"

"I'll take it from here, Gabe," Deputy Rawlins said, his desire for amusement apparently satisfied. "Call holding and have Libby Coombs brought to interview room 1."

"If you say so," said Deputy Longface, with a shrug of indifference.

Rawlins moseyed over to the counter and placed the sign-in sheet and a personal possessions box within my reach. "I'll need to see some I.D.," he said with a straight face.

"You're kidding."

"Do I look like I'm kidding?"

He met me as I passed through the metal detector and we followed the same path we had taken earlier in the day to arrive at the same interview room.

When we got there, the deputy planted his backside in the doorway, blocking my entrance to the room. "By the way," he said, resting one hand on the doorframe and the other on the crown of his nightstick, "Tommy Goings sends his regards."

My breath caught in mid-inhalation. "Oh?" I said, barely able to squeeze out the word.

"Yeah," he said, as if it were no big deal—greetings from a long-lost friend. "Tommy's my cousin. I spoke with him on the phone this afternoon and mentioned you were in town."

I felt my face grow hot. The pulse point in my temples throbbed. "How's Tommy doing?" I said in a creaky voice.

"He manages," Rawlins said. "Has himself one of those power wheelchairs. Goes all over town with it." He winked. "You should stop in and see him while you're here. Same house he and Gilbert lived in as boys. You remember it. You and Gilbert were just like this, right?" He held up crossed fingers.

I nodded. My mouth moved with the intention of making a verbal acknowledgment, but a stampede of thoughts clogged my brain and I could sort out nothing else to say.

Rawlins slapped the doorframe a couple of times before moving out of my way. "Have a nice visit with your sister," he said, and whistled his way back down the hall.

I staggered into the interview room and stood on rickety legs while the room dipped and swirled. I braced a hand against a wall for support and was still propped up that way when Libby rushed into the room and threw her arms around me.

"Thank you for coming back," she said, nestling against me. When I didn't immediately respond, she pulled back from me. "Are you okay? You look pale."

I forced a smile. "I'm fine. Just got a little dizzy for a moment. Too many hours on the road and too little sleep, I guess."

"Come sit down," Libby said, pulling me over to the table. She plopped down in a chair next to me. "Did you go see Mom?"

"I . . . uh . . ." was all I could get out as I fought to reestablish rational thought after suffering cognitive whiplash during my exchange with Deputy Rawlins about Tommy and his brother Gilbert. It was Gilbert and I who had sentenced Tommy to a lifetime of wheelchair use.

I gave my head a brisk shake in an effort to rid my mind of the voices calling me back to the past. *Stay in the present. Focus on the moment.* "Mom? Oh . . . yes. I went to see her. She's worried about you, of course. But I assured her you were okay and that the attorney is doing everything he can to get you released on bail tomorrow."

"Thank you. I know that couldn't have been easy for you, going back—"

"I went to see Bobby Hobson," I said, preferring to steer the conversation in a difference direction.

Libby's face shuttered.

"He didn't have much to say about what happened."

She sneered. "Pleaded total ignorance, I suppose."

"That's about it."

"And you expected otherwise?"

"No," I said. "I know Bobby better than that. But it was important that I talk to him if for no other reason than to let him know I'll not sit idly by and watch you go to prison on account of some tiff with him."

Libby didn't say anything.

I swung around in my chair and faced her squarely, my mind fixed now on the objective at hand—getting her to cooperate in her own defense. "Here's the thing, Sis. Bobby's not talking, and I don't think he ever will, which makes it all the more important that you tell me what happened between the two of you."

"Did you watch the DVD the lawyer gave you?"

I told her I had.

"Then you know what happened."

"But I don't know *why* it happened," I said. "And if I don't know *why*, I don't know how to help you." I tossed up my hands in frustration. "I don't even know where to start, and neither does your attorney."

Libby's lower lip protruded. "Please, Darryl," she said, her eyes pleading for understanding, "don't ask me to talk about it."

"But—"

"Please."

"Libby, I'm only trying—"

Her face became an emoji of woe.

I heaved a sigh. "Okay," I said, sensing the depth of her distress. Something big—and, for now, unbearable—dwelt at the core of this incident, something Libby couldn't yet bring herself to face up to. I identified with her plight and my heart went out to her. Things happen, awful things you don't want to think about, much less talk about. So you blockade the door to the memory of those events. You know what's behind that door and you don't want to open it. You simply want to forget.

I kissed Libby's forehead the way I used to when she was little. And in my mind, she remained that little girl—that rambunctious, freckle-faced kid who, whenever I tried to leave our parents' house without her, clung to my back like a Rhesus monkey until I promised to bring her home a surprise, by which she meant something sweet, preferably containing chocolate.

As a child, Libby was equal parts feisty and free-spirited. When she was in first grade, a boy sitting in the desk behind hers kept yanking on her ponytail and calling her names like *horse lips* and *pony face*. Instead of complaining to the teacher, she got a pair of Mother's sewing scissors and cut off her pony tail. She taped it to the back of a photo of herself and, the next day at school, gave it to the boy. "Is this what you wanted?" she asked him. The boy was so shocked by the *gift* and Libby's new boyish look that he burst into tears. "I didn't mean for you to do that," he said. "I know," Libby told him, "and I didn't mean to make you cry." The boy sniffled. "I'm not crying," he said, "and I don't want your dirty ol' hair." But he never taunted her again, and she never let her hair grow long after that.

I gave her another peck, this time on the cheek. "I'll let it go for now," I said. "But eventually you'll have to open up about what happened, or things could go very badly for you. Do you understand that?"

She drew up her legs and hugged her knees. "Yes," she said. "I'm not stupid."

Stubborn, yes. Stupid, no.

I got to my feet, the act seeming to take more effort than usual. "Are you going to be all right, spending another night in here?"

"It's not so bad," she said, obviously putting on a brave face for my benefit. "Earlier, a man in the holding cell next to mine was yelling and banging on the door, and that made me nervous. But after a while they took him out, and it's been quiet since."

"Well, hopefully, we can get you out of this place tomorrow. Mr. Broward says I can go to the arraignment, and I will. But I'll come back here in the morning to see you first."

"Thank you," Libby said, managing a fragile smile.

I was about to press the button on the wall, signaling the end of my visit, when my thoughts went back to my arrival at the sheriff's office minutes earlier.

"What do you know about Deputy Rawlins?" I said.

"Ted? Not much. Why?"

"This afternoon when I first got here, he knew who I was, but I don't remember him. And he said something to me just now that... surprised me."

Libby hitched her shoulders. "All I know is he moved to Grotin not long after you left—from Kansas City, I think. But I understand he has family here that he visited sometimes when he was a kid. So what did he say to you?"

"Nothing important. It just brought back memories of something that happened years ago, about the time you were born."

"Oh," she said, without probing for more of an explanation, for which I was grateful.

I took her hand and pulled her to her feet, noticing as I did that her fingernails looked more chewed than filed.

She noticed my noticing and balled her hands into fists, concealing her ragged nails. "A bad habit I've been trying to break," she said. "That's why I was carrying around the fingernail file—to keep my nails trim so I wouldn't chew on them."

Her comment called to mind something I'd been curious about but had yet to follow up on. "Where in the world did you get a pearl-handled nail file?"

"It was Mom's," she said. "Apparently, at one time she was into cosmetology."

"Yeah—thirty years ago."

"Well, I wasn't around then, so I don't know. But remember all those boxes stacked in the corner of the basement Mom told us to stay out of? I went through them once when she was gone from the house. What I discovered was all kinds of beauty supplies: combs and brushes, clippers and blowers, makeup kits, bottles of nail polish, creams and lotions. Enough supplies to stock a salon. That's where I found the fingernail file."

I would have thought that odd had I not known my mother so well. She just couldn't let go of the past.

I gave Libby a goodbye hug and punched the button on the wall.

12

I DROVE BACK to the Prairie Inn and parked in front of my motel room, but was unable to dislodge myself from behind the wheel. In front of me was a row of darkened windows—empty rooms waiting like discarded lovers for someone's return. Behind me, reflected in the rearview mirror, the motel's red neon VACANCY sign pulsed on and off like a beating heart.

I closed my eyes and felt the clutch of my exhaustion. Multiple body parts lodged complaints and my mind threatened to go on strike. A two-hour nap had not been enough. I wanted to return to my room and give myself over to the nothingness of dreamless sleep. But I knew that wasn't going to happen anytime soon.

Even if I went to bed and managed to doze off, there would be nothing peaceful in the dream world that populated my slumber. Tommy Goings and his older brother, Gilbert, would be there, as they were in the nightmares I'd had for months after the incident Deputy Rawlins had conjured up with his *regards* from Tommy. That was a long time ago. But regret has longevity, a fact that, for reasons of his own, Rawlins was happy to exploit.

Gilbert Goings had been my best friend at the time of the incident. Gilbert and I were nine years old. Tommy was three. It had happened on the day my sister Libby was born. My mother had gone into labor and Dad had taken her to the hospital. Gilbert's mom said I could stay at their house while my mom was in the hospital. Gilbert and I were at each other's house a lot so it was nothing new.

What was new was the handgun that Gilbert's mom had recently purchased. She and Gilbert's dad were divorced. There'd been reports of prowlers in the neighborhood at night. A few break-ins had occurred, and one woman living alone had allegedly been assaulted. Gilbert's mom decided she should have a gun for protection. She kept it in the drawer of the nightstand beside her bed. She hadn't told Gilbert about the gun, but he'd heard her talk about it on the phone with a girlfriend of hers.

The day my mother had gone into labor and I was sent to Gilbert's house was the day of Mrs. Goings regular monthly hair appointment. "I'll only be gone an hour or so," she told me and Gilbert. "You two stay in the house or the yard, and keep an eye on Tommy." We promised to do that.

As soon as his mom was gone, Gilbert said, "I want to show you something." He told Tommy to stay downstairs. I followed Gilbert up the stairs and down the hall to his mother's bedroom. He opened the nightstand drawer and there was the gun. It was small and silver and shiny and I thought it might be a toy.

"It's real," Gilbert said.

I shrank back from it, feeling a rush of terror, as if it were a snake about to strike, because that's what I envisioned it to be.

Gilbert reached for the gun.

I pushed his hand away. "Don't touch it. It might be loaded."

My mom never allowed guns in our house. I didn't know why at the time that she was so anti-gun. It wasn't until years later I learned that she'd had a brother who committed suicide when he was fourteen by putting a pistol in his mouth and pulling the trigger. As a result of that tragedy, my mother viewed guns as forbidden objects. I remember her saying to me, "You wouldn't want me to put a rattlesnake in your bed, would you? Well, that's what having a gun in the house is like."

"I'll be careful," Gilbert said, nudging me aside. "My dad has guns and lets me shoot them all the time."

I knew this to be true, because Gilbert's dad had invited me to go target shooting with them. The targets were beer cans and bottles he tossed into the back of his pickup after emptying them. But I never went with them, and I rarely visited Gilbert at his dad's house, because I knew about the guns.

Gilbert reached into the drawer and brought out the pistol. "It's not as heavy as my dad's," he said, hefting it in his hand. "I guess it's a girl's gun." He gripped the handle and aimed the barrel at a painting on the wall above the bed of a woman swinging on a swing that hung from a tree, her skirt puffed up by the breeze her movement created. "Bang," Gilbert said. He swiveled around and pointed the gun at a mirrored vanity, at my reflection in the mirror. "You're dead," he said. He grinned as he held the gun out to me. "Want to hold it?"

I shook my head and took a step back.

"Are you afraid?"

"No," I said, but my legs were quivering and I felt a compulsion to run. My mother had convinced me that guns and poisonous snakes were equally dangerous. I didn't want to handle either one. "I . . . I just don't want to hold it."

Gilbert put the gun flat against his hip, as if holstering it, then he jerked it up and aimed it away from his body, mimicking a quick draw. "If someone breaks into our house, my mother will shoot him dead."

"You better put it away before she comes home," I said, doing my best to keep the fear out of my voice. "I don't think she'd want you playing with it."

"She'll be gone at least an hour."

"Let's go outside," I said.

"You sure you don't want to hold it?"

"I'm sure."

"Don't be afraid," Gilbert said, grasping my wrist and pressing the gun grip into my palm.

Instinctively, I jerked my hand away.

Whose finger or what force caused the gun to fire, we never knew. But it went off with an earsplitting crack and enough recoil to cause it to come free of any hand and drop to the floor. Horrified, Gilbert and I both jumped back from it as if it *were* a poisonous snake. I stared at Gilbert's startled face as he stared at mine. Then, through the noise fog in our ears came the most sickening of sounds—the anguished moan of a child.

We looked toward the sound and saw little Tommy in the doorway, curled up in a ball on the floor. We thought he was downstairs.

The moment I saw the ribbon of blood on the carpet next to Tommy's twitching body, I screamed and ran blindly—down the stairs, through the foyer, out the front door of the house. That was where I ran smack into the mailman, who'd just stepped up onto the porch. "What the—" he said. I kept running and didn't stop until I got home, where I crawled under my bed and stayed there until my father found me six hours later.

"You have a new sister," he told me.

"We killed Tommy," I said.

"No," he said, but I didn't believe him.

Later I learned that he'd been telling the truth. The mailman, sensing something wasn't right inside the house, had investigated and found Gilbert upstairs sitting on the floor beside Tommy, crying. He immediately called 911.

The bullet, it turned out, had struck Tommy an inch below the belly button. It didn't meet much resistance until it reached his spine. He survived six hours of surgery, but never walked again.

Gilbert and I were never friends after that. When he was fifteen, Gilbert was arrested for selling pot and pills at school and was sent to a juvie facility in Salina for rehabilitation. Two years later, back at home, he overdosed on his mother's anti-anxiety medication and spent three days in a coma before waking up in his hospital bed and telling his mom, "Why don't you just shoot me." She reportedly slapped him. When he turned eighteen a few months before I did, he tried to join the army but was refused because of his history of using and selling drugs and his suicide attempt. In response to this rejection, he got one of his father's guns, a Glock 19, and shot up a military recruitment office in Beloit. Last I heard, he was serving time at Leavenworth.

I buried my face in my hands now as the antique pain of remembrance welled up inside me. If I could have, I would have plucked out my mind's eye. But memory is a diary whose pages cannot be torn out or rendered unreadable, and Deputy Rawlins was unkind enough to use this reality against me, as if I hadn't suffered enough already from the sting of regret.

I sat quietly for a time, trying unsuccessfully to harness my runaway emotions. Sleep was not an option for me now—not for a while anyway. And I knew that this was only the beginning of my wakefulness. Rawlins's sucker punch was merely one of many blows to my psychic suit of armor I could expect now that I was back in Grotin. Already the castle walls of my sweet forgetfulness were tumbling down, and intruders from my past were pouring in, prepared to bear me back in time to the nightmarish days of my youth.

I felt numb as I got out of my car. I shambled aimlessly around the parking lot. The night sky was pocked with stars that pulsed as they glowed. A nimble breeze carried on its back broken fragments of sound—voices coming from an occupied motel room, music from the radio of a passing car, a dog barking in the distance, the tinkling of wind chimes. I blundered toward the door to my motel room, but my legs had other plans. Without my conscious participation, they performed a military-style about-face and headed for the lighted OPEN sign across the street.

13

IT WAS ALMOST ten o'clock when I entered the Silver Platter Diner. To my surprise, Debbie was still on duty.

"It's my night to close," she said, fatigue tugging at her eyelids as she wiped down the worn Formica countertop. She glanced up at a clock on the wall. "One more hour."

I suspected it was not going to be a productive hour. Besides me, the only customer in the place was an old man in bib overalls and a conductor's cap, sitting at the counter polishing off an order of biscuits and gravy, some of which had not made it past his beard.

I took a seat in a booth near the door and ordered some coffee with cream, which Debbie promptly delivered. I sat there sipping occasionally from my cup and staring out the window, all the doubts of the day scudding about in my head like leaves swirling in a rogue breeze.

At some point I realized that Debbie was sitting across from me in the booth. She had brought the coffee pot and a second cup. The man at the counter was gone. The kitchen area was dark.

"I seem to be keeping you from closing up," I said. The OPEN sign in the front window had winked out. Time had flapped its wings without my noticing.

"Actually, I've locked you in," she said. She poured coffee into a cup and lifted it to her lips.

"Ah, so I'm your captive."

"Only as long as you want to be."

I nodded and smiled, and we both fell silent, allowing the moment to spool itself out in a direction of its own choosing.

"It's strange being back," I finally said, punctuating my remark with a sigh. "You try to put things behind you, but . . ."

"Don't I know it," Debbie said, her voice weighted with weariness.

I stared at a cream-colored swirl in my coffee cup and waited for her to say more.

"Sorry," she said, making a move to get up. "But you're not the only one in this town with regrets."

I reached over and touched her arm. "Please stay," I said, "I'd like to ask you something."

She settled back into the booth.

"Have you seen the video of the . . . uh . . . *incident* at the latest board of commissioners' meeting?"

Debbie grimaced, displaying her endearingly crooked front teeth. "I think just about everyone in the county has," she said. "And thousands of other people too. It went viral on the internet."

I groaned. "I guess I shouldn't be surprised. So, is there anything you can tell me that might help me understand why Libby would have done something like that?"

She ran a finger around the rim of her coffee cup as if it were a wine glass she was trying to make sing. "All I know is that Libby hasn't been the same since the accident."

My mind did a double take on those words. "What accident?"

"You don't know about the car accident?"

I shook my head.

"Hmmm," Debbie said in a melodic tone that conveyed surprise. She wriggled her mouth and nose in the rabbit-like gesture I'd seen her make many times in her youth. "Well, about six months ago, Libby and RuAnn Tolliver were coming back from a party in Thomasville. They were in RuAnn's Toyota but Libby was driving, when some old man in a pickup truck—drunk out of his mind, I'm told—ran them off the road. Just veered right into them. Libby swerved and they went off the road and overturned in a ditch. Libby wasn't hurt other than some bruises, but RuAnn suffered a head injury that messed up something in her brain."

"What do you mean *messed up*?"

"I don't know all the details, but RuAnn is like retarded or something now. No one knows for sure because her folks keep her at home all the time except for trips to an out-of-town rehab clinic. Libby is the only person they've let visit her since the accident. But I've heard that, mentally, RuAnn is like a child again."

I sat there wondering why Libby had never mentioned any of this to me. I knew that she and RuAnn Tolliver had been BFFs during their teen years and that their friendship had continued after high school when they'd both gone to work as interns at the local office of the Farm Bureau. They'd even shared an apartment in Grotin for a time. But recently RuAnn had moved back in with her parents (because of the accident?), and Libby, unable to afford the place on her own and uncomfortable with the idea of a different roommate, had moved back in with Mom.

I'd always been happy for my sister that she had such a fast friend in RuAnn, because I'd had nothing of the kind growing up. Yet I'd wondered about the differences in their family backgrounds and how that would ultimately play out.

Whereas the Coombs had a relatively brief and spotty history in the county, the Tollivers were well-known and well-respected members of the community. They were, in fact, direct descendants of Major Zack Tolliver, a Civil War veteran who was one of the original settlers in Harbin County. Also, the current Mr. and Mrs. Tolliver were both champion skeet shooters. Skeet shooting was a popular sport in these parts, although I'd never developed an appreciation for it myself. The Tollivers were apparently shrewd businesspeople as well. Despite owning some of the least productive farmland in the county, they had managed over the years to expand their holdings to include large tracts of land north of Grotin, well beyond the original Tolliver homestead.

My recollection of RuAnn herself was sketchy. She was in the same grade as Libby, which would put her in the third grade when I'd last seen her at a May Day event at the elementary school a few weeks before I left town. She and Libby were both scrawny kids back then.

As for the other members of the Tolliver family, it was RuAnn's sister, Ashley, I remembered most. Ashley Tolliver, who was a year behind me in school, was gorgeous. She had the kind of radiant beauty that, like direct sunlight, you could look at only so long before you had to turn away. She was a cheerleader and every boy in the school had a crush on her, me included, although I never had the courage to ask her out. But I remember that Bobby Hobson had asked her out—numerous times, I'd heard—and she turned him down every time. She may have been the only girl in school to say no to Bobby.

Debbie drank from her cup and set it down. "Like I said, Libby hasn't been herself since the accident. It's like she's mad at the world or something. She hardly talks to anyone anymore. I think she blames herself for what happened to RuAnn, even though the accident wasn't her fault."

I groped in my mind for the significance of what I'd just heard, but came up empty-handed. "Well, it would be just like

Libby to blame herself," I said, "especially if RuAnn did incur some brain damage in the accident. But what this might have to do with her stabbing Bobby, I can't imagine."

"Neither can I," Debbie said. She got up and began clearing the table. "But I can imagine myself home in bed, where I will pour myself a cup of sleep and dip in it with cookie dreams. But for that to happen, I'm going to have to kick you out of this place."

"No violence necessary," I said, rising. "Thanks for the talk."

Debbie's lips formed a labored smile. "Thanks for the company."

I was headed for the door when she called out to me. "I would have gone out with you, you know—if you'd asked."

I looked back at her, but experiencing a déjà-vu moment of embarrassment, became tongue-tied.

Her smile was bright and easy now. "I've always been a sucker for blue eyes and a bashful smile. Besides, you're a lot better-looking than you give yourself credit for."

"How . . . ?"

She laughed. "Girls always know."

14

IT HAS BEEN my experience that sleep does not always equal rest; it is not necessarily "the balm of hurt minds," as one Will Shakespeare has asserted. To the contrary, sleep is often an agitator, a thief of the sought-after sanctuary of slumber. After my late-night visit with Debbie, I crawled into bed in my motel room and, surrendering to my exhaustion, finally dropped off to sleep. I awoke the next morning feeling as if I'd been on a forced march all night. My legs cramped, my body was lathered in sweat, and my tongue was so dry and swollen I had trouble swallowing.

I sat up in bed and aimed my fuzzy vision at the red numbers of the digital alarm clock on the nightstand. The numbers wavered like flames in a fake fireplace, but I came to understand that it was a few minutes after eight o'clock. I needed to get moving. Libby's arraignment was scheduled for ten, and I had promised to come see her before then.

Doing my best to shed my delirium, I showered and dressed, and then dragged myself over to the Silver Platter. I ordered coffee and a double order of toast from a waitress I didn't recognize and who gave no indication of knowing me.

While I sipped coffee and waited for my toast, I called Charlotte. "Sorry to bother you at work," I told her when she answered, "but I needed to hear your voice."

"That bad, eh?" she said.

I filled her in on the events leading up to that moment.

"Is there anything you can do?" she said.

"I don't know. That's what I'm trying to figure out. Something's going on here and I need to get to the heart of it, but I don't know where to start."

"You'll think of something. After all," she said, her voice becoming light and saucy, "you're very resourceful."

I laughed, and that moment of levity was like a sip of oxygen-rich air. "That's only because you bring out my creative side," I said. "I don't think the people of Grotin are as susceptible to my charms as you are."

"I pity them."

My toast arrived. "I'll let you go now," I said. "I'll call you again soon."

I slathered strawberry jam on a slice of toast, took a bite, and after a few chews, washed it down with a swig of coffee. I consumed the remaining stack of toast in a similar manner, and as I did, my thoughts drifted back, longingly, to San Antonio, my city of refuge for the last ten years, and to Charlotte. Our relationship was such that we could go for days without seeing or talking to each other and reconnect as if time was never a bridge too far. But I missed her. Although neither of us had been willing to make a commitment that included disrobing our inner selves, she was the one constant in my life.

We'd met at work, and looking back I still wondered at our coming together, because it seemed so improbable at the time, but felt so inevitable now.

I was eighteen years old when I first stepped on Texas soil, too young and naïve even to appreciate the desperation of my circumstances. But I was determined to embrace my new surroundings. San Antonio is a big, amorphous town—multicultural, inclusive, at once raucous and reverent—a place where you can lose yourself in order to find yourself. And that's what I set about doing.

Within days of arriving in the Alamo City, I got a job as a flunky at a car wash and was invited to crash on the couch of a fellow employee, a young Mexican named Ricardo, who introduced me to mescal and told me he could arrange for me to sleep with his cousin. "She's a little overweight," he said, "and has a mustache, but she's very kind in bed, I'm told."

I declined his offer and as soon as I could afford it rented a room of my own near the local community college and began taking classes at night: accounting, with an eye toward getting a job; philosophy, out of a desire to make some sense of the universe. For the next few years, I did little more than work and study. With an A.A. degree in accounting in hand, I got a job keeping the books for a small engineering firm. I also enrolled in upper-division courses at UT San Antonio. For the next few years, again, I did little more than work and study.

It was on my current job at the accounting firm of Campbell and Associates that I met Charlotte. After getting my bachelor's degree, I'd been hired as a junior accountant, which meant I was given accounts none of the senior accountants wanted. During my second year at Campbell and Associates, Charlotte came to work there as an assistant in the accounts receivable department. Accounts receivable was on the third floor, while the cubicles for the junior accountants were on the second floor, so some months passed before I had any contact with her.

She came downstairs one day to confer with the fellow in the cubicle next to mine about his client billing hours. He was new and the rules for billing were confusing. Every minute of your time had to be accounted for: face-time with clients, telephone time, records review, research, posting, preparation of reports. Unless you wanted to spend all your time accounting for your time, you learned to allot hours to each client's account the way auto mechanics bill—by charging the typical amount of time it takes to perform a certain task instead of the actual time spent. That way each client sees his bill as reasonable even if it isn't accurate. What had to be accurate were the books kept and the reports and tax returns prepared.

I listened to Charlotte interact with the new guy. Her voice was leading and instructive, while devoid of condescension and criticism. She used words like *preferred* and *helpful* as opposed to *requisite* and *obligatory*. She was dosing medicine and somehow making it taste good. I thought, if I ever have to be reproved for any reason, I want it to be by this woman.

I watched her leave the cubicle and walk away. She didn't look at me, but I knew she knew I was looking at her. She moved fluidly, with an understated grace. Everything about her was understated. She was dressed modestly in a loose-fitting gray pantsuit. Her jet-black hair was pinned up in a neat bun at the nape of her neck. Her makeup was sparingly and subtly applied. There was a tucked-in neatness about her that suggested reticence and restraint. She was captivating, I thought. But hers was a veiled enchantment, shorn of ornamentation, willfully kept in check, as if she had done everything possible to camouflage her beauty, having seen the danger in displaying how lovely she truly was.

After that day, I went out of my way to catch further glimpses of this lovely creature who seemed intent on going unnoticed. I observed that, coming to work and leaving, she always took the stairs and not the elevator, and so I started using the stairs as well. I found reasons to visit the third floor. I didn't speak to her, just ambled through the accounts receivable department as if it were the only way to get to where I was going. She would glance up and nod politely before going back to her work.

One day I asked a coworker about her. His name was Caleb. He was short and stout and single and we occasionally had a beer together after work. "Charlotte Robinson?" he said. "Nice girl. Good-looking, too, in an Amish sort of way. But don't waste your time on her. She's married. Haven't you seen the ring on her finger?" I hadn't.

The next time I saw Charlotte I made a point of looking at her hands. Sure enough, she wore a wedding band, or what looked like a wedding band, on the ring finger of her left hand. How could I not have noticed?

I decided it didn't matter. My interest in her, I told myself, transcended mere romantic fantasy. Here was a genuine mystery: a beautiful woman who, by all appearances, wanted to make herself invisible.

During the months that followed, whenever the opportunity arose—at the compulsory all-staff meetings or the occasional bonus presentation or her sporadic visits to the second floor—I observed Charlotte's behavior with increasing fascination. What I noticed was that she spoke only when necessary to do her job, or as a matter of courtesy, never engaging in idle chatter. She neither gave nor asked for anything beyond what the situation called for. She was courteous but not friendly. She smiled, but in a detached manner. It was a smile that said, "Nice doing business with you, but please keep your distance." So I did. But I continued wondering what she was all about, and how someone so alluring could be so self-contained.

At the end of one workday, when I was exiting the building, it happened that Charlotte was walking ahead of me. As we crossed the gleaming terrazzo tile in the lobby, the heel of one of her shoes (she always wore flats, while most of the other women in the firm wore high heels) found something slick on the floor. Her foot went out from under her. Her body lurched to the side and she would have gone down had I not been able to reach out and get an arm around her waist.

I helped her regain an upright posture, then stepped back from her.

She pivoted and gazed at me, and what I saw in her eyes at that moment was vulnerability. The near fall had caused her to drop her guard, had unveiled her in a way that exposed some hidden yearning. I thought I must have learned something about her that she hadn't wanted to share, but I couldn't put my finger on what it was.

She recovered quickly. "Thank you," she said with a casual nod. She scraped the offending shoe on the floor, testing its traction, then continued walking toward the exit door.

For some time after that the memory of that moment lingered with me like an unsatisfied longing—the feeling of Charlotte's weight against my arm as I protected her from a fall, and in response her unguarded gaze that told me there was more to her than meets the eye.

I noticed after that a slight alteration in her demeanor toward me. Whenever our paths crossed, she made eye contact and sent a wisp of a smile my way. I never had the sense that she was flirting with me. On the contrary, she seemed to be thanking me for keeping my distance.

Which got me to thinking.

One day I decided to follow up on my line of thought. I left my desk a few minutes early and waited at the bottom of the stairs for Charlotte to appear. When she did, I fell in step beside her. She didn't say anything, just kept walking in her usual way, which is to say straight ahead, as if to prove that the shortest distance between two points is a straight line.

"You're not married, are you?" I said to her.

The thought had occurred to me that, despite the ring on her finger and her decorous behavior, Charlotte Robinson did not exhibit the tendencies of a married woman. It was no great insight into the feminine mystique that led me to this conclusion. I had minimal experience with members of the opposite sex from which to draw. As a teenager, I had viewed girls as a foreign country whose territory I had not the proper visa to explore. During my college years, having gained a measure of confidence in myself through my academic achievements, I was emboldened to enter the dating scene, which I did with mixed results—namely, I found the experience to be equal parts pleasure and pain. Dating, it seemed to me, served mostly to validate the difference in perception between men and women exhibited by the fact that they seldom give the same answer to the same question.

More recently, seeking a better grasp of the workings of the female psyche, I had done some reading on the subject. I recalled one article in particular that discussed the psychology of married women. The author of the article asserted that married women have no lesser need than unmarried women to feel attractive to men in general—that is, to men other than their husbands. I didn't understand why this would be so. But the author of the study was adamant in her thesis that married women crave romance as much, or more, than single women. That Charlotte Robinson did not seem to fit within this mindset got me to thinking.

"What did you say?" Charlotte said, pulling up short.

"I said, you're not married, are you?"

Charlotte regarded me for a long moment, as if turning over in her mind my motive for questioning her in this intimate way. Her lips parted as if she were about to issue a rebuttal to my remark. But she stopped herself—stopped herself, I suspect, from saying what any other woman would have said under the circumstances: *That's none of your business.*

Instead, she said, "No. The wedding ring was my grandmother's."

"Ahh, *she* was married."

"Why, yes," Charlotte said, and smiled as if in forgiveness of my impertinence.

The next day, after work, I asked her out. She declined. I asked her out again the following week, and the week after that. Again, each time, she declined.

"Why do you want to go out with me?" she said.

"You seem like a nice person," I told her. "I'd like to get to know you better."

"And what if you find out I'm not such a nice person?"

"Then I'll dump you like soured milk."

Her eyelids fluttered. "Well, that certainly is an honest answer."

"I believe in honesty at all cost," I said, "unless the cost is too great."

I don't know if it was my feeble attempts at humor or my persistence that won her over, but she finally agreed to go out with me. We went to dinner at a sidewalk café downtown along the river that runs through the city. We sat at a table under a colored umbrella that was in a line of tables under colored umbrellas situated along the riverbank. It was a Friday night in May. The River Walk was bustling with people. On the water, cruise boats glided by loaded with tourists beaming with delight. The evening air was full of music and light-hearted voices and the competing aromas wafting from the kitchens of the riverside restaurants.

I'm not sure what I expected of the evening, or what were Charlotte's expectations, but there seemed to be from the outset a mutual understanding that our coming together was solely about the here and now—the shared moment. Dispensed with were the rituals of dating. I didn't have to face the dreaded opening salvo of every other first date I'd had: *So, tell me about yourself.*

In fact, we talked sparingly as we immersed ourselves in the chaotic wonder of our surroundings.

"I love this town," Charlotte said.

"What do you love about it?"

"It's so full of distractions," she said, and she was right.

After dinner we strolled along the River Walk in company with the tide of humanity that flowed through the heart of the city this balmy night—although the scene was so aglow with light from the shops and restaurants on both sides of the river and the multitude of string lights draping the trees that you wouldn't have supposed it was night.

Charlotte let me hold her hand. I remember feeling happier than I'd been in a long time. I'd had a glass of wine with dinner, but now I was feeling punch-drunk on the pleasure of this beautiful woman's company.

We paused on a bridge that arched over the river and observed the gleeful faces of the pleasure seekers on a boat that was about to pass under the bridge. Not far away a mariachi band punctured the air with a rousing rendition of "Cuando Calienta El Sol."

Charlotte rose on her tiptoes and put her lips close to my ear. "Are we going to make love tonight?"

The question caught me off guard, and I was momentarily at a loss for how to respond. Was her question an invitation or a test? I knew that I wanted to make love to this woman. Had imagined it from the moment I first saw her. But how was I to respond to such a query?

"Absolutely," I said, feeling a rush of desire that loosened something deep inside me.

She squeezed my hand. "Good."

And we did make love that night, and on many succeeding nights. But in many ways, Charlotte continued to remain a mystery to me. We spent a lot of time together after that first glorious encounter, and I discovered many things about her. She was fun, she was smart, she was a great listener and an astute observer of the world around her. She kept up on current events and held her own in conversations involving a wide range of issues. But one subject she didn't care to talk about was herself. Referring to her own personal history, she would grin coyly and say, "My life was boring until I met you."

I couldn't help but wonder about her lack of openness about herself, why she was so quick to shut the door to any discussion of her past. I speculated that there must have been something in her former life—some tragic loss—that had caused her to create forbidden rooms in her mind that no one, not even me, was allowed to enter. But to press her on the issue would have been to open myself up to the same questioning, and I did not care to visit the boneyard of my own past.

So there was about Charlotte this reservation that never went away, except in the bedroom. There, she abandoned all sense of privacy. There, she was this amazing flower that seemed to bloom only in my presence. And we reveled in each other's sensuality because that is what we had to offer one another.

It was shortly after nine o'clock by the time I washed down the last morsel of toast and jam with a final gulp of coffee. I was still waiting for the caffeine to kick in when I paid my bill and left.

15

TEN MINUTES LATER, I entered the sheriff's office to find Deputy Rawlins back at the duty desk. He made eye contact with me and held it briefly before getting up and slogging over to the counter as if he were wearing ankle weights. Dispensing with the I.D. check, he slid the sign-in sheet across the counter.

"We'll be taking Libby to the courthouse in twenty minutes," he said, "so talk fast."

I nodded in acknowledgment as I began emptying my pockets.

When I stepped into the interview room, I was surprised to see Libby already there, sitting in a chair at the little table. She was bent over with her arms crossed at her midsection as if suffering from a stomachache. Her hair was matted down in the back and stuck out like ruffled feathers on the sides. Her jumpsuit sagged lower on one shoulder than the other, and there was a whitish stain breast high that I hadn't noticed before. Breakfast oatmeal dribble that hadn't been wiped off?

"Are you okay?" I said, pulling up a chair and sitting down next to her.

She looked at me with eyes plagued with misgiving. "The attorney says I might not get to go home today."

"When did he tell you that?"

"Just now. I mean, a little while ago. He was here and we talked—he talked anyway. Then he left. And I told the officer who was going to take me back to my cell that I wanted to wait here for you, and he said you'd better show up soon because they had to take me to the courthouse before long, and I said you'd be here any minute, and I was right. But we don't have much time."

She was babbling, her voice skating along the edge of panic.

I gave her knee a gentle squeeze. "Mr. Broward will do everything he can to get you out of here as soon as possible. But if you won't talk—"

She flailed her arms as if clearing the air of smoke. "I know, I know," she said. "That's what the attorney keeps saying. He wants me to make a statement in court. Tell the judge why I stabbed Bobby. But I won't do it." She pounded her thighs with her fists. "I *can't* do it."

I was inclined to push back against her obstinacy with a serious talking to, but something stopped me—a feeling that pressuring her at this moment would only make matters worse, would only tighten the knot of her resistance to assisting with her defense.

"Libby, why didn't you tell me about the car accident?" I said, hoping for movement on a different front.

She looked at me sharply. "Who told you about the accident?"

"Debbie Sprague, or whatever her married name is. She said you were driving RuAnn Tolliver's car and RuAnn was with you."

Libby responded by drawing her lips inward in a tight line.

"Please, Sis," I said. "You know I only want to help. Just tell me about the accident—that's all I'm asking."

She snuffled. "There's nothing to tell. Some drunk ran us

off the road. He came straight at us. I had no place to go but into the ditch."

"Debbie said RuAnn suffered a head injury."

Libby angled her face away.

"Possibly some brain damage."

"I don't want to talk about that," she said, then clamped her mouth shut so tightly her jaw muscles bulged.

"All right," I said, feeling a surge of irritation that had me kneading the heel of one hand with the knuckles of the other. "I can't force you to talk. But all this silence from you isn't helping . . . *anybody*."

Libby's face crumpled. "Oh, Darryl, please don't be angry with me."

"I'm not angry with you," I said, although anger was much akin to what I felt at the moment. I leaned into her and massaged her back through the coarse-fibered jumpsuit. "I'm just troubled because I don't know how to help you."

"Just your being here helps."

"But I can't stay here forever. And if you end up going to jail, I'll never forgive myself if there was something I could have done and didn't."

"I'm not sure anyone or anything can help me now," she said.

I was about to object when my words were preempted by knocking at the door. Her escort to the courthouse had arrived.

I gave her a last-minute hug. "Don't give up," I told her, but even to my ears the words rang hollow.

LIBERTY BAIL SERVICES is on the first floor of a converted boarding house across the street from the Harbin County Courthouse. The sign on the storefront promises SPEEDY, RELIABLE SERVICE. I looked around for a drive-through window but didn't see one. Not that speedy.

Inside, a young woman with purple hair and jade lipstick greeted me, took my name, and offered me a cup of tea, which I declined. "Jerry is with a client right now," she said, "but he shouldn't be long. Please have a seat."

It was Harvey Broward who had suggested I go see Jerry at Liberty Bail. "I'm sorry," he had said minutes earlier as we huddled in an alcove outside Courtroom B, on the second floor of the county courthouse, following Libby's arraignment. "I was hoping for a better outcome."

I hung my head. "So was I."

The proceedings had lasted a whole two minutes, and from where I sat in a mostly deserted public gallery, it hardly resembled a fair fight.

Following Libby's plea of not guilty to a charge of attempted murder, the judge—perched on his throne in his magisterial robe, wielding his authority like a scepter—listened with imperial indifference as the opposing counsels debated the issue of bail.

Harvey Broward, speaking first, argued that Libby should be released on her own recognizance. "She's nineteen years old, your honor. She's a lifelong resident of Grotin who lives with her mother. She has no criminal history; nor has she ever been in any kind of trouble. She's not a flight risk or a danger to herself or others."

The county attorney, a man of girth with a gravelly voice, was of a different opinion. "The state vehemently disagrees, your honor. We believe that, given the seriousness of the charge and the fact that the victim is a public official, the defendant should be held without bail pending trial."

"Your honor, that's absolutely uncalled for," Broward replied. "The CA's office knows it is overreaching when it comes to the charge brought against my client. The weapon in this so-called attempted murder was a fingernail file. Furthermore—"

But the judge had already made up his mind, and the gavel went down. "Your positions are duly noted, counselors," he said. "Bail is hereby set at $250,000. Defendant has forty-eight hours to post bail."

"But your honor, that amount—"

"Next case."

Libby shot a frightened look my way as the bailiff steered her out of the courtroom. Dazed by this lightning bolt of *justice*, I staggered to my feet, raised my hand in a pathetic wave, and mouthed "It'll be okay," as if I knew something she didn't.

As I turned to leave the courtroom, I was confronted by a young man with a notepad and pen in hand. He was of slight build, had spiked hair, and a nose too big for his face. He'd been the only other person in the public gallery during the arraignment, but I had paid him no mind, assuming he was there for a subsequent case. It was his T-shirt that caught my eye now. It was white with the image of a collar and a red-and-black-striped necktie imprinted on its front. A millennial version of business attire?

"I'm Roger Stokes with the *Harbin County Journal*," he said. "Can I get a statement from you regarding your sister's case? Can you tell me why she stabbed Commissioner Hobson?"

I could not, and would not if I could. "Thank you for your interest," I said, "but I have no comment at this time."

"Why are you in town? I understand you've been gone from Grotin for ten years."

"As I stated, I have nothing to say."

I brushed past the young man and met up with Harvey Broward as he came from behind the bar, looking as dejected as I felt.

"There's no way I can come up with that kind of money," I told the attorney as we conversed in the alcove outside Courtroom B.

He rifled through his briefcase and came out with a business card, which he handed to me. "Liberty Bail Services," he said. "Talk to Jerry. He's not a bundle of empathy, but he's honest." He rubbed the back of his neck. "In the meantime, I'll continue running a full court press on the county attorney. If I can get him to move off the attempted murder charge, then we should be able to get the bail reduced."

"That would be a good thing," I said, the figure $250,000 looming in my mind like a base-camp view of Mt. Everest.

"One other thing," Broward said. "Don't talk to Junior."

"Junior?"

"Young Roger Stokes. The kid with the notepad and the faux dress shirt and tie. He's the son of the publisher of the local newspaper. Fancies himself a latter-day muckraker. Wrong place, wrong century."

"Got it," I said.

I'd been sitting in the outer office of Liberty Bail Services for fifteen minutes when the door to Jerry's office opened and a middle-aged woman shuffled out, daubing her eyes with a wad of tissue. It wasn't an encouraging sight.

"Jerry will see you now," the receptionist said.

"I'm not sure how this works," I told the bail bondsman as I seated myself in the proffered chair in front of his desk. "My sister's in jail and the judge set her bail at $250,000. I'd like to get her released as soon as I can."

Jerry Renfro had a round face with fat cheeks. The soft flesh under his chin puffed out like the vocal sac of a frog. He rocked back in his armchair, studying me with one eye closed. I was sure he had heard my sad tale a thousand times and was doing his best not to exult in the fact that one man's misfortune is another man's gain.

"It's a straightforward business deal," he said, his chin-pouch flapping distractedly as he spoke. "Before setting your sister free, the court wants surety in the form of money or collateral that she will appear at any future court date. As a bail bondsman, I provide that surety. The courts here require 10 percent of the bail in cash and the rest in the form of a bond—a legally enforceable promise to pay if the terms of the bail are not met, which would be the case if your sister were to miss a future court date."

"She won't," I said firmly.

Jerry nodded. "Okay, then, in your sister's case the cash part of the bail is $25,000. That same sum is my fee for posting your sister's bail with the court. The fee must be paid up front and is nonrefundable. In addition, because of the hefty bond we're talking about here, you'll need to provide me with security in the form of assets equal in value to the full amount of the bail. This is my protection against the"—he made a swiping motion with his hands similar to that of a baseball umpire calling a baserunner safe—"*unlikely* event of forfeiture. Questions?"

"How the hell am I gonna come up with $25,000?"

Jerry Renfro tugged on one of his fleshy earlobes. "That, I'm afraid, I can't help you with."

I stared at the wedge of tissue billowing from the floral-patterned Kleenex box on Jerry's desk, but resisted its siren call.

16

A NEIGHBOR IN the apartment building where I live is a practitioner of scream therapy. Whenever she gets angry or frustrated or, as she puts it, needs to exhaust the emotional impurities that inevitably build up in one's psyche over time, she screams at the top of her lungs. She calls it *expunging the darkness*. "I go to some isolated place," she told me once, "to keep from raising the dead." This was after I had nearly broken down the door to her apartment one night to save her from some perceived horror.

I had just fallen asleep when I heard her murderous cries, so primal as to have emanated from the soundtrack of a slasher film. She opened her door, thankfully, before I broke my hand pounding on it. "I'm sorry," she said, gazing at me with the clear-eyed tranquility of a sanitized soul. "I should have gone out to my car—better soundproofing there. But I was already in bed and didn't want to dress."

"As long as you're okay," I said.

"Yes," she said. "Thanks for checking on me."

As I sat at the little table in my motel room, having arrived at a roadblock in my endeavor to help Libby, I was thinking that a primal scream might be in order. But the walls surrounding me now were no thicker than my apartment walls, and I didn't want someone calling the cops. So I sat there quietly holding in my emotional impurity in the hope that it would soon stop crying to be let out.

I was experiencing the concussive effects of having banged my head against the stone wall that was the issue of bail. Upon returning to my motel room following my visit with the bail bondsman, I had done an assessment of my resources to see how much of the $25,000 bail fee I could come up with. Between my checking and savings accounts, I had a whopping $3,000 in the bank. That was because most of my monthly paycheck went toward living expenses and student loan payments. I had a 401K currently worth about $12,000, but only half of that had vested and the maximum I could borrow was 50 percent of that, which would get me another $3,000. I could sell my car, which had a Kelly Blue Book value of about $6,000. In need of a quick sale, I'd be lucky to get $4,000 from a dealer. So, accruing every bit of cash I could in the time allotted by the judge, I would still fall $15,000 short of my goal.

The $250,000 in collateral was an even steeper hill to climb. I was not a man of property. I didn't own a home. Other than my 401K, I owned no other stocks or bonds. My mother, no doubt, would be willing to put up her house as security, but the old place couldn't be worth much more than twenty-five or thirty thousand dollars.

I hadn't even broached the subject when I'd called Mom to let her know Libby's release would be delayed for now.

"For *now*?" she said. "What in blazes does that mean?"

"I'm not sure, Mom," I said, knowing that no answer I gave would satisfy her. "I'll have the attorney call you and explain."

I pushed myself up from the little table now and padded restlessly about the motel room as the walls seemed to close in on me. My effort to help Libby had come to an inauspicious standstill. I couldn't raise the bail money. I couldn't convince my sister to talk to me. And I had no notion as to what to do next.

On impulse, I spread my arms and lifted my eyes to the heavens—to the motel room ceiling, anyway. "So, what the hell am I supposed to do now?" I said aloud, but not so loud as to raise the dead.

What I finally decided to do, for sanity's sake, was to set aside for the time being the issue of bail and concentrate on another matter critical to Libby's case—motive. The big question lingered: Why did Libby stab Bobby Hobson? Logic dictated that there must have been a reason for her to do what she did. You don't go around stabbing people out of boredom. But the only hint I had as to an explanation of her uncharacteristic behavior was that, according to Debbie anyway, Libby hadn't been herself since the car accident in which RuAnn had been injured.

I told myself that what I needed to do was to approach the question of motive as if it were a logic puzzle waiting for me to solve. The difficulty inherent in this strategy was that deductive reasoning was not my strong suit. I was an accountant, not a detective. I made entries in journals and ledgers following fixed rules, the underlying principle being *X minus Y must equal Z or you've screwed up*. But on the plus side, I reminded myself, I was a reasonably intelligent man, had played the game Clue as a kid, and had paid enough attention in school to be able to construct a basic syllogism. This didn't exactly qualify me for induction into the Sherlock Holmes Investigative Hall of Fame, but it would have to do.

Having thus fortified myself with this pathetic dose of positive thinking, I took up pen and memo pad and began making notes. First I listed everything I knew relative to Libby's case, which wasn't much. Then I wrote down the questions that each of these facts called to mind. Needless to say, I ended up with more questions than affirmations.

When finished, I reviewed my list:

(1) Libby stabbed Bobby Hobson with a fingernail file during a Harbin County Board of Commissioners' meeting. (Questions: Why did she stab him? Why with a fingernail file? And why would she have done such a thing during a public meeting she must have known was being recorded? Did Libby and Bobby have a history—as in, a prior relationship?)

(2) Libby and RuAnn, who have been the best of friends for many years, were in a car accident in which RuAnn suffered brain damage. Libby reportedly has not been herself since the accident. (Question: What if anything does this have to do with the stabbing?)

It wasn't much to go on, but it served to get my deductive juices flowing. I decided to concentrate on one question at a time, starting with the one I thought I could answer based on what Libby had already told me: Why had she used a fingernail file when assaulting Bobby?

When, initially, I'd asked my sister about the stabbing, assuming her weapon of choice had been a knife, she'd informed me otherwise. She hadn't stabbed Bobby with a knife, she told me. She'd used "the only sharp object" in her purse—a metal fingernail file. I had found this amusing at the time, but now, having figuratively donned my deerstalker cap, I considered the implications of this disclosure.

What it told me was that she had not *planned* to assault Bobby, at least not at the time and place she did, or she would have been carrying a knife or some other weapon for the express purpose of doing him harm. That she had resorted to stabbing him with a nail file suggested that the attack was a spur-of-the-moment decision—an impulsive act of violence. Which meant that something must have happened just prior to the assault that caused Libby to lash out at Bobby in this recklessly aggressive manner. Something had provoked her. But what?

To search for an answer to this question, I decided to replay the DVD of the board of commissioners' meeting. When I'd viewed it earlier (in an anxiety-ridden, sleep-deprived state), I had concentrated on the drama that had occurred during the moments surrounding the stabbing itself, giving little thought to the substance of the meeting—that is, to the issues that had been discussed and, in some cases, voted on. None of that had seemed relevant at the time. What mattered was that there had been a roomful of eyewitnesses who could be called upon to testify as to Libby's transformation from ingénue to slasher.

Knowing this would take some time, I propped myself up in bed with pillows, balanced my computer on my lap, and with pen and notepad at the ready, inserted the DVD. Each time the air-conditioner compressor kicked in, I had to boost the volume on the weak-throated computer speaker.

It didn't take long for the tedium of a civic meeting to chloroform my senses. An hour or so into the proceedings, I took a break to clear my head. Needing an energy boost, I hit up the vending machines in the motel lobby. Then I roamed the mostly empty parking lot, swigging Pepsi from a can and munching Cheetos that turned my fingers orange. The midday sun dazzled in a pale blue sky. It was a heat lamp aimed at the earth. My bare head was a solar panel. By the time I returned to my room, my face waxed poetic—it had bloomed like a red, red rose.

Altogether it took me two and a half hours to go through the video of the board of commissioners' meeting and notate its contents. It turned out to be an enlightening enterprise.

During the meeting, the board had addressed five agenda items. The first issue discussed was the proposal to allow overnight camping in specific county parks. The next item taken up involved the question of what to do about a county roads project that was considerably over budget. Then came the reading and passage of a proclamation in honor of Jeanine Router, the county school district's teacher of the year. The fourth agenda item had to do with a building project that had been abandoned by the developer and was now seen as a hazard in need of cleanup. The final item deliberated, the one discussed and voted on in the minutes leading up to Libby's unforgettable appearance, was a proposal by a citizens committee to adopt zoning regulations for land use in the county.

It was this last issue that prompted the most, and the most passionate, audience participation. A tag-team of citizens left their seats and made their way to the microphone up front to address the county commissioners and make their views known. During my initial run-through of the video, I had fast-forwarded through this part. But on this second viewing, I listened to every word of the public comment, then went back over it a second time in order to take it all in.

What I learned was that the impetus for the zoning proposal was a desire by its backers for the county to more strictly regulate wind farms. I was vaguely aware of the increased use of wind power nationwide to generate energy. Even in Texas, where oil is king, wind turbines had been springing up weed-like, especially in the wind-ravaged areas of the Panhandle.

What I was unaware of was the recent proliferation of wind farms in many of the rural areas of the midwestern states, including Kansas, and the problems reportedly caused by these gigantic windmills for residents of homes in the vicinity. Also news to me was that, over the last five years, a wind farm consisting of several hundred turbines had been built on land north of Grotin, which made Harbin County a hotspot for complaints from those living near the windmills.

As I watched the video of this part of the meeting, I was struck by the stories of those who came forward to speak in favor of the adoption of a (heretofore nonexistent) countywide zoning ordinance that would allow for the tighter regulation of wind farms. Echoing one another's sentiments, they spoke fervently about how their lives had been negatively impacted by living near the massive turbines.

One woman, a schoolteacher who said her name was Tina Martin, was particularly eloquent in conveying how the peace and quiet of the rural setting she and her family had once enjoyed had been stolen from them. According to her, the noise generated by these huge turbines—a sound she described as a deep, pulsating hum—was far greater than AltEnergy, the operators of the local wind farm, had promised it would be. During the day, the constant din assaulted one's ears, leading to agitation and anxiety, she said. At night, the reverberation from the ever-churning blades made it difficult if not impossible to sleep. No amount of soundproofing could block out the low-frequency vibrations emitted by the turbines, she asserted. And it wasn't only humans that suffered from the noise. Her two dogs habitually pawed at their ears in a futile effort to rid themselves of the clamor that never stopped.

Another woman who lived near one of the windmills came forward to decry the phenomenon known as shadow flicker. At a certain time of day, she said, the sun cast a shadow of the rotating turbine blades on her home. The flicker—the continuous, alternating pulse of shade and light—produced by the spinning blades invariably caused her to experience headaches and nausea, and on one occasion prompted her to have an epileptic-like seizure.

An older man took to the lectern and told of an incident in which a Life Flight helicopter had been summoned to airlift a woman injured in a car accident on a road located within the boundaries of the AltEnergy Wind Farm. The helicopter pilot refused to enter the area, deeming it unsafe on account of the air disturbances created by the churning windmills. The woman subsequently died of her injuries.

Several other citizens came forward to express concerns about the loss of property values on homes located near the windmills. One man attested that not only had he tried in vain to sell his home, he couldn't even get an appraiser to place a value on his property because of its proximity to a wind turbine.

As I listened to the testimony of these citizens, I was appalled by what I heard. I had no idea any of this was happening to people living near wind farms. Why had none of this been front-page news before now? Was the situation truly this bad? Whatever the answer to this last question, it seemed obvious to me that the adoption of zoning regulations for land use was a reasonable approach to resolving the citizens' concerns, and, in fact, no audience member at the meeting spoke against the proposal.

At the end of the public comment period on this issue, a motion was made by the female commissioner to establish a committee made up jointly of commissioners and citizens to draw up the specific zoning regulations. She glanced at her fellow commissioners in turn, but no second to her motion was forthcoming. She glared at Bobby Hobson, who avoided her gaze.

"Absent a second—" the chairman said.

"I call for a vote nonetheless," the female commissioner said.

"As is your right," the chairman said. "My views on this issue are well-known. Further comment from either of you before we take a vote?"

Bobby shook his head.

The female commissioner said, "Just one last remark—a question for my fellow commissioners: Were you even listening to what these people had to say just now?" She snatched up her water bottle and began unscrewing its cap. "I ask for a roll call vote."

A roll call vote was taken. The result: one vote in favor, cast by the female commissioner; two votes against, cast by the chairman and Bobby. As a result, the proposal failed.

I was clearly not the only one surprised by this outcome. Audible on the recording of the meeting was a general murmur of discontent among the audience members, many of whom shook their heads and fidgeted in their seats.

This was the point in the proceedings at which Libby strolled to the front of the room and shocked everyone by stabbing Bobby in the neck with a fingernail file—the only sharp object in her purse. Again, I cringed as I witnessed the attack.

I put aside my computer, got up from the bed, and stood gazing out the motel room window. It was well after noon by now. Eastward slanting shadows were attached to upright objects in the parking lot. Young Dolman, having emerged from the motel office, was one of them. His shadow moved in lockstep with him as he leaned into the task of dragging a lengthy water hose toward a planter bed near the motel entrance. I reckoned it was wasted effort. I had walked and driven past that bed several times. My assessment was that the flowers in it had already transitioned from temporary wilt to permanent tilt. He might as well water a grave.

I thought about my review of the board of commissioners' meeting and considered what I had learned. I came to three conclusions: One, there is nothing pettier than small-town politics. Two, nothing brings out the bile in the hearts of our citizenry more than an assault on their way of life. And three, although I'd never known Libby to care a whit about politics, and she lived nowhere near a wind turbine, it appeared that the regulation of wind farms was somehow connected to her case, making the issue ripe for inquiry.

17

THREE-THIRTY THAT AFTERNOON, I sat on a pew-like bench in the vestibule outside the offices of the Harbin County Commissioners, which were located on the first floor of the courthouse building, hoping for the opportunity to speak with Carl Peeples. Peeples was commission chairman and one of the two *no* votes at the recent board of commissioners' meeting on the proposal to adopt countywide zoning regulations for land use. I'd had to play back the voting portion of the video of the meeting a couple of times in order to make out the names of the two commissioners unknown to me as they were shouted out by the clerk during the roll call vote. Voting yea: Kay Bacchus. Voting nay: Carl Peeples and Bobby.

I didn't know anything about Peeples other than his voting record at one meeting of the Harbin County Board of Commissioners, but that was enough for me to believe he could answer some of the questions engendered by my review of the proceedings. A female voice answering my phone call to his office had informed me that, yes, Commissioner Peeples was in and, yes, he was willing to see me without a prior appointment as long as I was willing to sit and wait for an opening in his busy schedule.

Unlike the grandeur and seeming timelessness of the stone-block exterior of the Harbin County Courthouse, the interior of the building is a study in outmodedness. Considered sumptuous in its day, the building's inner decor today more closely resembles that of a rundown old hotel with chipped tile flooring, patched lath and plaster walls, and ceilings that seem hard-pressed to uphold the weight of the building's copious chandelier lighting. The staleness of the air inside the building adds to the overall sense of decay, as if time ravages from the inside out.

I had been closeted in the waiting room for going on a half hour when Mr. Peeples appeared in the doorway of his office and invited me inside. He was a trim, silver-haired man, distinguished-looking in his gray slacks and pale-blue dress shirt. He greeted me with a Goldilocks handshake—not too weak, not too firm. His hand was soft and his fingernails neatly clipped. I guessed he was an attorney or a salesman. "I have another meeting in fifteen minutes," he said, directing me to a chair in front of an antique-looking oak desk, "so we'll need to keep it brief."

I introduced myself, and if he was surprised by my visit it didn't show in his demeanor. "As you know, my sister is in jail for stabbing Bobby Hobson."

"Yes," Peeples said as he seated himself behind his desk, "a disturbing turn of events."

"I'm trying to find out why."

"*Why?*"

"Why she stabbed him."

"Ahh," he said. "I assume you've tried the direct approach—asking your sister that question."

"I have. It appears she has taken a vow of silence on the issue."

The commissioner furrowed his brow. "That would be a stumbling block."

"I don't suppose you know why she assaulted Bobby."

"I'm sorry," he said, "but I haven't an inkling. And it seems that neither does Bobby."

"You've talked to him?"

"I went to see him this morning. Fortunately, it appears he will recover from his wound."

Despite a primitive urge within me that favored an opposing point of view, reason dictated that I concur with his sentiment, which I did with a token nod. "Can I ask you about another subject, then?" I said, mindful of the time constraints in play here. "The zoning proposal that was voted on during the commissioners' meeting—why did you vote against it?"

The commissioner rocked back in his chair and laced his fingers at belly-button level in front of him. "That question I can answer. I voted against the proposal because I think it's the wrong approach to solving the problem at hand. The issue we're faced with here is how best to respond to the complaints of a few of our citizens whose quality of life may have been adversely impacted because they live near a wind turbine. We currently have an ordinance in place for the purpose of regulating wind farms. We don't need zoning to solve the problem. What we need is to modify our current wind farm ordinance so that it better protects those living in the vicinity of the turbines. Specifically," he said, denoting each item with a raised finger, "we need to revisit the issue of setbacks, require noise-level monitoring, and restrict nighttime operation of the windmills when certain noise levels are exceeded. We can do all that without resorting to zoning, which I see as a slippery slope leading to an undesirable erosion of our property rights."

"So zoning is overkill."

"Exactly. You don't need a sledge hammer to squash a bug."

"And is this also how Bobby Hobson sees it?"

Commissioner Peeples's expression clouded. "That's the thing," he said. "Before last Monday night's board meeting, I would have bet that Bobby was going to come down on the side of zoning. This is Bobby's first year on the board, so he doesn't have much of a voting history. But when he campaigned for office, he represented himself as pro-zoning. If I recall correctly, what he said back then was that he was *open* to the idea of zoning as a means to regulate land use. That left him some wiggle room. Still, I was surprised when he voted against the zoning proposal, especially since there'd been a recent upsurge in public opinion in its favor."

So there was one more question to add to my list: Why had Bobby done an about-face on the issue of zoning for land use?

I thanked Mr. Peeples for his time and courtesy in meeting with me and left him to his busy schedule. He'd been open and honest with me, I thought, in answering my questions. But as I began retracing my steps to the courthouse building's main entrance, I had the unsettling sense that I'd become caught up in a high-stakes game of Whac-A-Mole. Every time I nailed down the answer to one question, another one popped up that required my attention. And if the analogy held true, the pace of the game I was being forced to play was only going to get more frenetic.

"HEY! WAIT A MINUTE!"

The courthouse lobby was straight ahead of me, only a few more paces along the last of the corridors I'd traversed on my way out of the building following my meeting with Commissioner Peeples. The voice I heard came from behind me. I paused and glimpsed back in that direction.

The only person there was a young man dressed in gray work clothes like maintenance men wear, which made sense in that he gripped a mop handle whose head end was submerged in a rolling bucket at his feet. He had apparently come out of a restroom behind me. A yellow easel-style CAUTION WET FLOOR sign stood near the restroom entrance.

"Aren't you Libby Coombs's brother?" the man said.

"I am," I said, puzzled that he knew me by the back of my head—or at all. He was no one I remembered having met.

"I'm David Pierce," the man said as he rolled his bucket toward me, using the mop handle as both push pole and rudder. The wheels of the metal trough clattered over the uneven tiles, jiggling the soapy water inside, frothing it to a head. "I saw you sitting in the waiting room at the commissioners' offices."

"And you knew who I was because . . . ?"

When he got to where I stood, he propped the mop handle against the wall, retrieved a shop rag from a back pocket, and wiped his hands. "I used to go out with Libby sometimes. She showed me a picture of you on her phone."

"Oh." I didn't recall Libby ever mentioning a David Pierce, but I didn't want to say as much. "Pleased to meet you," I said, extending a hand. The hand I shook smelled of Pine Sol or some such heavy-duty cleanser. If I'd had a cold, one whiff of that scent would have cleared my sinuses. I waited to see if there was more to this chance meeting than a chemical handshake.

"Is Libby going to prison?" Pierce said.

I took a keener measure of the kid as I considered my response. He looked about Libby's age. He was close to my height, although he had on work boots with more heel than my Reeboks. His hair was long and limp on top and buzz-cut nearly to the skin on the sides, as if to mimic the mop in his bucket. A small hoop earring dangled from his right earlobe. He had a wide mouth and a patrician nose.

"What makes you think that?" I asked.

Young Pierce looked at me without blinking. "I've seen the blood."

I felt a sudden chill. I knew what he meant, but I asked the question anyway. "What blood?"

"In the meeting room. Commissioner Hobson's blood. They wouldn't let me clean it up—the cops."

That made sense; the room was a crime scene. The police would want all the evidence preserved until they were done with their forensic analysis. But Pierce was a janitor; he would want to clean it up as soon as possible.

"Were you at the meeting?" I asked.

"No, and I'm glad I wasn't. But I've seen the video." He made a sucking sound as he inhaled through bared teeth. "Why would Libby have done that?"

I sighed. "That's the question of the day, David."

I was about to bid the young man goodbye when a thought struck me. Where it came from, I wasn't sure. Latent morbidity? A Sherlock Holmesian moment? A true conviction that there was something to be learned that could help Libby's case? I blurted the thought without settling on its origin or intent. "Can I see the blood too?"

Pierce looked at me with the light of surprise in his eyes. "For real?"

"For real," I said, hammering out a rationale on the fly. "I've seen the video of the meeting, but it might help me understand things better if I could take a look inside the actual meeting room." I played on whatever feelings he still had for my sister. "I'm sure you don't want Libby going to prison any more than I do."

Young Pierce chewed on his lower lip as he mulled my request, his eyes dancing to the rhythm of his thoughts. It didn't take him long to land on a decision.

"Come with me," he said, steering his mop bucket back down the hallway. He rolled it into a janitor's closet and shut the door.

I hustled after him as he continued down the corridor. He turned a corner, strode along an adjoining passageway, then ducked into a stairwell and headed down a flight of stairs. "We'll have to go in the back way," he said. "The cops have the public entrance to the meeting room closed off, and they'd know if we broke the security seal." The key ring on his hip jingled a note of caution with each descending step he took.

I stopped him as we reached basement level, suddenly having second thoughts about our little escapade. "Look, David, maybe this isn't such a good idea after all. I don't want to get you in trouble, and I certainly don't want you losing your job." *And I don't want to join my sister as an inmate in the Harbin County Jail!*

He shrugged off my concern. "No worries. I'm an info systems major at UK. This is a minimum-wage job I took because my mom wanted me home for the summer. What's to lose?" He grinned. "Besides, I already took two buddies in there earlier today."

At the end of a long hallway, we climbed a flight of stairs that took us back to ground level. We went through a fire door and emerged inside a short corridor with doors at either end. "That door," David said, nodding to his right, "leads to the outside. It's so the commissioners can go in and out of the meeting room without having to use the public entrance." He gestured toward the door on our left. "That's the back entrance to the meeting room. It's kept locked, but each commissioner has a key." He held up his key ring and jangled it. "And so do I."

The back-entrance door opened onto a small office. From there, another door led us directly into the meeting room, dais level, American flag side. In front of us was one end of the skirted table behind which the commissioners and a clerk sat during board meetings. Four padded office chairs were pushed up against the table. There was just enough gap between the chairs and the wall behind them to allow passage to the opposite side of the room, where the Kansas state flag was posted.

"The blood is over there," David said, pointing in that direction. "Some on the table and more—a lot more—on the floor."

The only light in the room was indirect sunlight coming in through a row of transom windows high on an outside wall, giving the effect of twilight. There was also a transom window above the entrance door.

"I can't turn on the overheads," David said. "Someone walking by might look up through the transom and notice."

"Not necessary," I told him. "I can see well enough."

I surveyed the audience section. The room was smaller than it looked on video. There were seven rows of unpadded stadium-style seating, ten seats to a row—five on either side of a center aisle. Forty-one of the seats had been occupied that night, including the one Libby had filled. Plus three commissioners on the dais, and a clerk. Forty-five people total at the meeting: Libby, Bobby, and the forty-three witnesses Harvey Broward had referenced.

"You want to see the blood?" David said.

"In a minute."

Stepping down from the dais, I walked between it and the first row of audience seating to the center aisle. I moved up the aisle to within a few feet of the sealed public entrance and turned around. This was the viewpoint from which I had seen the action on the video. The camera was mounted on the wall behind me, blinded now by a dust shroud.

I gazed out over the room and tried to replay in my head the video of those fateful moments during the recent board of commissioners' meeting. Libby must have been seated along the left side wall, toward the back of the room, out of camera range. I imagined her sidling between two rows of seats to reach the center aisle. She moved casually, unhurriedly down the aisle. When she approached the dais, she bypassed the public-comment lectern and went to stand in front of Bobby. A few seconds passed. Then her right arm flew up—

Voices arose behind me, in the hallway outside the main entrance door to the meeting room. I stood still. Listened. Waited. The voices trailed off down the hall.

"We shouldn't stay too long," David said in a husky whisper that took some of the shine off his earlier bravado at bringing me to this place.

I returned to the front of the room and positioned myself behind the lectern with the gooseneck microphone.

David was still on the dais, on the commissioners' side of the raised table. He edged his way along the wall to where Bobby had been sitting. "See all the blood," he said, indicating dark-brown blotches and smears on the tabletop. "And over here." He moved to the end of the table, near the Kansas state flag, and pointed down at the floor at a sepia-toned splotch whose shape resembled that of the continent of Africa. "This is where they laid him down. A lot of blood here."

I hadn't really come to see the blood. I wasn't sure why I had come, or what I'd expected to find. Some vital piece of evidence the police had missed? Some clue as to the *why* behind my sister's action? Some top-of-the-mountain insight into what this whole mess was all about? If any of this was what I'd hoped for, I had failed miserably. Sherlock Holmes I was not.

But neither was I totally without discernment. And what registered with me in that moment was that I was standing exactly where Tina Martin had stood during the last commissioners' meeting when she'd delivered her impassioned remarks about how living near a wind turbine had wreaked havoc on her family's quality of life. Such passion, it seemed to me, should not have been dismissed out of hand.

"I see, yes, lots of blood," I said. "We'd better go."

In the hallway outside the janitor's closet where David had

stowed his mop bucket, I thanked him for showing me the meeting room.

"I hope Libby doesn't get in too much trouble over this," he said.

"You seem to really care about her."

He nodded. "I like her a lot."

He seemed sincere. I felt I should say something encouraging to him. "Well, maybe after all this is over, you two can go out again sometime."

"Maybe," he said. "But I'm pretty sure that all we'll ever be is friends."

"Oh? Why do you say that?"

He stuck his hands in his pockets and shifted his feet. "Let's just say, I don't think I'm her type."

The look in his eyes told me there was more to it than that. But I was not inclined to pursue the matter further, especially not with a boy I had just met.

I shook young Pierce's hand again. "Good luck with your schooling."

"Yeah," he said. "Can't wait to get out of this town for good."

I knew the feeling.

18

ON MY DRIVE out of town to visit Tina Martin, I traveled through a landscape of far-reaching meadows and expansive crop fields: wide swaths of heavy-headed wheat ripe for harvest, seemingly endless rows of cornstalks beginning to tassel, broad carpets of lush green soybean foliage. The slanting sun spilled its glow onto the scene, glazing it in velvet hues of brown and green and gold.

Nearer my destination, as open prairie began to dominate the landscape, I encountered a far-flung forest of energy-producing wind turbines. From a distance the windmills looked harmless, majestic even, their super-sized blades tracing graceful arcs in the sky at a seemingly measured pace. I was soon to encounter a much different perspective.

After leaving the courthouse, I had called the number for the only listing the 411 operator had for a Tina Martin with a Harbin County address. Getting no answer, I left a message on Ms. Martin's answering machine. I was fueling my Explorer at the Sinclair station at 6th and Main when she called me back.

"You say you're Libby Coombs's brother," she said. "I didn't know Libby had a brother."

Ah ha! Someone in Grotin who doesn't know I exist. "I don't live around here. I used to, but not anymore. But you do know Libby?"

"She was in my sophomore English class."

I remembered then that Tina had introduced herself at the board meeting as a teacher at Grotin High.

"So," she said, "what did you want to talk to me about?"

"Wind farms," I said. "I watched the video of the latest board of commissioners' meeting. Your comments at the meeting got my attention. I'd like to learn more."

"What's the nature of your interest?"

"I'm not sure. I'm just in town looking to help Libby."

Silence. Then: "Why don't you come out to my place and see—and hear—for yourself."

Tina Martin lived in a white clapboard house off Norton Road, one of the many country lanes that crisscrossed the county in a grid-like fashion. Her home, it turned out, was located at ground zero inside the AltEnergy Wind Farm called Clement Ridge. The wind farm had sprung up in a ten-mile radius around her property north of Grotin, on a natural uprising of land that gave it enough profile to catch the wind from every direction.

As I drove up the gravel drive leading to the address I'd been given, Tina came out of her house to meet me. I got out of my car and shook the hand she offered. She was smaller than she looked on video. In appearance, she reminded me of Rita Moreno, not from *West Side Story* but from her later roles on television. Same quick smile. Same darting dark-brown eyes.

She made a sweeping gesture with her right arm, drawing my attention—as if it needed to be drawn—toward the object rising from the grassland behind her home. "There it is," she said, "in all its glory."

What was there, looking so out of place as to have been planted in the ground by aliens, was one of AltEnergy's wind turbines.

With my eyes, I traced the bone-white trunk of its tubular tower up to the massive rotating blades. "It's huge," I said, astounded by the enormity of the thing when viewed up close.

"That one is 410 feet tall from base to blade tip at its apex," she said. "About the height of a forty-story building. Its tower is 262 feet tall, and each blade is 148 feet long. And the only time it stops turning is when there is no wind, which is almost never, and when it's taken offline for maintenance, which around here is a cause for celebration. Otherwise it goes day and night."

We lingered, listening to the sound the turbine made as it churned. It was a repetitive drone loud enough to have to raise your voice to talk over.

"How far away is it from the house?"

"Twelve hundred fifty-two feet," Tina said. "Fifty-two feet above the minimum setback. That's one of the problems with the current regulations. The setback should be from the property line, not from the residence."

I glanced over at the weather vane on the roof of her house that indicated a light wind from the northwest. The day had cooled slightly and the breeze was like a warm caress.

She read my mind. "If the air is moving at all down here, it's gusting up there. And it doesn't matter the direction of the flow. Northerly, southerly, easterly, westerly—it's all fodder for the ever-spinning head of that beast."

"How many turbines in this wind farm are located near homes?" On my approach to Tina's house, I had spotted numerous windmills but only a few other homes.

"About fifteen," she said. "That doesn't sound like much—unless yours is one of the homes affected."

I nodded.

"Come inside," she said, "and take in the ambiance there."

I followed her into the house, where we sat down on a brown leather sofa in the living room. The whooshing sound I'd heard outside, although muted, was still evident. But indoors, the noise wasn't the most noticeable effect of the gyrating turbine; it was the tremoring.

"You feel it, don't you," Tina said, reading my facial expression. "The sound waves emitted by the turbine cause a vibration of the walls and floor that makes everything inside the house tremor." She shuddered. "It's like insects crawling under your skin. It's like that feeling of motion that stays with you for a time after you've completed a long drive or a train ride. Only it never goes away. We wear earplugs at night, but that doesn't block out the vibration."

A teenaged boy dressed in cut-off jeans and a Def Leppard T-shirt came bustling through the front door of the house, two panting border collies at his heels.

"My son, Donny," Tina said.

"Hey," Donny said by way of greeting. He and his companions skittered through the living room and down a hallway to another part of the house. A door closed. Moments later, loud music emanated from that direction.

"It's Donny's way of coping with the noise. He puts Mutt Muffs on the dogs."

"Understandable," I said, recalling my own amped music days. Although, in my case, it was mostly the noise in my head I was trying to drown out. "How long have you lived out here? You're what, twelve miles from town?"

"Six years," she said. "And, yes, it's almost thirteen miles to Grotin, which appealed to me back then. We'd lived in Kansas City before that—before my divorce. But I'd always dreamed of living in the country. I yearned for the quiet, the solitude. And it was a dream fulfilled for about a year. That's how long it was before AltEnergy started putting up the turbines in this area. If we'd known then . . . well . . ."

She sighed. "What can I say? It's just so frustrating. The wind farm reps will act sympathetic when you call them and complain. They'll promise to send someone out to measure the noise level, and then they don't. The people who do come out—the reporters and the politicians—they come and stand directly beneath the turbine and listen. Then they go back and report that the windmills don't make that much noise. That's because the sound is broadcast outward. You have to stand back a few hundred yards from a spinning turbine to really hear and feel the reverberation. Those folks need to come out here at nighttime when the wind is blowing in this direction and try to sleep. Hell—try to think."

She hung her head. "I'm sorry. But I'm about at my wits' end over this. My daughter, Beth, is a junior at K-State. She spent two days here last Christmas break and then went back to Manhattan because she couldn't take, as she put it, *that infernal throbbing*. I'd move if I could. But even if I could sell this place—which is doubtful—I couldn't recoup enough of my investment to buy a home somewhere else. Hell, nobody wants a house inside a wind farm."

I felt terrible for Tina and her family. No one should have to live this way. "Would it have helped your situation if the zoning proposal had passed?"

She pursed her lips. "Probably not. Zoning or no zoning, they're not going to uproot that colossal noisemaker and move it away from my house. And they're not going to pay to have my house moved farther away from that thing. But zoning restrictions could keep other people who live in rural areas of the county from suffering the same fate as us."

"Commissioner Peeples told me that all the county needs to do to solve the problem is to draft a stricter wind farm ordinance."

Tina scoffed. "The problem with that is the county doesn't enforce the wind farm regulations they have. It's all lip service, because the county has no clout. They'd have to take AltEnergy to court to force compliance, and the commissioners don't have the will, or the money, for that. You need to put zoning restrictions in place to stop these things from being built near homes in the first place." She massaged her temples as if seeking to soothe a headache. "That's why the vote the other night was so disappointing."

It seemed like a good time to ask the question I'd wanted to ask from the beginning of my visit. "Do you have any idea why Bobby Hobson voted against the zoning proposal? I've heard he was a pro-zoning guy."

"He was," Tina said, throwing up her hands in a gesture of dismay. "At least he pretended to be when he ran for office. We knew Carl Peeples was going to vote against the proposal. He's anti-zoning, period. Talking with Kay Bacchus, we were convinced she would vote our way and she did. And we thought Commissioner Hobson would too. But we hadn't been able to get a commitment from him because he declined to meet with our committee. Too busy, he said. All the same, his past statements indicated a willingness to implement zoning regulations for land use, so we expected him to support the proposal."

"But he didn't. And you don't know why?"

She hesitated. "Not . . . really," she said, leaving the words suspended in midair as targets for speculation.

"Care to venture a guess?"

Her head rocked side to side as if in flux between magnetic poles of indecision. "This is just conjecture, mind you. But it could have something to do with his connection to Cyrus Tolliver."

Cyrus Tolliver? The mention of the name sounded a dissonant chord in my head. Cyrus Tolliver was RuAnn Tolliver's father.

"Why would you think that?"

"Money," she said, this time without hesitation. "Tolliver owns most of the land on which the Clement Ridge wind farm sits—land that, over time, has proven to be agriculturally unproductive. Which means that he is making a helluva lot of money off AltEnergy by leasing them land that's not much good for anything else. The last thing he wants is for the county to adopt zoning regulations that put restrictions on the use of his land."

"But what's Hobson's connection with Tolliver?"

"They're poker buddies," she said, the inflection in her voice conveying a lack of appreciation for the concept of male bonding. "Tolliver hosts a poker game at his house on Thursday nights, and Hobson, I'm told, is one of the regulars."

I thought about that for a moment, but the thought didn't take me anywhere because I had no launching pad for supposition.

"Do the Tollivers still live out on Pheasant Lane, past the hunting lodge?"

"They do. And, funny thing," Tina said, expressing mock surprise, "you won't find a wind turbine anywhere near their place."

I thanked her for seeing me and drove back to town discomfited by my encounter with Tina Martin. I had new information to work with, and another player in Cyrus Tolliver. But along with this additional information came more questions (*Whack! Whack! Whack!*)—questions I was sure Bobby Hobson could answer, but probably never would.

19

I ATE A LATE dinner at the Silver Platter and then went back to my motel room with the intention of taking a quick shower before returning to the jail to see Libby.

It didn't happen.

After showering, I was unable to summon the energy to dress and go out again. My body's furnace had flamed out, leaving me inert. I was also feeling vulnerable, cut off as I was from everyone and everything that for the past ten years had formed a protective shield around me. I missed Charlotte. I missed my life in San Antonio. *What am I doing here?*

Lying on the bed with a damp towel wrapped around my waist, I used my cell phone to call Charlotte's cell. She was home, settled in for the evening, she said, with a good e-book for company.

"How's it going there?" she said.

I told her about my day.

"Sounds like you might be on to something."

"I don't know," I said. "I feel as if I'm stumbling around in a fog while all around me there's a weighty conflict going on that I can't see or hear. Like it exists in some alternate reality."

"All you can do is keep digging."

She was right of course, but at the moment it all seemed so pointless. I felt like poor Sisyphus, that fellow in Greek mythology forced by the gods to push a boulder up a hill, only to watch it roll back down, then fated to repeat the process time and again for eternity. What I needed most right now was to put it all out of my mind, even if just for an hour—for a minute.

"What about things there?" I asked. "How're you doing?"

"I'm fine. As long as I don't run out of books on my Kindle."

"And at the office? Am I in danger of being fired?"

"Don't worry about that," Charlotte said, assuring me that all my clients were being well taken care of by my fellow employees.

There was a lull in the conversation while I reflected on something that had been bothering me ever since my arrival back in Grotin. "There are some things I should tell you," I said, giving voice to my thoughts. "Things I should have told you long ago." For some reason, I was feeling the need to unburden myself.

"What things?"

"Things that happened to me growing up in Grotin. Things I've wanted to forget, to quash from memory forever, but that have only become more deeply etched in my mind because of my presence back here." I had fought to keep the memory genie in the bottle, but it was obvious to me now that that was not going to happen.

A long moment of silence ensued and I thought I might have lost the connection with Charlotte. The battery on my cell phone was low and I needed to recharge it. But that wasn't it.

"Some things exist only because you talk about them," she finally said. "If you want to forget something, never talk about it."

"I'm not sure I can do that anymore."

"The past can be a dangerous place to visit," she said. "Are you sure you want to go there?"

"I don't know. All I know is that I haven't been forthcoming with you about my past, and I'm thinking I don't want to keep things from you anymore. Not if—" I was going to say, *not if we're going to have a future together*, but something held me back—a sense that I might drive her away with too much openness.

There is an intimacy in sharing with someone your inner life—an intimacy that goes beyond a physical embrace, beyond a kiss, beyond sex, even. It was that kind of intimacy that Charlotte and I had never shared with each other, and it was that kind of intimacy I now felt the need for. But what if my need to bare my soul did not mesh with her lack of desire to sit opposite me in the confessional box?

"Not if what?" Charlotte said.

I evaded the question by asking one of my own. "Don't you ever wonder how people got to be who they are? What happened in their past to shape their personalities?"

"Darryl," she said, "you're a sensitive, caring guy. You're fun to be with and you're a considerate lover. And you don't ask too much of me. I'm glad you are who you are, but I'm not all that curious about how you got to be that way."

I let it go then, dropped the subject of my past, because I didn't have a comeback for her kind assessment of me. "Okay," I said. "I'm glad you feel that way." And I added, "That's how I feel about you too."

"Good," Charlotte said.

Confession might be good for the soul, but in the world according to Charlotte Robinson, that obviously wasn't the case.

We talked about some other things then. The last thing she said to me before hanging up was, "You're a good man, Darryl Coombs."

I lay there thinking about that. If I was such a good man, why didn't I feel like one? Why didn't I feel decent, upright, worthy? Why did I feel exactly the opposite? In truth, I knew why—I knew it had everything to do with my being back in Grotin. I just didn't know what to do about it.

I jettisoned the damp towel, plugged my phone into its charger, and doused the lamplight.

I drifted off to sleep only to be awakened by the ringtone I had assigned Charlotte's cell. I glanced at the clock as I groped for my phone and disconnected it from the charger. It was 2:06 a.m.

"Hello," I said, slurring the word like a drunk.

"Tell me."

"Charlotte?"

"I'm sorry," Charlotte said, her voice husky and nasally, as if she'd been crying. "You're hurting, and I wasn't there for you. You wanted to tell me something and I cut you off. That was selfish of me. If you need to talk, I'm listening."

"It's okay, Charlotte. I understand, and I don't want to push you away."

"No, it's *not* okay. I care about you, Darryl, and I want to be here for you. I'm just not sure how. This is very difficult for me, because . . . well . . . it just is. But I want to hear what you have to say. So talk to me."

"Now? In the middle of the night?"

"Yes, now. I'm listening. You said you wanted to tell me about some things that happened to you when you were growing up in Grotin. Okay, tell me."

"Are you sure?"

"Yes."

I sat up in bed with my knees steepled under the top sheet. My thoughts were a mishmash of psycho-tornadic debris. Where to begin? Dark images from a bygone existence flooded into my consciousness. "There was a club—" I said, then had to pause to clear phlegm from my throat. I tried again: "There was a club for boys in Grotin called the Water Tower Club." My heart was drumming a dynamic beat inside my chest. I took a shuddering breath and continued.

THERE WAS A CLUB for boys in Grotin called the Water Tower Club. It was an unofficial club and only the kids in town knew about it. There were no dues or meetings or anything like that. It was more of a rite of passage. The minimum age for joining the club was twelve; the maximum age, fourteen. It was a source of pride to be a member of the club, and the boys who weren't members got picked on by the boys who were.

The way you joined the club was this: After dark on a moonless night, you had to climb the city water tower, stand against the railing of the catwalk that ran around the rim of its massive tank, and take a piss over the side. This feat had to be witnessed by at least three current members of the club, who, using battery-powered spotlights, lit up each novitiate during his climb and at the moment he let loose his urine stream. Invariably when it got around that, on a given night, one or more boys would be attempting to join the club, a crowd of youth—club members and the merely curious of both sexes—gathered at the base of the tower to witness the event, and to praise the courage of those who succeeded and to ridicule those who did not.

Bobby Hobson and I, and most of the other members of our sixth grade class, turned twelve the same year. That summer, a handful of the twelve-year-old boys wanted to join the Water Tower Club. Bobby was one of them. I was not. The water tower in Grotin is 165 feet tall. To get up to the catwalk you had to climb over a security fence, then ascend an open, nearly vertical, 130-foot metal-rung ladder attached to one of the tower's support posts. The idea of scaling that sky-tall ladder appealed to me about as much as cutting off one of my arms. I knew I'd be taunted if I refused to climb, but I didn't care. My fear of climbing—or, more accurately, of falling in an attempt to climb—was greater than my fear of ridicule.

In mid-July, under a new moon, Bobby and four other boys—one thirteen-year-old included—succeeded in becoming members of the Water Tower Club. "Nothing to it," Bobby boasted later. "If you never look down, you might as well be two feet off the ground." He swaggered as he hitched up his trousers. "Hey, I'm a poet." That was Bobby.

I did indeed take a ribbing for a time after that by some members of the club. They'd flap their arms like wings when they saw me and make cackling sounds that I pretended to shrug off even as inside I was stung by their mockery. I salved the hurt by applying the reasoning that it was stupid to think that just because you climbed a tall ladder and took a piss from on high, you were more courageous than others.

This was the mindset I clung to as another year passed and, during the summer following my thirteenth birthday, a fresh crop of twelve-year-olds and a late bloomer or two joined the Water Tower Club, again without my participation.

But upon my turning fourteen, with the deadline looming for me to join the club, there came an alteration in my thinking on the matter. I felt a mounting pressure to make the climb, not from outside sources—for I had reconciled myself to the taunts of others—but from an excruciating inner conflict regarding my own self-worth.

The sad truth was that, growing up, I had embraced a dim view of myself as a person. I can look back now and analyze why I was so withdrawn and lacking in self-esteem. But at the time, this sense of worthlessness I felt seemed like a natural state of existence, one I was born into, as if I were a human pupa waiting quiescently for the metamorphosis in my self-image that would come with or without my active participation.

What I ultimately concluded was that my cocoon of isolation and self-debasement was not going to crack open on its own. I had to break out of it myself, and the way I would do it was by joining the Water Tower Club.

When, that summer, on the designated night for the water tower climb, word circulated that timorous Darryl Coombs was going to participate, a larger than usual crowd gathered at the base of the water tank. There must have been fifty kids already milling about in the dark when I arrived. I heard a hushed voice say, "He's here—Darryl's here." And flashlight beams hit me like shock waves from different directions. "I didn't think he'd show," another voice said.

There were six of us prepared to climb that night: four twelve-year-olds, one thirteen-year-old, and me. The older club members, meaning the fourteen-year-olds, decided that we would climb according to age, the youngest first—which meant I was to go last. That suited me fine, since already I was having second thoughts about my decision. Standing there, encumbered by the immense darkness, I felt my strength, along with my resolve, draining from me. My legs were rubbery. My stomach was a churning mass of dread. The night was unseasonably cool, but I was sweating nonetheless. I kept wiping my hands on my pant legs. The rungs on the ladder I had to climb were nothing more than bare metal rods, and I feared I wouldn't be able to maintain a grip on them with sweaty palms.

"Benny goes first," said Bobby Hobson, taking charge of the scene as he was accustomed to doing. "He just had his twelfth birthday. Then Lamar, then Conrad, then Monty, Trevor, and Darryl."

"I'm a month older than Monty," Conrad said.

"All right then," Bobby said, "he goes before you." He clamped a hand on Benny's shoulder. "Now remember, wait until everyone's up there before taking a whiz. We want to light up everyone at once."

"What if I don't have to pee when I get up there?" Lamar said.

"You should worry more about pissing your pants on the way up," Bobby said.

Everyone laughed except those of us preparing to climb.

Benny DeMont was a small kid, but wiry and nimble. He had two older brothers with whom he wrestled all the time, and that rough-and-tumble sibling combat had toughened him. He had no trouble scrambling over the chain-link security fence. He ascended the tower's ladder as if he were Spider Man.

Lamar Higgins was a pudgy kid, overweight and not all that coordinated, and it took him considerably more time getting over the security fence. He paused at the base of the ladder, looking up as if reassessing, before beginning to climb, slowly and deliberately. Someone spotlighted one of his hands as it clenched a rung of the ladder: white knuckles gleamed beneath pink skin.

Monty went next with Conrad following close behind. They were both farm boys who, even at twelve years old, were accustomed to driving farm equipment and jumping out of hay lofts. Neither was intimidated by the task at hand.

"Where's Trevor?" someone said. "He's next."

Flashlight beams danced around erratically, slicing up the darkness like light sabers, but to no avail. Trevor was nowhere to be found.

"Chickened out again," someone said.
"Same as last year."
"Went home to mommy."
"Probably sucking tit right now."
Hoots all around.
"Okay," Bobby said. "Forget Trevor. Darryl, you're up."

I didn't feel up. My limbs quivered. My insides had turned to mush. My pulse revved like a car engine with the gas pedal stuck to the floor. I stumbled forward and seized a handhold on the chain-link fencing. My mind seemed to disengage from my body as I struggled to mount it, my shoe-tips slipping repeatedly on the skimpy footholds provided by the gaps between the links. I was gasping for air when I dropped to the ground on the other side.

I located the base of the ladder in the dark and gripped a head-high rung with my right hand. The rung felt wet. I drew back my hand and wiped it on my shirt, realizing only then that I had gashed my palm on the exposed wire-ends atop the fence. Blood oozed from the wound and trickled down my wrist.

"Get on with it, Coombs," Bobby said. "The others are waiting."

Shafts of light poked and prodded me.

Ignoring the blood, the pain, and the fear that wanted to overpower me, I grasped a rung of the ladder and began to climb. The rungs were about a foot apart, which meant I had to mount approximately 130 of them. I had not intended to count them as I went, but I found myself subconsciously doing exactly that. One, two . . . five . . . ten. *Don't do that*, I told myself. But a part of my brain had gone off on its own, and it kept counting—and calculating. Ten rungs—ten feet off the ground. Twenty rungs—twenty feet off the ground. Forty rungs—forty feet off the ground.

If you never look down, you might as well be two feet off the ground.

When I was seventy-eight feet in the air, according to my involuntary step-count, a wash of light off to my right caught my attention. Glancing in that direction, I saw that the glow was coming from the bell tower of St. Mary's Cathedral, which was always illuminated at night. At my current height, I was at eye level with the bells of St. Mary's.

Don't look down. Don't look down.

I don't remember looking down. But to this day, I have imprinted in my mind a tableau, in gauzy black and white, of an aerial view of the town of Grotin. It was as if I were Gulliver looking down on Lilliput at night. Only, if I took one false step, it wasn't a Lilliputian in danger of being flattened.

I ascended one more rung of the ladder and froze.

I don't know how long it was before the voices broke through to my consciousness, for I had all but blacked out. When I became aware of my body again, I found that I was clinging to the ladder with both arms—the crook of one arm locked around a rung and the other arm clamped around an upright—the way a boxer whose legs are gone clutches his opponent.

A spotlight lit me up from below. A voice—Bobby's voice—said, "Darryl, what's the matter with you? Either go on up or come down, you cowardly slug."

And shouts descended from the darkness above. They started out as words of encouragement: "Come on, Darryl, you can do it!" They soon turned into threats: "Get your ass up here, Darryl, or I'll come down there and kick it!"

I heard the outcry—the cajoling, the encouragement, the threats—from above and below, but none of it spurred me to action. When fear grips you, it takes total control, and that was what happened to me that night. Fear paralyzed my body and stupefied my mind. I was as closed off from outside influence as a clamshell that can't be opened without smashing it to bits. I wasn't about to move one more step up or down. In my mind—at least the way my mind was working at the time, which wasn't with any semblance of logic—I was stuck exactly where I was as surely as if I'd been welded there.

During the minutes that followed, I was only vaguely aware of the commotion going on above and below me. The shouts continued in a cacophony of voices that fell on deaf ears. Then there occurred a time of quiet during which I thought it must have started to rain. But it wasn't rain. The boys above me—Benny, Lamar, Conrad, and Monty—were making their admission to the Water Tower Club official by pissing from the catwalk. They were also making a point: they wanted me out of their way. Four streams of urine jetted down, all aimed at me. Much of the piss went awry, but enough of it hit its target to soak my hair and dampen my shirt. I puked—not from the smell, but from the humiliation.

But the ordeal was far from over.

One by one, the boys began descending the ladder. I could hear their chatter above me as they urged each other along. The ladder vibrated with the shifting weight of their descent.

Monty reached me first. "Move, Darryl," he barked. "Go on down. You're blockin' the way."

When I didn't respond, he put a shoed foot on my head and pressed down. "Go!"

I didn't go—couldn't go.

He extended a leg farther down and kicked at me, the blow landing on my shoulder. I tightened my arm-lock on the ladder. He kicked me again, harder. I didn't say anything, didn't do anything.

A voice from above Monty—Benny's voice—said, "Make him move."

"I'm trying," Monty said. "But he won't budge."

"Dumbass Darryl!" Benny said. "All right, climb down past him then."

"I don't know if I can."

Lamar's voice from higher up: "Move, guys. I'm getting really tired. I need to get down."

"*Okay. Okay*," Monty said. "Move aside, Darryl. I'm coming down past you. If you fall, it's not my fault."

He stepped on my arm that was locked around a ladder rung. I winced from the pain of his full body weight treading on me. His other foot scraped down my ribcage and found a footing on a lower rung. Then, using his shoulder as a battering ram, he shunted me aside as he made room for himself between the uprights. My only recourse to becoming disconnected from the ladder was to poke a leg between two rungs and achieve a knee lock on the lower one. With my backside hanging out in midair, I clung to an upright with all my might, because that was all I could do.

"You better stay up here for the rest of your life," Monty said as he descended past me, "because when you come down, I'm going to beat the crap out of you."

Before I could reclaim space on the ladder rungs, Benny was there nudging me aside. "You're a real turd head, you know."

Conrad clambered down next, again forcibly occupying the face of the ladder while I hung precariously over the side.

By now my physical resources were all but depleted, and I knew that if I was going to save myself from falling I had to regain a position of stability on the ladder. As Lamar was about to descend past me, I swung my body around and reoccupied the space between the uprights.

"Get out of my way," he said. "I'm coming down."

A person can take only so much humiliation lying down—or in my case, clinging desperately to a ladder—and a sense of defiance welled up inside me. I had been pissed on and kicked and pummeled enough, and I wasn't going to take it anymore.

It turned out that Lamar was as spent as I was. When he attempted to force me out of his way, I used every ounce of strength I had left to maintain my attitude on the ladder. Lamar kicked at me repeatedly—at my head, my arms, my shoulders. And when I didn't give up an inch of ladder space, he kicked harder.

Too hard.

When one of his leg thrusts missed its target, hitting nothing but air, he lost his handhold on the ladder, and with a fearful cry came crashing down on top of me. Suddenly it was as if I had a hundred-and-fifty-pound monkey clinging to my back, and I knew I couldn't hold on.

When my arms gave way, my upper body wrenched violently backward. Lamar let out another cry, this time a long, keening scream that lasted from the time he lost his clawing grip on me until he hit the ground.

I dangled there—seventy-nine feet in the air, semiconscious, one leg hooked on a ladder rung—for what seemed like an eternity, until a fireman ascended the ladder, fastened a harness to me, and using a rope and pulley, lowered me to the ground. I was told that my rescue, witnessed by almost everyone in town, was quite a spectacle.

21

"THAT'S TERRIBLE," Charlotte said when I had finished my story. "But you have nothing to be ashamed of, or to blame yourself for. You were just a boy—a frightened boy—and the others treated you cruelly. What happened was not your fault."

"I've been telling myself that for years," I said.

"Well, it's time you started believing it."

My heart was still hammering in my chest. "It's not that easy."

Charlotte didn't immediately respond, and when she did there was melancholy in her voice, as if she'd peered down the dark tunnel of her own past and was not fully at peace with what she saw. "I know," she said.

"I'm sorry," I told her, feeling guilty now for having unburdened myself at her expense. "It's the middle of the night and I've upset you. Go to sleep now or you'll be a mess at work tomorrow."

She let out a long sigh, and I imagined her breath brushing past my cheek, carrying with it the fragrance of her unique essence. "I'll try," she said.

I gave out a sigh of my own. Was it longing or fatigue? Both, I decided. "Thank you for listening," I said.

"Thank you for reaching out to me."

"Yes, but will you thank me in the morning?"

"We'll see," she said. "Now *you* go back to sleep."

THE NEXT MORNING, lacking an appetite, I skipped breakfast. Having recalled seeing a coffeemaker and a FREE COFFEE sign in the motel lobby, I headed in that direction. A few minutes later, as I loitered outside the lobby entrance sipping from the world's worst cup of coffee, I put in a call to Harvey Broward's office. His assistant put me through to him without delay.

"I'm glad you called," he said. "I'll be heading to the jail in a few minutes to speak with Libby. I'd like you to be there. She is, shall we say, more receptive when you're there."

"That's good," I said, "because I wanted to see her this morning, but I didn't know if she was still in holding."

"She was as of last night, but my understanding is she'll soon be moved to a cell in general population. Exactly when, I don't know."

We agreed to meet at the sheriff's office in fifteen minutes. I located the nearest trashcan and disposed of my coffee.

It was approaching nine o'clock by the time the attorney and I had been checked into the jail by a dour Deputy Rawlins and escorted to one of the interview rooms. When Libby arrived moments later, she rushed over and gave me a lavish hug. Then she hung onto me like a counterweight as we shuffled over to the table. I scooted two chairs together and we sat down, with her maintaining a grasp on me as secure as a wrestling hold.

"I wanted to update the two of you on the status of Libby's case," Broward said as he seated himself. His gaze turned gloomy. "I'm sorry, but it's not good news. It appears that the county attorney is determined to play hardball with this case. He insists that he will not back off from the charge of attempted murder."

"Damn," I said, feeling an urge to go a few rounds with a punching bag. "So what does that do to our chances of getting the bail amount reduced?"

The attorney shook his head disconsolately. "I've petitioned the court for a rehearing on the bail issue, but relief is not likely to be granted as long as the charge stays the same."

I grunted in exasperation.

Libby squeezed my arm. "It's all right, Darryl," she said, but the nervous flicker in her eyes suggested otherwise.

"We need to get you out of here," I said. She'd been locked up for almost seventy-two hours, and I worried about the physical and emotional toll her confinement was taking on her.

"I'll keep the dialogue going with the county attorney," Broward said. "It's possible I can get him to soften his position, but I wouldn't hold your breath. If we can't work something out on the bail issue, then the best we can do is ask for an early trial date." He stood to take his leave. "I wish I had better news."

I broke free of Libby's clutch, rose, and shook his hand. "Thank you for your efforts."

"I'll let the deputy know you'll be staying a while longer," he said as he exited the room.

I rejoined Libby at the table and we sat mutely for a time, shoulder to shoulder, leaning into each other as if in need of propping up. I longed to share some comforting words with her, but I knew there was nothing I could say that would alter the harsh reality of her situation.

Not wanting to squander the time we had left together, I spoke what was on my mind. I'd been thinking about what Tina Martin had told me about the connection between Bobby Hobson and Cyrus Tolliver, and the implications of it nagged at me. Also, it seemed too much of a coincidence that the name *Tolliver* had popped up again.

"Libby, did you know that Cyrus Tolliver and Bobby Hobson were poker buddies?"

She straightened in her chair as if she'd been poked with a pin. "So?"

"So, I spoke with someone recently who thinks that Bobby's relationship with Tolliver may have played a role in the way Bobby voted on the zoning proposal at the recent board of commissioners' meeting. It happens that Tolliver has a good reason for not wanting zoning regulations in Harbin County. Restrictions on the use of his land could cut into the revenue he receives from AltEnergy, the wind farm company. It's also the case that until recently Bobby professed a willingness to support zoning regulations for land use, yet he voted against them at the meeting. But then, you know that because you were there."

"Again—so?" Libby said, projecting an adolescent *whatever* attitude that annoyed me.

"So, do you have anything to say about all this?"

"Why should I?" she said, turning her face away.

"Look at me," I said.

After a delay that further irritated me (*Why was she making this so much harder than it needed to be?*), her head swiveled until her eyes met mine, and what I saw in them was a glass-eyed emptiness.

"Listen, Sis," I said, intent on breaking through to her awareness, "I'm gonna get to the bottom of what's going on here sooner or later, so you might as well tell me now what's driving your antagonism toward Bobby. I know you don't care about county politics, so it has to be something else. *What is it?*"

She bit her lip and fell silent.

"Talk to me, for God's sake!" I said, slapping the tabletop hard enough to make my palm sting.

She flinched. Her face twisted in pain. Tears flooded her eyes, and somewhere inside her an emotional dam broke. "It's all my fault," she said, letting out a pitiful wail. She covered her face with her hands and sobbed.

"What's your fault?"

"I can't... I can't," she said, wagging her head. "It's too awful."

"What's too awful? Tell me."

"It's no use!" she cried. "There's no one to blame but me." She shook her fists in the air. "Don't you see? It's done. You can't help me now."

No, I don't see! I wanted to scream, but I held my tongue and waited for her to calm down.

When at last she quieted, I brushed tears from her cheeks with my fingertips. I stroked her hair. "I love you," I said, "and I'm going to do everything in my power to get you out of here. But, at some point, I'm going to need your help."

She sulked. "There's nothing—"

I put my fingers to her lips to hush her. Another emotional eruption wouldn't do either of us any good. "I'm going now. But I'll be back. Okay?"

She nodded, but there was such anguish in her eyes I couldn't help but give credence to her despair, and wonder, *What is this awful thing that has snuffed out her capacity for hope?*

22

I FOUGHT TO rein in my frustration as I walked out of the county jail. For all my determination to make sense of things, to create order out of chaos, I had managed only to become more confounded by what I'd learned since arriving in Grotin. All my questions kept coming back to mock me, reverberating in my head as if I were shouting them into an echo chamber: *What is going on here? What is going on here? What is going on here?* I needed somehow to break the logjam of unknowns that clogged my pathway to understanding. *But how?* Libby wasn't talking. Bobby wasn't talking. And I was doing entirely too much talking to myself.

I got in my car and started driving with no particular destination in mind.

Even taking a meandering route, it doesn't take long to circumnavigate the width and breadth of Grotin. From the jail, I headed east for several blocks then turned north on a road that took me past the high school. The school's interconnected wings were shuttered and silent, as doubtless also were the minds of the students on summer break. A pickup game was in progress on the school's baseball field. An outfielder was chasing a ball hit in the gap between left and center fields. I doubted he would catch up to it before the batter circled the bases.

I ventured west on a cross street that led to the opposite side of town, where I cruised past the fairgrounds. They, too, were deserted. The Harbin County Fair, a mid-July event, would already have taken place. The exhibit halls had gone back to being empty warehouses. The open-air livestock shelters waited for their next opportunity to play host to would-be blue-ribbon hogs and heifers and their Future Farmers of America nursemaids.

Making turns at random, I wound my way south through residential streets so familiar to me during my youth that I could tell if a house had been painted a different color in my absence, or had been remodeled to an extent that altered the look of the exterior. I noticed that some streets had been improved, sidewalks and gutters installed, an occasional streetlamp erected.

Jimmy Parsons lived there. Joey Baker's house was across the street; his sister had epilepsy. That's the Reynolds's house. Mr. Reynolds almost killed his fourteen-year-old son Charlie when, besotted, he drove his pickup through the garage door, behind which Charlie kneeled as he worked to install a new chain on his Roadmaster bicycle.

Seemingly every other block, I passed a church—all Christian, mostly Protestant. On this corner, the Church of the Nazarene. Two turns away and midway down the block, Grace Baptist. Up ahead, First Presbyterian. And two streets over, the one Catholic church in town: St. Mary's with its high bell tower, always lighted at night—a beacon, like the Star of Bethlehem, to show us the way to the Christ Child.

I skirted downtown. I had traversed that hub of shoestring commerce enough times going to and from the jail for its foreignness to have worn off; I didn't like the feeling.

It was the sight of the Harbin County Community Hospital that finally halted my progress to nowhere—that put me back on a heading with intent. I pulled into a space in its parking lot.

"Someone," I muttered to myself, "had better start talking."

I STRODE DOWN the hallway in the hospital's General Care Unit, propelled by a renewed determination to lay bare the truth about what was going on behind the scenes in this *Libby Versus the Commissioner* melodrama. I was done with being Mr. Nice Guy. I wanted some answers and I wanted them now.

When I got to Bobby Hobson's room, I rushed in through the door like a predator ready to pounce.

The room was unoccupied.

Not only that, there were no signs of a current tenant. I looked around, confused. The bed was freshly made. All the life-support equipment was silent and disengaged. On a side wall, the patient's whiteboard had been wiped clean. Had I gotten the room number wrong? Or could Bobby have been moved to another room? *In the Critical Care unit?*

I walked back to the nurses' station.

"The doctor released him last evening," the nurse behind the counter informed me.

I should have been relieved. Bobby's release confirmed that his injury was not severe. This had to be good for Libby. Then why wasn't I pleased?

"Do you have a telephone book I can look at?"

According to their phone book listing, Bobby and Janelle Hobson lived on Cloverdale Drive in southeast Grotin. Libby had mentioned that Bobby was married, which had come as somewhat of a surprise to me, given his juvenile record as a serial lady-killer. It was Debbie who'd informed me of the identity of the lucky bride: the former Janelle Weaver. I only knew Janelle in passing. She was two years behind me and Bobby in school. But from what I remembered of her, she fit the profile when it came to Bobby's interest in members of the opposite sex: she was beauty-queen material whose intellectual lantern threw off little light.

The Cloverdale Drive area of Grotin is upscale only in relative terms. It's referred to as *the newer part of town*, because most of the homes there were built in the 1970s and '80s, the last era during which the town experienced anything resembling development. They are ranch-style homes set on large lots, with curbing and concrete driveways. Brickwork and stucco replaced the clapboard siding typical of the older homes in town. A number of white-collar government workers live in the area, along with the more successful businesspeople and their families.

By the time I pulled into the driveway of the well-maintained red-brick home on Cloverdale, I had managed to dial back my intensity level a notch or two. Being combative with Bobby wouldn't advance my cause, even though what I really wanted to do was to cudgel him into submission.

Janelle opened the door on the second ring of the doorbell. She was even prettier than I remembered. She had sea-green eyes and a sprinkle of freckles across her nose and cheeks. Her golden blond hair was pulled back in a ponytail. She had on a tank top and a pleated miniskirt, as if she'd just returned from a tennis match, and I pitied any male opponent of hers who had to keep his eyes on the ball when all they wanted was to be on her.

She cocked her head and looked at me with a questioning expression. Then, as if some unpleasant memory stirred in the back of her mind, her countenance dimmed like a dying sunset.

"I'm Darryl Coombs," I said. "I stopped at the hospital to visit Bobby and was told he'd been released. So I thought I'd drop by and see how he was doing."

"Bobby is resting," Janelle said in an icy tone.

"I certainly don't want to disturb his rest," I said, "but if I could speak with him briefly, I'd very much appreciate it. It's important, and I'm only going to be in town a few days."

"He's asleep."

"Then how about I come back in an hour?"

Her green eyes flared. "Look," she said, "I know who you are and why you're here. You're Libby Coombs's brother and you're here to make trouble for us the way you always make trouble for everybody. So, please go away and don't come back."

She was swinging the door closed when I heard Bobby's voice calling from inside. "Who is it, Jannie?"

I poked my head in the doorway, hoping not to get guillotined. Thankfully, Janelle resisted the urge to carry out my execution, halting the door's progress inches short of my exposed neck.

"Bobby, it's Darryl Coombs," I hollered into the house.

"Well, come on in," Bobby hollered back.

Janelle stood firm, cutting me to shreds with her eyes. Finally, she stepped aside and allowed me to enter.

Bobby was sitting tipped back in a recliner in the living room with a pillow behind his head. He was wearing plaid pajamas and moccasin slippers. He'd combed his hair but had yet to take a razor to his face. The side of his neck was bandaged, but there were no other signs of infirmity. In his hand was a remote control, which he'd apparently used to mute the wide-screen television mounted on the wall opposite his chair, its silent screen flickering with the action of what appeared to be a Civil War drama. On a TV tray beside his chair sat an empty porcelain mug and a dessert plate littered with crumbs.

"Haven't seen you in ten years," he said, bringing his chair to an upright position, "and now you've come to visit me twice in one week. You must care."

"I care about a lot of things."

"Sit down, Darryl. Jannie, honey, get my friend here some coffee and one of those famous scones of yours. She makes the greatest blueberry scones."

I waved off the offer. "Thanks anyway," I said, and remained standing. "I can't stay long. Maybe next time."

"Don't know what you're missing," Bobby said.

Before leaving the room, Janelle gave me a final stare, this one the equivalent of a dagger through the heart. I didn't bother pulling it out.

"Look, Bobby," I said, "this is not a social call."

"What is it, then?"

"You know damn well what it is," I said, feeling my blood pressure rise in spite of my desire to stay cool. I was tired of Bobby's feigned comradeship and pretend ignorance in the matter at hand. When he played for Grotin High's football team, he could juke his way through a host of defenders and, when he reached the end zone, be rewarded with a frenzy of chest bumps and helmet slaps. I wanted no part of his celebrated evasiveness. "This is an opportunity," I told him, "before things go from bad to worse, for you to come clean about what's going on between you and Libby that compelled her to lash out at you the way she did."

"You have it wrong, Darryl." He brushed some crumbs off his pajama top. "There's nothing going on between your little sister and me. And like I said before, I don't know why she did what she did."

I stood there smoldering inside, my anger stoked by the realization that all I was going to get from Bobby was pushback when what I needed was answers. "Tell me one thing then,"

I said. "At the last board of commissioners' meeting, why did you vote against the proposal to implement zoning regulations for land use, after purporting to support zoning earlier?"

"You've been talking to my critics."

"Actually, I've been talking to Commissioner Peeples, who was as surprised as anyone when you flip-flopped on the issue. So, why did you?"

Bobby smiled the smug smile of a man experienced in shading the truth. "Because it was the right thing to do."

"Bobby," I said, having none of his BS, "I've known you a long time, and I've never known you to concern yourself with doing the right thing."

He shrugged. "People change."

"I doubt you're one of those people," I said, and stalked out of the house.

As I drove away, I almost missed it. But a last glance back and there it was, barely detectable within a slender half-moon opening in the curtains covering a front-room window: the catlike glint of two green eyes.

23

THERE IS A SAYING attributed to St. Augustine that asserts, "The truth is like a lion. You don't have to defend it. Let it loose. It will defend itself." Since arriving in Grotin I had been on a quest to let loose the lion of truth—that is, to disclose the *why* behind Libby's assault on Bobby Hobson—in hopes that the truth would provide at least some measure of defense against the severity of the criminal charge brought against my sister. Even so, I was not fully at ease with this approach to her defense. For what St. Augustine's analogy does not take into account—and what worried me now as I pressed forward in my search for answers—is that, once set free, the lion of truth in defending itself is liable to eat you alive.

These and other thoughts were going through my mind as I drove out to the home of Cyrus Tolliver. It was unlikely I could extract any more information from Mr. Tolliver than I'd gotten out of Bobby, but I was at a loss as to where else to go for answers to my questions. I was like the stupid kid at the zoo, rattling the cages of the big cats and expecting something positive to happen. More likely than not, I'd simply get my fingers bit off.

But I couldn't shake the feeling that Tina Martin had hit on something when she'd suggested that Bobby's *no* vote on the proposed zoning regulations might have had something to do with his connection to Tolliver. The Bobby I knew did favors for people only if he got something in return. In this case, the one person who benefited most from Bobby's change of heart on the zoning issue was Cyrus Tolliver. It only made sense that Tolliver had done something for Bobby in return. I wanted to know what that something was.

There was another reason I wanted to pay the Tollivers a visit: RuAnn. Since learning about the car accident, I'd been curious about the extent of her injuries and wondered why Libby was so adamant in refusing to talk about RuAnn or the accident. What was it she didn't want me to know? Was there a connection between the car accident and the stabbing? It seemed implausible, but nothing about this whole affair made sense to me at the moment. Which left me with only one thing to do—keep rattling cages.

The current generation of Tollivers lived on a sprawling estate located several miles northwest of Grotin. The Tolliver name was well-known to the residents of Harbin County, since the Tolliver homestead had a narrative that was woven into the official history of the county. In the early 1870s, Major Zack Tolliver, a Civil War veteran, taking advantage of the Homestead Act, had settled on land along the bank of Turkey Creek, north of town. He built a cabin for himself and his new bride overlooking the creek and set about tilling the bottomland and having children. As it turned out, he didn't have the heart for farming, which he discovered requires a spiritual attachment to the land. As a former soldier, he was more comfortable with shooting guns than planting seeds. So it wasn't long before he gave up farming and took up hunting as a means of livelihood. Fortunately for him, the grasslands typical of the countryside thereabout yielded plenty of pheasant, quail, prairie chicken, turkey, and deer.

Subsequent generations of Tollivers tried their hand at farming with varying degrees of success but continued to rely on hunting for much of their subsistence. It was Cyrus's father, Delvin Tolliver, who went all in on hunting. He leased much of the family's landholdings to others for farming or use as pastureland but retained exclusive rights to hunt on the land. Then he built a hunting lodge near the site of Major Tolliver's original cabin and began hosting hunting parties.

The venture turned out to be quite profitable. Young Cyrus worked for his dad at the lodge and, when he was old enough, began guiding the hunting parties. When Delvin Tolliver died, Cyrus took over the entire operation. As an adjunct to his hunting business, Cyrus built a first-class skeet shooting range and began hosting skeet shooting tournaments. It was a good move on his part, as governmental regulations in the form of license fees, kill limits, and species protection eroded the popularity of hunting for sport. Another shrewd move Cyrus made was to sponsor and provide financial support for a skeet shooting class at Grotin High, which became an incubator for skeet shooting enthusiasts and, of course, a boon to Tolliver's business—at least until one student got careless loading his shotgun and blew off half of one foot. That ended skeet shooting instruction at Grotin High.

The Tollivers' home was about a half mile up the road from their hunting lodge and was built in a similar style—with stacked log construction, a green metal roof, and multiple gabled dormers. The Tollivers, I'd heard, had their own private skeet shooting course, and as I drove up the long driveway to their residence, evidence of this fact presented itself in the form of what sounded like explosions occurring in bursts of two at regular intervals.

I parked my Explorer behind a red pickup with mud flaps, got out, and approached the front door of the house. I knew I was taking a chance no one would be home, but I hadn't wanted to call ahead for the simple reason that I suspected announcing my visit would have resulted in my being disinvited. Bad news travels fast. In a small community like Grotin it travels at the speed of light. I didn't consider myself to be bad news—or a troublemaker, as Janelle Hobson had cast me—but then it wasn't my cage being rattled.

I had rung the doorbell three times and was prepared to abandon my enterprise when the door opened and a woman appeared. She was dressed in tan jeans and a western-style blouse with pearl snaps down the front and on the breast pockets. She looked to be in her mid-fifties, as evidenced by the streaks of gray in her shoulder-length hair. She was tall and sinewy in an athletic way and had an outdoor face—that ruddy, uneven facial skin tone characteristic of someone who has spent a lot of time in the sun while foregoing protection from UV rays. Nowhere on that face or in her eyes was the hint of a smile.

I had seen photos of the Tollivers in the newspaper and on fliers for skeet shooting events, but ten years and much white-washing of my recollection of the past had occurred since then, and I wasn't sure who this woman was.

She didn't give me a chance to inquire. "He's out back," she said in a prickly tone of voice, not bothering to hide her annoyance at my presence on her doorstep. She tossed her head to the side. "Go around and through the gate. Follow the noise." She shut the door.

I assumed that the *he* she was talking about was Cyrus Tolliver, and that, in her own way, Mrs. Tolliver had introduced herself to me—for what other woman than the woman of the house would have treated a visitor so brusquely, not caring who I was or why I was there, only assuming that I was not there to see her.

I followed her instructions and ventured around to the back of the house. The explosions I'd heard grew louder as I rounded the corner, and at that point I was able to identify their source. A hundred yards or so beyond the house, in a clearing ringed by a copse of trees, a man stood with his back to me. I watched as he raised a long gun to his shoulder and pointed it at the sky. Moments later, two quick blasts of gunfire shattered the brief interlude of quiet.

Edging closer to the action, I noted the two skeet houses, the high one on the left and the low one on the right, from which clay targets were being launched like birds in frantic flight. The acrid smell of gunpowder hung heavy in the air. With uneasy fascination, as if observing a scheduled demolition, I watched the man shoot several more volleys from different positions on the skeet layout. Each time he fired, the clay disk exploded in a shower of shards that, as they caught the sunlight, gave off the effect of fireworks. He quickly broke open the gun to eject the spent shells and reloaded the breech with fresh cartridges.

When eventually he missed a target, the man stomped his foot and cursed. With a semaphoric hand gesture, he signaled to the trap operator that he was done. He emptied the breech of his gun, shouldered it, and began striding toward the house with the resolution of someone who's late for an appointment. He would have walked past me without acknowledging my presence had I not stepped into his intended path.

His eyes sparked. "What?" he said, extracting his earplugs.

Cyrus Tolliver was a big man. He had a barrel chest and a sandbag belly. His meaty face continued up his forehead in rows of cranial wrinkles that gave way to thin, graying hair combed straight back on top and on the sides. He was wearing scuffed high-top boots, khaki cargo pants, and a shooting vest over a T-shirt dark with sweat stains at the armpits. His girth and bearing were reminiscent of a man I'd once seen in a circus act wrestle a bear.

"Mr. Tolliver," I said, already feeling intimidated by his presence. "I'm Darryl Coombs. Libby Coombs is my sister. Can I have a few minutes of your time?"

I knew then that Cyrus Tolliver was a good poker player, because there was not a flicker of reaction in his eyes to my request, not a tick of cheek or tweak of brow.

"This way," he muttered, and I hustled to keep pace with him as he marched toward a small outbuilding connected to the back of his home by a breezeway.

I had never been in a gun shop before. When we entered the building, the scent of gun solvent was pervasive, its rank sweetness attaching itself to the soft tissue at the back of my throat. To keep from gagging, I swallowed frequently, which did my stomach no favor.

Tolliver laid his shotgun, a 12-gauge over and under, on a workbench. He took off his vest and hung it on a peg on the wall, alongside other hanging vests. My eyes went to an adjoining wall lined with shelves laden with skeet shooting trophies, testaments to this family's facility with guns. Beneath the array of trophies stood a broad Browning gun safe with an elk-head emblem on the door. Inscribed below the emblem were the words KEEP IT SAFE. A warning to be heeded, I knew all too well.

"Are you a shooter, Darryl?" Tolliver said.

"No, sir. Can't say that I am." I didn't say what I was thinking, that my mother was anti-gun and I had good reason to be her ally in that cause, and that in high school I had opted for the sport of badminton over skeet shooting.

He opened a drawer in the workbench and withdrew some rags, along with a can of gun solvent, a box of cleaning pads, and a ramrod. "Shooting's a good stress reliever," he said. He squirted solvent onto the barrel of his gun and began rubbing it down with a rag. "You feel yourself gettin' stressed out by your job or your personal life. You want to kick and scream, punch your fist through a wall, or beat the crap out of someone who's been giving you a hard time. You could do those things, but you'd probably regret it later. It's much better to get yourself a gun, preferably something that kicks like a cannon and sounds as loud when you pull the trigger. Then you go to your local shooting range and have at it. You load up, draw a bead on your target, and fill it so full of holes the only thing it's good for when you're done is confetti. Poof!" he said, "no more stress." He blew some lint from the action of his gun. "Hell, every one of those clay pigeons I blew to smithereens today lowered my blood pressure a half point."

He loaded a pad onto the end of his ramrod and doused it with solvent. "Now, what can I do for you, Darryl?" He inserted the rod into the top barrel of his gun and began working it back and forth. "This is about your sister, I'm guessin'." He shook his head. "Troubling incident."

By this time the smell of gun solvent had nauseated me and all this talk about shooting had set my teeth on edge. I was also realizing how far out of my element I was here, confronting this man who obviously had a gunslinger mentality. But it was too late to back down now. "The truth is, Mr. Tolliver, I'm struggling to make sense of a lot of things that have gone on around here lately, including my sister's actions, and I was hoping you could help me out by answering a few questions."

"Fire away," Tolliver said. He winked and added, "in a manner of speaking."

I swallowed for the twentieth time. "I . . . uh . . . I'd like to ask you about AltEnergy. I understand they've erected a number of wind turbines on land you own."

Tolliver withdrew the cleaning rod, changed to a fresh pad,

and continued working at an efficient but unhurried pace. "Darryl, I understand you've been gone from Harbin County for a number of years."

"Ten, to be exact."

"Well, I'm sure I don't need to tell you that a lot of things have changed during that time, not just in this county but nationwide. One of those changes has been the growth of wind power as a source of energy. It just so happens that wind is something we have in abundance around here. So, yes, I've allowed windmills to be placed on some of my land. But I fail to see how that's any concern of yours."

"Maybe, it isn't," I admitted. "But nothing happens in a vacuum, and Libby's stabbing of Bobby Hobson happened at a time and place where the perceived need for stricter regulation of wind farms was under discussion—with strong opinions voiced by a number of citizens. I'm just trying to understand what this debate is all about."

Tolliver arched an eyebrow. "Awright, then, I'm gonna indulge you on this. But only because I got nothing better to do while I finish cleaning this gun"—he'd gone to work on the second barrel—"which'll take me about three more minutes."

"I'll be direct then."

"Good. It's always better to aim before you shoot."

"Yes . . . well . . ." There was no doubt who had the upper hand here. I cleared my throat and tried to let go of some of the tension that had built up inside me. "Am I correct in assuming that you oppose zoning regulations for land use—regulations that could inhibit the future installation of wind turbines in the county and possibly restrict the operation of those currently in place?"

"You are," Tolliver said. "And I make no excuses for that stance. I've always been an advocate for private property rights.

I don't think the government should be able to tell me what I can and cannot do with my land."

"And does Bobby Hobson feel the same way?"

Tolliver shrugged. "You'd have to ask him that."

"But he's your friend, isn't he? Surely the two of you have talked about the issue."

"We've talked about a lot of things."

"During your Thursday night poker games?"

Tolliver paused his cleaning action and peered at me through narrow eyes. "What are you angling at, Coombs?"

"Is Bobby a good poker player?" I asked.

"He holds his own."

"Wins a lot of big pots, does he?" It dawned on me that I might have uncovered the quid pro quo I was sure existed: Tolliver loses large sums of money to Bobby at the poker table in exchange for Bobby's *no* vote on the zoning issue.

Tolliver guffawed. "Nah, Bobby goes home a loser more often than not. If you don't believe me, talk to his wife." His aspect hardened. "Look, why don't you just come out and ask me what you really want to know: Did I buy Bobby's vote on the zoning issue?"

"Am I that transparent?"

"As a bakery case."

"So, did you—buy Bobby's vote?"

Tolliver let out a derisive snort. "Didn't have to," he said, giving his ramrod a few final thrusts before withdrawing it. "Bobby came to his senses long ago on that issue. He didn't need no prompting from me."

I was feeling more and more like that stupid kid at the zoo as I watched Tolliver stow his cleaning supplies. He retrieved a container of gun oil and a rag from a separate drawer. He applied oil to the rag and began wiping down his gun.

I was about to be dismissed.

At that moment, the shop door opened and a beautiful young woman came rushing in. "Daddy," she said as she ran over and hugged Tolliver around the middle the way a child would, "look what Mommy got me." She proudly displayed a stuffed giraffe.

"Be careful, Ru. I got gun oil on my hands."

"Mom says I get to name it."

"That's nice, sweetheart."

RuAnn? Could this be the same girl who'd been Libby's friend all these years? The last time I'd seen her in the flesh she was nine years old and as distinguishable from other girls her age as one blade of grass from another. Since then, I'd viewed her likeness in photos Libby had sent me via Instagram. But in the photos, the two of them were always clowning around, hanging off one another's shoulder, mugging for the camera—girls being girls. And because my eyes were always drawn toward my sister's image, I hadn't paid attention to the transformation that had taken place over time in RuAnn's physical appearance. And it had been a while since Libby had shared any photos of the two of them together.

Seeing RuAnn in person now was a shock. At nineteen, she was a beautiful woman in full flower. She had a curvaceous figure, long flowing flaxen hair, and the face of a magazine cover model. But what struck me most was how much she'd grown up to look like her older sister Ashley. I hadn't seen Ashley in ten years either. Libby had mentioned that she'd gone off to college in California and stayed there. But I would have sworn that she was standing here before me at this very moment, the resemblance was that uncanny.

The other surprising aspect of RuAnn's appearance was that she didn't look damaged in any way. Her body had survived the car crash unscathed. Only her mind had been scrambled.

"Hello, RuAnn," I said. "You probably don't remember me. I'm Libby's brother."

She looked at me uncertainly for a moment before turning back to her father. "Daddy, Mom says to tell you—" She scrunched up her face, apparently trying hard to remember the rest of the message. "You got a meeting," she announced, smiling broadly at her achievement.

"Awright, honey," Tolliver said. "You go on back to the house and I'll be along soon." When RuAnn hesitated, he waved her on. "Go on now."

"Okay, Daddy," she said, and left.

Tolliver wiped his hands with a clean rag, then tossed the rag onto his workbench. He opened the big Browning safe and placed his shotgun on a rack inside. "Darryl," he said, turning the full force of his attention on me. "I know life hasn't always treated you fairly. No doubt you were smart to put this town behind you. And you'd be smart to go back to wherever it is you call home these days." His eyes bored into me. "You're an outsider here now. As I said, a lot of things have changed in the last ten years, but one thing that hasn't is that bad things have a way of happening to you here. The longer you stay in Grotin, the longer you put yourself at risk."

"Is that a threat?" I said, knowing full well it was.

"No, son. It's the voice of experience speaking."

"I have to do what I can for my sister," I said, trying to sound bolder than I felt.

He nodded musingly. "Yeah . . . *Libby*. Always liked that girl. Can't imagine what got into her, stabbing Bobby like that in front of all those . . . witnesses." He made a clicking noise with his tongue that sounded enough like a gun being cocked to make my gut twitch. "Best let the lawyers handle that." He rolled his shoulders and straightened his back. "Now, if you'll excuse me, I got some business to attend to."

He exited the gun shop, leaving me with a roiling stomach and the all-too-familiar feeling of helplessness. But at least I still had all my fingers.

24

I CAME AWAY from my meeting with Cyrus Tolliver feeling more stymied than ever in my quest to help Libby. Despite all the digging I'd done over the last couple of days, I had failed to unearth answers to any of the questions that lay at the heart of this (as Tolliver had labeled it) *troubling incident.* Like a room too full of furniture, my mind was cluttered with uncertainties useful only for tripping over. Why had Libby attacked Bobby Hobson? Why had Bobby done an about-face on the zoning issue? If it wasn't for money, what then? What part, if any, did Tolliver play in this muddy-watered drama?

To my lament, I was not one candela closer to enlightenment regarding these vexing questions. In fact, the only thing I'd accomplished by confronting Cyrus Tolliver was to make myself cannon fodder in a political skirmish I was not a party to. Tolliver was right: bad things always happened to me here. Now they were happening to Libby, and my attempts at intervention had served only to fan the flames of hostility toward me and my sister.

It was well past lunchtime by now and I hadn't eaten anything all day. But I was too worked up to feel hunger pains, so I headed back to the jail to see Libby. Maybe—just maybe—she was ready to open up to me, for I was sorely in need of some breadcrumbs to lead me out of this jungle of confusion I found myself in.

Inside the sheriff's office, a deputy I didn't recognize sat behind the duty desk. He was an older fellow with a gray-stubbled chin and droopy eyelids. His uniform was crumpled and ill-fitting, as if it had been rented from a costume shop. I told him who I was and that I wanted to visit Libby.

"You're here at the wrong time, pal," he said. "Visiting hours are over for the day."

I muffled a sigh. Another hard case.

"That may be," I said, "but your records will show that I have permission to visit my sister while she's in holding, and I understand there are no set visiting hours for holding."

"You understand correctly," he said with a hyperbolic nod. "The thing is, your sister is no longer in holding. She was moved to a cell in general population about an hour ago."

I flinched as in my head I heard the bang of the judge's gavel striking its sounding block.

"I see," I said, taking short quick breaths in an effort to keep a lid on my simmering disappointment. "In that case, when is the soonest I can visit her?"

The deputy poked a finger at a bulletin board on the wall behind me. "Daily visiting hours are posted there."

I reviewed the listed hours: MONDAY, WEDNESDAY, FRIDAY—9:00 a.m. to 11:00 a.m., and 1:30 p.m. to 3:00 p.m.; TUESDAY, THURSDAY, SATURDAY—9:00 a.m. to 11:00 a.m. only. NO VISITATION SUNDAY. Today was Thursday—visiting hours had ended at eleven. The earliest I could see Libby was the next morning at nine o'clock. I cursed the day, the minute, the hour, and every other temporal element I could think of.

As soon as I was out of the building, I called Libby's attorney.

"I just found out myself," Broward said. "It was only a matter of time before a bed opened up in general population. And it's probably for the best. Libby won't be so isolated. She'll have a roommate and access to a commons area and a telephone."

"I can call her?"

"No. Outgoing calls only, and limited times of the day. And she'll need to have a phone account set up for her before she can make any calls. How are you doing on raising the bail money?"

I admitted that I'd given up on that approach for the time being. "I can't raise the up-front fee much less come up with the required collateral."

"Well, do what you can," the attorney said. "The judge in the case has granted my petition for a rehearing on the bail issue, so there's still a chance we can get it reduced."

"By how much?"

"I'd rather not speculate," the attorney said, and I knew why. He didn't want to feed my hopes with bloated optimism.

Nursing a bout of despondency, I returned to my motel room and sat on the edge of the bed with my head in my hands. *Do what you can*, the attorney had told me. But to what end? So far, no action I'd taken since coming back to Grotin had produced a positive outcome. All I'd succeeded in doing was to revive dormant animosities and peel the scab off old wounds. Now I was charged with delivering on what amounted to a ransom demand in order to rescue my sister from confinement.

Twenty-five thousand dollars! At best I could come up with $10,000. But how would I get my hands on the rest? I'd have to go out and rob a bank. Yet even that would take more skill and courage than I had. Besides, I was no thief, although I had once been branded as one. And who had held the hot iron to my flesh? None other than Bobby Hobson.

After all this time, it still made me furious to think about it. You'd figure that in twelve years you could slough off the hurt and shame of something like that. Time is supposed to heal all wounds, but sometimes it only allows them to fester.

IT WAS DURING the summer following my sophomore year of high school that I'd been branded as a thief. I had gone to work as a stock boy at Hobson's Farm Supply on Northwest 2nd Street. I swept floors, stocked shelves, and helped customers load fertilizer, seed, and livestock feed into their pickups and onto their flatbeds. The first few days I wanted to quit because my shoulders and back ached from hoisting sacks as heavy as wet hay bales. But I took doses morning and evening of Extra Strength Tylenol and stuck with it, and after a week or so my body adjusted to the hard work.

Hobson's Farm Supply was family owned and operated. Mr. Hobson and his wife, Rebecca, both worked at the store full time, as did Rebecca's brother Jerod. The Hobson children—Jason, MaryAnn, and Bobby—helped out at the store afternoons and weekends. Summers, the younger Hobsons worked extended hours. When Jason joined the Navy and MaryAnn got married and moved to Colorado, Mr. Hobson started hiring local kids to fill in at the store during the summer. That's how I got a job there, working alongside Bobby, the youngest of the Hobson kids.

Bobby being Bobby, he presumed that whenever we worked together he was my boss, even though he had no more status at the store than I did, other than on one account: he'd been entrusted with a key to the cash register so that he could cashier on the occasions that his mom, dad, and uncle were all busy or away from the store, which was usually during lunchtime or when they were meeting with their various suppliers. It didn't matter to me that I wasn't allowed to cashier. But Bobby acted as if it gave him the cachet of a rock star. He stood erect behind the cash register with his chest puffed out, grinning as if he was king of the world.

While on the job at Hobson's, I avoided Bobby as much as I could. And he mostly ignored me, unless it happened that some odious task needed done that he felt was beneath him, like cleaning up spills of pesticide or removing dead chicks from the incubator. Then he was in my face with *orders from headquarters* to drop what I was doing and *take care of it*. I needed the job, so I did as I was told, even though I didn't like who was doing the telling.

I'd been employed at the farm supply store for about three weeks without incident, when one morning not long after I arrived for work Mr. Hobson called me into his office and directed me to a chair opposite where he sat behind his desk. He was a nice man with a ready smile who'd always treated me fairly. I had heard that his wife was less charitable, and so I'd done my best while she was at the store to stay out of her way. So when Mr. Hobson called me into his office, I didn't think much about it until I noticed he wasn't smiling.

"Darryl," he said, eyeing me over the top of his wire-rimmed glasses, "I know things are tight for your mother, and you've been helping her out, but stealing is not the way to do it."

Stealing? What . . . ? My mind went blank. It seemed that I had come too late to this conversation to pick up on its true meaning. "I don't understand, sir."

Mr. Hobson's eyes turned cold. "Darryl, we know you've been taking money from the till."

"But . . . sir . . . ," I said, staggered by the accusation. I felt dizzy and sick to my stomach. "That's not true. I haven't stolen anything. It's not how I was raised."

Mr. Hobson wagged his head the way a disappointed parent would. "When Bobby first told us he'd seen you pilfering from the cash drawer, we didn't want to believe him. We've never had need for surveillance cameras in the store. This is an honest community. People don't steal from their friends and neighbors. But after cash started going missing from the till, even though it was small amounts, we decided we had to do something about it." He made a *tsking* sound with his tongue. "Darryl, we have you on video getting into the cash drawer."

"But... but..." I was too shaken and confused by what I was hearing to be capable of further response.

Mr. Hobson rested his forearms on his desk. "Now, Darryl, I don't want to involve the police in this if we can help it. So here's what we're going to do. I don't know how you got a key to the cash register. But you give us the key, pay back the money you stole, and we'll call it square. We'll have to let you go, of course."

I sat there open-mouthed for a time before I could get out any words. "I... I don't have a key to the cash drawer," I said, "and the only time I ever—"

That was the moment I knew I was screwed. I was a fly caught in a spider web. I was a mouse that had triggered the trap. There was no use in continuing to claim my innocence. They had *undeniable proof* of my guilt. Any protestations to the contrary would fall on deaf ears. Any explanation I offered would prompt cannon blasts of denial from Bobby. Who were they going to believe? Not me.

"As I said, son, we have you on video using a key to open the cash drawer."

"How much money did I steal?" I said.

"Don't be impertinent."

"I wouldn't think of it, sir."

Mr. Hobson scowled. "In case you just happened to lose count, during the time you've worked here, the sum of one hundred sixty-five dollars has gone missing from the till. And that's the amount you will need to repay."

I was sixteen years old at the time. By then I was well aware that life is a sweet-and-sour dish sometimes served with immoderate measures of vinegar. I had tasted life's bitterness more times than I cared to, and I should have been prepared to drink my next cup of gall with dispassion. But that was not the case. As I sat there contemplating my situation, I felt the hurt and anger building inside me like floodwaters rising behind a dam. Hot tears streamed down my cheeks. My fingernails dug into my palms as my hands tightened into fists. I trembled uncontrollably.

"I'm sorry, son," Mr. Hobson said, and I believed him.

I was sorry too, but not for any wrong I had done—rather for my stupidity, for allowing life to stomp on me again, because I should have known better. I should have seen it coming. One of Bobby's buddies said to me later, "You're such an idiot to have fallen for that." And he was right.

There was a reason the receipts at Hobson's Farm Supply had come up short on occasion that summer. And there was a reason I'd been *caught on video* with my fingers in the till. But in neither case was it because I had been stealing. It was because I was at hand when Bobby needed a patsy.

It so happened that during those times when Bobby cashiered, he'd been selling goods to his friends using favorable terms. It went like this: They paid for their purchases with cash, and Bobby gave them change. The thing was, when they paid with a five, he gave them change for a ten. If they paid with a ten, he gave them change for a twenty. The sales registered correctly, which was important for keeping the inventory accurate, but at the end of the day the receipts came up short. Bobby didn't do this every day, and not with just anybody, only on occasion and only for a few of his best buddies.

Bobby must have known his scheme had a limited lifespan, although I doubt he'd thought it through that far. In the end,

I think it was just, once again, Bobby being Bobby. When he learned that his father, having become concerned about the receipts shortages, had installed a surveillance camera, he began looking around for a scapegoat. And there I was.

On the afternoon that I was captured on video allegedly stealing, I was at the store stocking shelves. The store was closed, but we had received a shipment of goods earlier in the day that needed stocking and I had agreed to stay late to do the job. Bobby was supposed to be helping, but I wasn't surprised to find myself working alone.

I was in the garden section, racking hand tools, when he appeared at the end of the aisle. He was with a girl and they were talking and laughing. I ignored him as I always did. Towing the girl by the hand, he sauntered up to me and said, "Hey, Coombs, your little sister came into the store earlier looking for you, but I didn't know where you were. She had a note for you from your mother. Said it was important. Wanted me to give it to you."

"What are you talking about?"

What he was saying didn't make sense. Why would Mother have sent Libby to the store with a note for me? If Mother had something important to tell me, she could just call the store and ask for me. Then again, if she'd let me have a cell phone, like most other kids my age—

"You want the note or not?" Bobby said.

"Yeah. Sure. Let's see this note." I held out my hand.

He didn't have it on him, he said. When Libby had given it to him, he hadn't wanted to lose it, so he'd put it in the cash register drawer—"for safekeeping."

I asked him to get it for me.

"Hey," he responded, bracing up against the girl, "don't you see I got better things to do?" He handed me a key. "Get the note yourself. I put it under the twenties."

I took the key but didn't feel right about it. Despite Bobby's prompting, getting into the cash drawer myself didn't seem like a good idea. I deliberated on my options for a time before deciding on a course of action.

I broke off from my work and went to the front of the store to look for Mr. or Mrs. Hobson or Jerod to ask for their help in the matter.

Nobody was around.

I lingered there, jiggling the key in my hand as if it were a pair of dice, as I gazed at the cash register and pondered what to do. I still couldn't figure why Mother would have sent me a note, although I saw no reason for Bobby to lie about such a thing. But even if there was a note, I was loath to access the cash drawer to retrieve it.

I had a thought. I would call home and ask my mother if she had sent me a note, and if she had, what it said. Problem solved.

I used the wall phone behind the front counter to dial our home number. No one picked up. I let the phone ring and ring. Still no answer. I hung up and dialed again with the same result. Mother wasn't home, and neither was Libby. I wondered why, and not knowing why worried me.

Maybe Bobby was telling the truth. Maybe there *was* a note. And maybe the note would tell me why Mother wasn't home to answer the phone.

Feeling a sense of urgency now to turn these *maybes* into concrete answers, I made one more sweep around the store in search of a senior Hobson to consult. When I found none, my need to resolve the issue reached critical mass. If there *was* a note, I needed to know what it said!

I went to the cash register and used the key Bobby had given me to unlock it. I opened the cash drawer, dug beneath the twenties, and pulled out a note. I unfolded it and read it—all one word of it.

FOOL

"Very funny," I said to Bobby when I returned the key to him, but he was too busy groping the girl to respond.

It wasn't until the following morning when I was called into Mr. Hobson's office and accused of being a thief that I realized how big a fool I'd been, and it angered me. And as I sat there with my fists clenched and tears gushing from my eyes, my anger grew exponentially—by the factor of my stupidity, by the factor of my hatred at that moment for Bobby, by the factor of the humiliation my mother would once again have to endure because of me.

I barely recall what I did next. Looking back on it later, I thought I must have had an out-of-body experience. As I stumbled out of Mr. Hobson's office, it was as if I were viewing the action from above.

I wandered throughout the store, moving mindlessly up and down the aisles, looking for Bobby. I couldn't find him. I kept searching, because there was nothing else for me to do. At last, I found him in the stockroom.

"Hey," I said, walking up to him.

"Not now, pal. I'm busy. Got all these pre-orders to pull. On second thought," he said, shoving a bundle of order slips at me. "Here. You pull them."

I took a half-step forward and hit him in the face with my fist as hard as I could. The blow dropped him to the floor. As he lay there squealing, blood streaming from his nose, I kicked him in the ribs.

Then I floated, or so it seemed, back to Mr. Hobson's office. "You'd better call the police after all," I told him. And he did.

I BELLOWED IN frustration now, not because of the fool I'd been back then but because of my current ineptitude in helping my sister. I needed to get her out of jail, and stewing about old hurts was not going to further that cause. So I tossed aside the useless memories, shook myself into a state of resolve, and began making phone calls—to a representative at my bank, to an account administrator for the company managing my 401K, to used car dealers within a fifty-mile radius—with the purpose of putting together as much bail money as I could. Would it be enough? I had no idea.

25

I CALLED CHARLOTTE that evening. She had become my lifeline to normalcy—such as it was. And I missed her much more than I'd thought I would. I felt an emptiness at my center that I had never experienced before, and it confused me. Charlotte and I had been a couple for going on three years now, but we had kept the liaison low stakes, as if we'd set a betting limit on our future prospects. Neither of us wanted to be a big loser in the romance game. So our relationship sailed in shallow waters and always near the shore. We never uttered the word *love*, never spoke of marriage, never made plans for the future. We simply enjoyed each other's company, reveled in the touch and taste of each other's flesh, and never asked for more than what was offered out of hand. We had drawn a line in the sparkling sand of our mutual affection and never crossed it. Ours was a bond without a promise, and both of us had wanted it that way.

So when I talked to Charlotte that evening, I didn't convey to her this deepening sense of longing I felt for her, for fear of breaching our unspoken accord. I imparted instead a hazy truth. "I miss you," I said. "I've been gone only a few days and it seems like a month."

"I know what you mean," she said. "It's been terribly quiet around here without you."

I had already filled her in on my latest efforts to help Libby, and vented my frustration at being thwarted at every turn. At this point in our conversation, I wanted to keep things light.

"So that's what I am to you," I said, "a noisemaker."

Charlotte laughed, a rich delicious laugh like chocolate pudding. "Among other things."

"Well, maybe that's what I ought to be doing here in Grotin," I said, "making noise."

"Maybe you should."

"Let's see," I said, going with the flow. "I could get my hands on a bass drum and march down Main Street banging it—at three o'clock in the morning."

"Who knows, you might start a parade."

"Or get shot."

"There is that possibility."

"Maybe something a bit more subtle?"

"That's probably advisable."

"I'll sleep on it," I said.

And I did.

THE NEXT MORNING, I showed up at the county jail a few minutes before the commencement of visiting hours. I quickly learned that visiting someone lodged in general population was a much less personal experience than interacting with them in an interview room. I might as well have been Skyping with Libby from the International Space Station.

Following the check-in procedure at the front desk, a uniformed deputy escorted me through a series of steel-plated doors and into the visiting area, which was nothing more than a wide corridor sectioned off by partitions. Within each partitioned space was a molded plastic chair facing a fixed, wire-reinforced window. A corded desk phone without a keypad sat on a narrow counter below the window. The person you were there to visit would take a seat on the opposite side of the glass in a space that mirrored your own, and you would talk to them via telephone.

"You'll have fifteen minutes from the time you pick up the phone," my escort said as I seated myself and waited for Libby to arrive.

When she did, I was startled by her appearance. Her hair was a rat's nest of tangles, her face was pastry puffy, and there were dark half-moons under her eyes. Her body had a ragdoll stoop. She flopped down in her chair with her arms dangling at her sides as limply as if they'd been robbed of their bones. Libby's attorney had expressed the opinion that she would be better off in general population than in holding. Clearly that was not the case.

I picked up the telephone receiver on my side of the window, and she did the same on hers. "What's wrong?" I said.

"Nothing," she said, shaking her head. "It's just that . . ."

"What?"

"The girls in here are so . . . mean."

"What did they do?"

Her face flushed. "They're just so rude and crude. They have filthy mouths and they're always looking to pick a fight with you. I don't know—maybe it's just because I'm the new girl. But I don't like it. And if one of them lays a hand on me, I'm gonna claw her eyes out." Her eyes glistened from the tears I knew she was holding back.

"I'm sorry," I said, furious with myself for not having done more to help her.

"It's not your fault."

"Mom wouldn't agree with you. And she's right. I should have been here for you."

Libby shook her head. "It wouldn't have mattered. There was nothing you could have done to stop me from doing what I did."

"That's what I don't understand," I said, unable to quell my vexation over her dismissal of the central question in her case. "Why *did* you do what you did? Until I know—"

I stopped when I saw the tears spilling from her eyes. She swiped at them with the back of her hand.

I sighed and moved on; the clock was ticking on our time together. "I went to see Cyrus Tolliver yesterday," I said. "RuAnn was there."

Her eyes widened. "You saw RuAnn?"

"Yes."

Like the sun when eclipsed by a fast-moving cloud, the light of acknowledgment on Libby's face suddenly gave way to a dark expression of sorrow.

"What's the matter now?" I said.

"They won't let me see RuAnn anymore. Not since—"

"Not since what?"

She turned away, but I could tell from the convulsing of her chest she was crying.

"Libby," I said, sensing a crack in her closemouthed attitude toward her legal jeopardy, "don't you get it? You need to tell me what this is all about. Either that or you'd better start making nice with your cellmates. Because if you don't start talking, you're not getting out of here for a good long time. And if you go to trial on the attempted murder charge and are convicted, you're likely to spend years in a state prison. And I don't think your cellmates there will be any more hospitable than your current ones. Is that what you want?"

She remained speechless for a time, sobbing softly. At length, having calmed, she faced me again. Mucous seeped from her nostrils. She sniffled several times, then wiped her nose on the sleeve of her jumpsuit. "They blamed it on me," she said, "but it wasn't my fault."

"The accident?"

"No. RuAnn's pregnancy."

My head snapped back as my mind did a backflip in midair. "RuAnn is pregnant?"

Harsh noise came through the phone as Libby unclogged her throat. "She was. She had a miscarriage."

"Wait a minute," I said. "You've lost me. RuAnn had a miscarriage because of the accident?"

Libby flapped her free hand. "No, no. She wasn't pregnant when the accident happened. She had the miscarriage four months later."

I rapped my knuckles on the window between us for no reason other than to emphasize my confusion. "What are you talking about? I saw RuAnn yesterday. The accident definitely damaged her brain. She was like a child. How could the child she is now have had a romantic relationship with anyone?"

And that's when the thought hit me, its aspect so hideous I wanted to turn away from it. *It's not possible; no one with a soul would have done something so base, so repulsive.* But there it was—the most unimaginable and yet most logical explanation for everything that had happened. "Bobby Hobson?" I said.

Libby looked at me with the agony of one who has taken on herself the sins of the world. She gave an almost imperceptible nod.

"Are you sure? How . . . ?"

"I don't have proof, like DNA or anything," she said. "But I'm sure in my heart."

"Libby, please . . . *please* . . . tell me everything you know."

She leaned toward the glass that separated us. Her eyes, glossy from her tears, grew round with recall. "When the car accident happened, I didn't know how bad RuAnn was hurt.

She had a lump on the side of her head, but she wasn't bleeding or anything. When I asked her if she was okay, she didn't respond. She looked dazed. I thought she must be in shock—had a concussion or something. I was just glad we were both alive. It never dawned on me that RuAnn had suffered brain damage."

She closed her eyes for a moment and took a deep breath before continuing. "I called 911, and it wasn't long before an ambulance came and took RuAnn to the hospital here in Grotin, where the ER doctors treated her. But instead of admitting her, they transferred her to a hospital in Manhattan for follow-up care. I was worried sick about her and wanted to visit her, but the Tollivers had told the hospital 'no visitors but family.' A week later, RuAnn was moved to a rehab facility, also in Manhattan, with the family-only visitor restriction still in place. It was almost a month after that when the Tollivers finally brought her home.

"But they still wouldn't let me see her or even talk to her on the phone. I called RuAnn's cell and got a *no service* message. Whenever I called the Tollivers' home number, the answering machine picked up. It was maddening. I couldn't understand why I was being shut out of RuAnn's life. Were they blaming me for the accident?

"Then, talking to other people, I found out that it wasn't just me they were keeping away from RuAnn; it was everybody. Later, it became obvious to me that they hadn't wanted anyone to know about the brain damage. I think they were hoping RuAnn's condition was only temporary."

Libby blotted the remaining tears from her eyes. Now that she'd opened up about the circumstances surrounding her assault of Bobby Hobson, she seemed determined to share every detail of the story no matter the emotional cost.

"Anyway, during this time, RuAnn was still getting treatment. Twice a week her mother took her to an outpatient rehab clinic in Beloit for therapy, even though there's a similar facility here in Grotin. At some point the therapist at the clinic recommended that RuAnn be allowed to spend time with some of her friends from before the accident, hoping the interaction would help her get better. RuAnn's parents didn't like the idea, but they eventually gave in and started letting me come to the house to visit her. But they made me promise not to tell anyone about her condition, how damaged she really was. After a while they allowed me to take her to her therapy sessions.

"One day when we were on our way to a session, we happened to see Bobby Hobson. He was getting out of his car in the parking lot at the hunting lodge. When RuAnn saw Bobby, she giggled. I asked her what she was giggling about. She said, 'He's my boyfriend. But don't tell anyone. It's a secret.'

"I laughed it off. I thought, you know, with her brain not working right, she could be imagining all kinds of silly things. Then a few weeks later, when I went to visit RuAnn, her mother wouldn't let me see her. She was crazy mad at me. 'You horrible girl!' she screamed, getting in my face. 'What have you done?'

"I had no idea what she was talking about. 'Who is he?' she demanded to know. 'Who raped my little girl? I'll kill him! I'll kill the son of a bitch!'

"Again, I didn't know who or what she was talking about. But she kept on like that, psycho ranting and demanding answers, and it frightened me. I'd never seen her like that. She'd always been nice to me, although RuAnn had told me that her mother had a temper—that when she got torqued off with RuAnn or Mr. Tolliver, she would sometimes go rageaholic, screaming and throwing things. It scared me to be on the receiving end of her anger, because I thought, wow, she really could kill someone, and that someone could be me."

As Libby spoke, the fingers of her free hand feverishly twiddled the telephone cord. "All I could do was keep repeating that

I didn't know what she was talking about. Finally, she yelled at me to get out and never come back, and I did."

She exhaled forcefully. "I was really shook up and didn't know what to do, or whether I should talk to anyone about it. About a week later, I went to a movie with another friend of mine, Heather Porter—I've told you about her—and afterwards she came over to the house and we baked a frozen pizza. Heather works as a nurse's assistant at Community Hospital. While we were eating, she whispered to me, although there was no one else around to hear because Momma had gone to bed. 'Can you keep a secret?' she said. Well, there's only one good answer to that question. 'Of course I can,' I told her. That's when I found out why Mrs. Tolliver was so PO'd at me that day."

By now, I was sitting with my face so close to the window that my breath had formed a cloud of moisture on the glass. I listened to my sister in rapt silence, not wanting to interrupt her even for a second. Finally, the jumbled facts surrounding her case were beginning to take shape.

Libby's tone became conspiratorial. "Heather wasn't supposed to tell anyone because of the hospital privacy rules and all, but she told me anyway. What happened was, a few days before Mrs. Tolliver's tirade against me, she had rushed RuAnn to the hospital because she'd started bleeding... you know... down there. Mrs. Tolliver, realizing it was way more flow than her regular period, thought it must be because of some internal injury from the accident. But it turned out that RuAnn was pregnant and something went wrong. She had a miscarriage right there in the hospital.

"Poor RuAnn was scared to death, Heather said. She was crying and asking if she was going to die. And Mrs. Tolliver made an awful scene, yelling at everyone as if there'd been a conspiracy against the family. When everything was over and they'd gotten RuAnn sedated—and they wanted to sedate

Mrs. Tolliver too, but she wouldn't let them—anyway, when everything was over, Mrs. Tolliver took RuAnn home.

"Then I guess she got to thinking about things and came to the conclusion that I was to blame for RuAnn getting pregnant, because I was the only one besides her who ever took RuAnn out of the house. She must have convinced herself that I'd left RuAnn alone with someone who'd taken advantage of her.

"But I never did that. I was as shocked as anyone by RuAnn's pregnancy. I didn't understand how that could have happened. Then I remembered how she'd giggled when she'd seen Bobby Hobson, and how she'd said he was her boyfriend, and I hadn't taken her seriously. I don't think she really understood what was going on. I knew about the poker game at the Tollivers' on Thursday nights, and that Mrs. Tolliver doesn't like being home when all the men are around, so she usually goes out those nights with some girlfriends."

Libby's voice wavered. "I think that's when Bobby . . . spent private time with RuAnn. And Mr. Tolliver allowed it."

The quid pro quo. I let out a rush of air, suddenly aware that I'd been holding my breath to the point of light-headedness. "So that's why you attacked Bobby."

Libby nodded. "That evening of the commissioners' meeting, I was going to confront him and drag the truth out of him. That's why I went to the meeting, to talk to him afterwards. Then, during the meeting, when he shocked everyone and voted the way he did on the zoning proposal—which had been the hot topic of conversation in town leading up to the meeting—I knew the truth. I knew he was doing a favor for Cyrus Tolliver, because Tolliver had done a favor for him."

She suddenly looked stricken, as if only now coming to the full realization of what had occurred at that point in the meeting. "I just lost it after that, I guess. I hardly remember stabbing him. The last thing I remember is thinking, *This man—who did this* horrible thing to RuAnn—*is going to walk away from this as if it never happened!* Because I knew in my heart that Bobby would never admit what he had done. Even if I spoke up, no one was going to believe me. They would think I was crazy, accusing him of committing such an unthinkable act." She cringed. "Of course, now they think I'm crazy anyway."

"That's . . . mindboggling," I said. And again, I thought, *Can this be true?* Would any father allow his daughter, especially one mentally incapacitated, to be so taken advantage of? And how could any self-respecting man go along with it? Then I remembered how Bobby had made a fool of himself over RuAnn's sister, Ashley, and how much RuAnn looked like her sister. Was this Bobby's way of fulfilling his fantasies about making love to Ashley? It was too grotesque even to imagine.

I heard a buzz in the line. A digital voice said, "One minute remaining."

"I have to go now," I told Libby. "But I'll be back." I placed the palm of my free hand flat against the window and Libby matched it on the other side of the glass with hers. "You hang in there," I said. "One way or another, I'm going to get you out of here."

"Be careful," Libby said. "Don't do anything crazy. Promise?"

"I promise."

But in truth, I had no idea what I was going to do.

26

MY MIND BUZZED with uncertainty as I paced the parking lot outside the jail, contemplating what to do with the information I had received from my sister. The air vibrated around my face in concert with the droning going on inside my head. Overhead, the sky was signaling a coming change in the weather. There were reports of a storm front approaching from the west, and already the endless blue transparency that had defined the preceding days had given way to a gauzy haze—a kind of visual ambiguity.

Libby was right: if Bobby Hobson had done what we thought he'd done, he would never admit it. And you could bet your life that Cyrus Tolliver would never own up to his part, for it seemed certain he had played a role in this ugly drama.

I considered marching back into the sheriff's office and telling them everything Libby had told me. I didn't know anything about the rape laws in Kansas, but surely it was against the law to have sex with someone who was incapable of giving consent because of age or mental defect. Did this apply to RuAnn, who, although she had the body of a Playboy pinup, had the mind of a kid who gets excited about a stuffed animal?

But who was I kidding? No way would the authorities be receptive to such bizarre accusations aimed at two prominent citizens of the community, especially from the likes of me. They wouldn't believe me any more than they would have believed Libby.

Still, I judged it imperative that Bobby be exposed for the creep he was. To my way of thinking, his actions were so revolting they had to be disclosed. If people knew what he had done, how could they possibly blame Libby for stabbing him? Hell, they'd probably want a shot at him as well. The question was how to go about bringing this sordid affair into the light of day.

As I gazed up at the condensing sky, I thought about the previous evening's conversation with Charlotte, and I suddenly knew what I had to do. And it didn't involve the police. It had been proposed in jest, but what is humor if not insight in gaudy wrapping? If I was going to get anywhere in my quest to help Libby, I had to make some noise—lots of noise.

But how best to do it?

I decided to start by acquiring a bass drum—of sorts.

I took out my cell phone, and after consulting Directory Assistance, dialed the general number for Harbin County Community Hospital. I asked the woman who answered to please page Heather Porter and give her a phone number to call, and tell her it was important. When the receptionist asked my name, I said, "Just tell Heather it's about her application. She'll know what I'm talking about." The woman surprised me by agreeing to do as I asked.

I went back to my motel room, and while I waited for the call I hoped would come, I did my best to screw my courage in place and plug my ears against the denizens of doom crying out inside my head: *The lion will surely eat you alive!*

It probably will, I acknowledged with gut-wrenching resignation. But equally evident to me was that, if I failed to mount an effort to expose the wretched truth, I would be dead to myself anyway, and Libby was sure to lose her freedom. I had no choice but to set aside my fear and stay the course. Sometimes you have to pretend to be something you are not in order to become the someone you want to be.

Ten minutes later, Heather called me back. I fessed up at once to the application ruse and told her who I was.

"Oh," she said, expressing surprise but not annoyance. "I wondered, *what application?* But I figured I should call anyhow in case there'd been some mistake and by chance someone lost out on a loan or a scholarship or something if I didn't call."

"That's what I was counting on," I said.

"So, what did you want to talk to me about?"

I did my best to sound offhand. "I just need some information regarding hospital policy, and I thought you might be able to help me since you work there."

"What information?"

I mentally held my breath as I continued. "What I want to know is what the hospital does with waste human tissue—for example, tissue left over from surgeries, or placental tissue expelled after a woman gives birth."

My question was met with a heavy silence that gained weight the longer it lasted.

"Look, Heather," I said before the silence hardened into obstinacy. "I know you're a friend of Libby's, and there's no way I want to get you in trouble. It's nothing more than general information I'm seeking here. No specifics, and no one will ever know we spoke."

More silence. Then: "Will it help Libby if I tell you?"

"It might," I said, recognizing an opening I needed to rush through. "That's why I'm asking."

"All right, then," Heather said, "here's what I know: One of two things can happen. One is that the waste tissue is deposited in a special receptacle along with other medical or so-called biohazard waste. Then once a week a medical waste disposal company comes and picks it up."

"And what do they do with it?"

"Incinerate it, I think."

"Okay. What's the other thing that can happen?"

"In some cases, a patient will have signed a consent form to have their leftover tissue preserved and sent to a tissue bank, where later it can be used for research or some other beneficial purpose. In those cases, the tissue is sent to our pathology lab, where it's examined and processed. I'm not sure how that works, or who decides what tissue is preserved. I just know it happens. Is that what you wanted to know?"

"That's exactly what I wanted to know, Heather. Thanks so much. And again, this was just between me and you."

"Good. And, Darryl, I'm so sorry about Libby. I've been worried about her, but I haven't known what to do."

"I understand the feeling."

I thanked her again and let her get back to work.

As I reflected on my conversation with Heather, I concluded that it was almost certain the fetal tissue from RuAnn's miscarriage had gone the way of medical waste. There was a slim chance it had been preserved and sent to a tissue bank, but I had no way of finding out.

But neither, I surmised, did Bobby Hobson.

I had my bass drum. Now what I needed to do was to beat it as loudly as I could.

I FELT LIKE an avenging angel as I drove across town to Bobby's house.

Before I could put a finger to the doorbell, Janelle Hobson wrenched open the front door and accosted me with a withering look.

"He's not home," she blurted.

I wasn't sure I believed her. Reason dictated that Bobby should have been home convalescing. "Where is he?" I demanded to know.

"I don't know," Janelle said, sounding more hurt than angry. "He didn't say where he was going."

I considered whether to force my way into the house to satisfy myself she wasn't lying.

Janelle made it easy for me. She swung the door wide open. "Come in and see for yourself if you don't believe me."

After a moment of hesitation, during which my mind played bumper cars with itself, I decided to believe her.

In the throes of anxiety, I sat in my car in the Hobsons' driveway and agonized over what to do next. Above, the sky grew darker as an armada of ponderous clouds sailed in from the west. The storm was definitely coming.

I don't know how or why the conviction came to me, but I was suddenly sure I knew exactly where Bobby had gone.

Gripping the steering wheel tightly enough to wring its neck, I backed out of the driveway and headed for my next confrontation.

27

WHEN I APPROACHED the Tollivers' house, I saw that my intuition regarding Bobby's whereabouts had been correct. Parked in the driveway was a dark-blue SUV with a personalized license plate that read COMMISH. I doubted either of Bobby's fellow commissioners was vain enough to sport such a plate. The time apparently had come for Bobby and Cyrus Tolliver to circle their wagons in preparation for an assault on their integrity.

"You again," said the woman who answered the door—the same woman who'd stood at this threshold on my previous visit and dismissed me as if I were a Bible-toting bell-ringer.

"I'd like to talk to your husband," I said, without bothering to introduce myself.

Again, she didn't seem to care who I was. "He's in the den," she said, stepping back and allowing me to enter.

I followed her through a slate-tiled foyer into a high-ceilinged living room whose decor suited more a well-appointed New York loft than a lodge-style home (a conjugal compromise?). She gestured toward closed twin doors at the end of a short corridor on her left. "Through those double doors."

If the living room reflected Mrs. Tolliver's esthetic sensibility, the den was all Cyrus. It was mannish and imposing. It had rough-wood paneled walls and an open-beam ceiling. The three walls not dominated by a massive stone fireplace were festooned with mounted heads of various beasts, some of which I recognized as local game and some that must have been taken on safari in Africa or some other faraway continent. At least I'd never known lions or gnus to roam the prairies of north-central Kansas. It was all quite impressive, but the big game I was interested in were the two men sitting in overstuffed leather chairs conveniently situated near a wet bar toward the back of the room. Both men fastened their gaze on me as I approached.

"I see you're not very good at following advice," Tolliver said.

"I guess not," I said, glancing in Bobby's direction. His face looked freshly shaved, and he had swapped his pajamas for blue jeans and a high-collar sports shirt. The bandage on his neck was hardly noticeable. The contempt in his stare, however, was unmistakable.

"What's on your mind today?" Tolliver said, without inviting me to sit. That was fine with me. I hadn't planned on sitting.

"I'm glad you're here, Bobby," I said, "because I have something to say to both of you."

Tolliver had a highball glass in his hand, though it was not yet noon. He sipped from his drink (a Bloody Mary?), then wiped his mouth with the back of his free hand. "So say it," he said.

On my way to the Tolliver place, I had decided on a strategy for making noise—one prompted by my encounter with *Harbin County Journal's* would-be muckraker, Roger Stokes, Jr., and given resonance by my talk with Heather Porter. I had no idea if it would work. And if it didn't—if I were exposed as the paper tiger in fact I was—my prospects of helping Libby would be set back to the Dark Ages. But it was a gamble I knew I had to take. Even so, my insides roiled with doubt.

"Mr. Tolliver," I said. "I know how you compensated Bobby for his *no* vote on the zoning issue. Or perhaps I should say what illicit favor you did him. And when I leave here, I'm going directly to the newspaper office in Grotin and I'm going to tell the publisher a very ugly story that will become tomorrow's front-page news."

Poker player that he was, Tolliver batted not an eye. "Which is?" he said.

"I'm going to tell him how, for financial gain, a father allowed a certain local politician to sexually abuse his brain-damaged daughter. And how that daughter became pregnant and ultimately had a miscarriage."

As I spoke, I glanced back and forth between the two men. Tolliver remained impassive throughout my declaration. Bobby, on the other hand, was definitely breathing more heavily.

Tolliver smiled, but his eyes were two ice crystals. "And you think anyone will believe such a story?"

I felt my heart rate kick up a notch as I made my play. "They will when the fetal tissue from RuAnn's miscarriage is sent to a lab for analysis and comes back with a DNA match to Bobby's."

Bobby sat bolt upright in his chair. "I didn't give any DNA sample."

"Shut up, Bobby," Tolliver said.

"You didn't have to," I said. "Your blood was on the fingernail file Libby stabbed you with and on the shirt you were wearing at the time, both of which are in police custody."

Tolliver's face darkened. He set his drink down on a side table. "Darryl," he said, his voice fraught with menace, "you'd best stop right there before you go over a line you don't want to cross. Because you have no idea how deep the water is you seem eager to jump into." His nostrils flared. "First of all, nobody's gonna believe your cockamamie story because it isn't true. And even if it were true, you can't prove it. You can't prove a damn thing." He bent forward in his chair and placed his hands on his knees in a crouch-like gesture of aggression. "So, what you need to do is to get the hell out of my house before I throw you out. And if you know what's good for you, you'll keep right on going back to where you came from."

Now I was the one breathing hard. My entire body tensed in response to a hot rush of adrenaline. It was fight or flight time, and I was determined to stand my ground. "You can threaten me all you want," I said, "but I'm not leaving town until it's widely known what the two of you did. I owe it to Libby and to RuAnn."

The words were barely out of my mouth before Tolliver was on his feet and in my face. He brought his big bulldog head close enough for me to get a whiff of the liquor on his breath. His eyes were fireballs of fury, and his neck muscles bulged and twitched. "Get out of my house," he growled, pointing the way with a thick index finger. "Get out while you're still able to walk out on your own."

Just then the door to the den opened.

Mrs. Tolliver, purse in hand, stood in the doorway with RuAnn at her side. "Sorry to interrupt, but I—" She cocked her head at the sight of her husband standing toe-to-toe with me in a combative posture.

Tolliver quickly composed himself. "It's all right, dear," he said, putting a hand on my shoulder in a comradely way. "We're finished here. Young Mr. Coombs was just leaving."

Mrs. Tolliver stepped into the room, eyeing me with curiosity. "Darryl Coombs?" she said, as if seeing me for the first time. "Libby's brother?"

If I have learned anything from life, it is that there are moments of opportunity to be seized without hesitation, moments that with the slightest vacillation will be lost forever in the tidal surge of the human drama. The telling moments of our lives do not repeat themselves.

I gazed at Mrs. Tolliver and at RuAnn, who remained in the doorway, and it became clear to me what I had to do. I shirked away from Cyrus and moved over to stand next to Bobby. "RuAnn, look who's here," I said. "Come in and say hi to your boyfriend."

"Shut up, Coombs," Tolliver said.

RuAnn giggled and hid her face in her hands.

"Don't be bashful, RuAnn," I said. "Bobby is here to see you."

"I said, shut your goddamn mouth," Tolliver said, taking a step toward me, then checking himself.

Mrs. Tolliver gave her husband a puzzled look. "Cyrus, what is this all about?"

"Nothing, dear," Tolliver said. "Darryl is just lookin' to stir up trouble, because that's what he does. I'll take care of it. Now you go on with your errand."

"Mrs. Tolliver," I said, speaking rapidly now, "I know about the pregnancy and the miscarriage, and I know who's responsible."

Mrs. Tolliver's face drained of color.

"Damn you, Coombs!" Tolliver said, rushing toward me. I recoiled, certain I was about to be attacked. But again, he stopped short—a vicious dog hitting the end of his leash. Turning to his wife, he said in a calm voice, "Now, Angie, you go on about your business like I said."

Mrs. Tolliver went to the doorway and steered RuAnn out into the corridor. "RuAnn, honey, you go up to your room and wait for me there. I'll be along in a little while."

When RuAnn was gone, Mrs. Tolliver came back into the den and shut the door. She approached the three of us and stood there with her arms akimbo. "Now, Darryl, you were saying?"

Before I could get out any words, Cyrus grabbed me roughly by the arm and, as if I were an arrestee being hustled into a police van, began shunting me toward the door. "He wasn't saying anything."

Mrs. Tolliver stepped in front of us.

"Move out of the way, Angie."

"No, Cyrus," she said, standing firm. "I want to hear what Darryl has to say."

"No, you don't."

"Yes, I do!" Mrs. Tolliver shouted, her face suddenly a gargoyle of anger, and I understood in that moment why Libby had been frightened of her.

Tolliver's jaw clenched. His face reddened. He maintained his tourniquet-tight grip on me, but held his peace.

"Now, Darryl," Mrs. Tolliver said, "say what you have to say."

"Mrs. Tolliver," I said, my voice pinched on account of the pain in my arm, "you thought my sister was responsible for RuAnn's pregnancy, believing she had allowed someone to have sex with RuAnn. But the real culprits are right here in this room."

"Don't listen to him, Angie," Tolliver said, shaking me as if I were a baby rattle. "He's a loser and a lying scoundrel, and he doesn't know what he's talking about."

But Mrs. Tolliver, undeterred by her husband's comments, kept her eyes fixed on me. "Go on, Darryl."

I was laboring now to keep my wits about me what with the manhandling I was being subjected to. "Mrs. Tolliver," I said, "I'm telling you that on those Thursday nights while you were out with your girlfriends, Bobby was doing more than playing poker with your husband and his pals, he was playing house with your daughter."

Mrs. Tolliver's spine stiffened. She glowered at her husband. "Cyrus, is any of this true? Did you allow Bobby to take advantage of our daughter?"

Tolliver scoffed. "Of course not."

"He did so," I said, using all the force I could muster to wrest my arm free of Tolliver's grasp. "In school, Bobby had a thing for your daughter Ashley, but she rejected his advances. Taking advantage of RuAnn was his way of getting what he wanted. And in return, he gave your husband what *he* wanted—a *no* vote on the zoning proposal at the last county commissioners' meeting. Think about it," I pleaded, desperate to be believed. "However preposterous it sounds, it's the most plausible explanation for RuAnn's pregnancy."

Mrs. Tolliver glared at me, then at Bobby, then at her husband—as if she wanted to kill us all—before rushing out of the room.

As soon as she was gone, Tolliver grabbed hold of me again. "You worthless son of a bitch," he said, and swung a big fist at me. I saw it coming, getting bigger and bigger as if being viewed on a 3D movie screen. I jerked my head back so that the blow collided with my face with less than full force. Even so, it was enough of a wallop to buckle my knees and send me reeling. I landed on my backside on the floor with my head spinning and lights flashing behind my eyes.

"Get him out of here, Bobby."

Bobby, who'd been as dynamic as a duck decoy all this time, got up from his chair and bent over me. He hooked his forearms through my underarms and struggled to pull me to my feet, but the punch had rendered me nearly senseless and I was dead weight.

"Well?" Tolliver said.

"I'm trying," Bobby said, while making little progress.

"Chrissakes," Tolliver huffed. He came over and the two of them jerked me upright. I was too out of it to resist, but also too woozy to stand on my own. They were dragging me to the door when they faltered in response to a piercing yell.

"*Stop!*"

It was Mrs. Tolliver. She was standing in the doorway, wielding a double-barreled shotgun.

"Now, Angie," Tolliver said, "put that thing down and move away from the door."

Mrs. Tolliver advanced into the room, still brandishing the gun. "Let him go."

"Sweetheart, listen to me—"

"No!" Her eyes glittered with fierceness. "You listen to me! *Let. Him. Go.*"

Time seemed to stand still then, as if the four of us had been placed in suspended animation. Mrs. Tolliver's eyes were locked on the three of us, and our eyes were locked on the barrel of her shotgun. Action resumed only when the two men finally let go of me. My knees were weak and I wasn't sure they would hold me up. I wobbled in place but managed to stay vertical.

"Now sit down," said Mrs. Tolliver, the steeliness of her voice leaving little doubt as to who was in charge here now. "All of you."

"You're not thinking clearly, dear," Tolliver said. "If you'll just let me handle this—"

She aimed the shotgun at her husband and gave him a fiery stare. "Sit down, Cyrus."

At this point, I welcomed a place to sit. After some hesitation, Bobby and Cyrus resumed their places in the big leather chairs by the bar, and I staggered to a settee nearby. I had recovered enough now to sense pain. I swiped a hand across my mouth and came away with blood. The blow from Tolliver had split my lower lip. I stared at the blood for a groggy moment before my attention was pulled back to the drama playing out in front of me.

Mrs. Tolliver stepped over to where Bobby sat, wide-eyed and ashen-faced, and leveled the shotgun at him. He pressed himself back into the chair as far as he could.

"Bobby," Mrs. Tolliver said, "did you have sex with my little girl?"

"Don't answer that, Bobby," Tolliver said.

"Shut up, Cyrus," Mrs. Tolliver said. "I've got two shells in this gun and I'll use them both if I have to."

She brought her attention back to Bobby. "Now answer me," she said in a commanding voice. "Did you have sex with my daughter?"

Bobby sported his palms in a gesture of entreaty. "Now, Angie," he said, flourishing a smile worthy of a saint, "why don't you put the gun away and we can talk this through peaceably?"

"Answer me!" Mrs. Tolliver screamed. She was panting now and her words came out in fitful bursts. She pressed the muzzle of the gun against Bobby's chest. "Did my husband allow you to violate my daughter?"

Bobby's eyes widened. His face paled and every trace of a smile disappeared. "Yes," he said in a paper-thin voice. "I'm sorry."

"Shut up, Bobby," Tolliver said. "Don't be such a coward."

"Angie," Bobby said, the corners of his mouth twitching, "I know now that it was a terrible thing I did, and I'm so sorry."

Mrs. Tolliver wheeled around toward her husband, her face a red mask of horror. "How could you?" she cried. Her body quavered, as did the shotgun she held that was once again directed at her husband.

Tolliver, looking more piqued than fearful, waved her off as if shooing a swarm of flies. "Get that thing out of my face, Angie. You're not going to shoot anybody and you know it."

But she kept the gun trained on him, as if its barrel were the snout of a hunting dog on point. "You let Bobby have his way with our RuAnn?" she said in a voice rent with agony.

"What if I did?" Tolliver said. "What did it hurt?"

"What did it hurt!" shrieked Mrs. Tolliver, tears of indignation coursing down her face. "Are you out of your mind! She's a child!" And as if not certain she'd made her point, she cried out again, madly, "She's a child!"

Tolliver sneered. "She's not a child. She's a grown woman. It's not like she was a virgin. You think she wasn't having sex before?"

"That's different!" Mrs. Tolliver bawled, stomping her feet. "Before, she had a choice."

"Well, I don't see how it matters," Tolliver said. "Hell, probably do her some good to be reminded what it feels like to be a woman." He emitted a self-satisfied chuckle. "Although, next time we'll need to make sure the fellow uses protection."

When the gun went off, I don't know who was the most surprised—me, Bobby, Mrs. Tolliver, or Cyrus. The blast was deafening. Cyrus's body slammed back in his chair. Blood splattered in all directions, like a burst of fireworks. A gaping hole opened up in Cyrus's chest and more blood gushed out of it. He moaned. His eyes bulged. He opened his mouth but the only thing that came out was bloody froth. He slumped sideways in his chair, still breathing—or trying to breathe—in broken, raspy gasps.

Mrs. Tolliver stood motionless, as if frozen in place, the gun still pointing at her husband.

My mind and body had locked up as well.

Bobby was the first to move. He rose in slow motion from his chair, his eyes glued to the gun in Mrs. Tolliver's hands, took a few tentative steps, then bolted for the door.

Mrs. Tolliver paid him no mind.

Regaining some sense of awareness, I went to her and took the shotgun from her grasp. She didn't resist. I laid the gun on the floor. I took her by the arm and guided her out of the den, along the brief stretch of hallway, and into the living room.

"What happened?" she said, gazing about in confusion.

"It's okay," I said, easing her down onto a sofa. "You sit here and rest."

"Momma?"

I turned and saw RuAnn standing at the bottom of the stairs that led to the second floor. "Your momma's all right," I said. "Why don't you come and sit with her."

RuAnn hesitated, her eyes bouncing back and forth between me and Mrs. Tolliver. Then, making up her mind, she rushed to her mother's side.

"Oh, baby," Mrs. Tolliver said, enfolding her daughter in her arms.

I went back into the den and closed the door. Cyrus Tolliver had stopped breathing, but his eyes remained open. I thought I could still see shock in them. I was sure there was still shock in mine. I took out my cell phone and dialed 911.

28

IT WASN'T LONG before the Tollivers' home was overrun with first responders—sheriff's deputies, paramedics, troopers from the state highway patrol—all of whom rushed to the scene with sirens blaring. Radios squawked, shoes squeaked, officers and paramedics conferred with one another in the hushed tones of a funeral parlor as they traipsed in and out of the den. The medical examiner arrived, followed by a state forensics unit that cleared most everyone else out of the room. The paramedics went outside to wait until they were needed, which I guessed wouldn't be until the medical examiner released the body for transport. A member of the forensics team came out of the den carrying the shotgun Mrs. Tolliver had used to shoot her husband. It was sheathed in a clear plastic bag.

In the meantime, I'd been ushered into the dining room, where I was instructed to sit and wait, presumably for someone to come and question me. A state trooper wearing a Smokey the Bear hat watched over me with the stoic resoluteness of a Buckingham Palace Guard. I sat in one of the slat-back chairs situated around a distressed-wood dining table, pressing a blood-dappled handkerchief against my lip as I viewed the comings and goings of the first responders. The wound had mostly stopped bleeding, but I could still taste the saltiness of blood in my mouth.

Two opposing arched openings provided access to the dining room. One of them presented me with a partial view of the doorway to the den. The other afforded a line of sight into the living room, where Mrs. Tolliver and RuAnn still sat huddled together on the sofa, under the watchful eye of a sheriff's deputy.

When a female state trooper entered the living room and said something to Mrs. Tolliver that I couldn't hear, she became upset. "No!" she cried as the trooper took RuAnn by the hand and assisted her to her feet. Mrs. Tolliver clung to her daughter for a time, initiating a futile tug of war with the trooper, before finally giving up and letting go. "She'll be all right, Mrs. Tolliver. I'll take good care of her," the trooper said as she shepherded a frightened RuAnn out of the room. Mrs. Tolliver gazed after them with a look of despair on her face, as if envisioning a kind of separation worse than death.

Shortly thereafter an officer from the sheriff's department entered the dining room. "I got him, Lewis," he said to my bodyguard. The state trooper nodded and strode away.

"I'm Sergeant Wilkens," the officer said as he sat down across the table from me. He wasn't someone I'd seen before at the sheriff's office or the jail, but I had noticed him coming and going from the den earlier. He was stocky. He had a shaved head, the probing eyes of a skeptic, and biceps that looked as if any moment they might burst through the sleeves of his uniform.

He shoved aside the table centerpiece, a vase of dried cattails and reeds, and gave me an armor-piercing stare. "Darryl," he said, "a man died here today. A good man. We need to find out why."

By now I had calmed down some, but there was still a

fist-sized knot in my stomach that didn't want to loosen its grip on my insides. And my mind had yet to stop swirling with kaleidoscopic images from those last insane moments in the den when a shotgun blast had fashioned a bloody crater in Cyrus Tolliver's chest.

"I'll tell you what I know," I told the officer.

"Good. The first thing I'd like to know is what you were doing here today at the Tollivers' house."

"I . . . I came here to talk to Mr. Tolliver." I found myself sucking on my damaged lip as I spoke so that the words came out the side of my mouth.

"About what?"

My mind stumbled over how best to answer that question. Was I about to stick my head in the mouth of the lion of truth?

The sergeant's eyes turned flinty. "Here's the way it is, Darryl. The best thing you can do for yourself right now is to tell me exactly what happened here. Because if you refuse, or worse, if you lie to me, this investigation will not go well for you. Do you understand?"

"Yes, sir," I said, swallowing the lump of apprehension that had formed in my throat.

"Then answer my question. Why did you come here today?"

I blurted the first thing that came into my head. "I came here to tell Mr. Tolliver that I knew what he had done, and that I wasn't going to keep quiet about it."

"And what had he done?"

"It's actually what he and Bobby Hobson did."

"Go on."

I experienced a cold moment of panic as I struggled to arrive at a starting point in a convoluted narrative. *In the beginning God created the heavens and the earth* was not going to fly. "It's complicated," I said.

Sergeant Wilkens interlaced his beefy arms across his chest. "Uncomplicate it for me."

But it wasn't that simple. It wasn't like unraveling a knotted ball of twine. I was being asked to synopsize *Crime and Punishment* in all its psychological aspects. My only chance of making sense of what happened was to get it all said at once in a way that demonstrated how that shotgun going off in Mrs. Tolliver's hands was the culmination of a causally linked series of events that started before my return to Grotin. Even then, I was certain that anything I said would be met with the blunt end of suspicion.

"It all started," I said, knowing how crazy it sounded, "when Bobby Hobson and Mr. Tolliver made a diabolical deal. In exchange for Bobby's *no* vote on the proposed zoning initiative, Mr. Tolliver allowed Bobby to take sexual liberties with his daughter RuAnn, even though she was brain damaged because of the car accident she'd been in."

I paused to search the sergeant's face for his reaction. Detecting none—maybe he played poker too—I rushed on with my story. "When RuAnn got pregnant and had a miscarriage, Mrs. Tolliver blamed my sister for what happened, because Libby was the only person allowed to take RuAnn out of the house after the accident. But"—I struggled to connect the dots—"Libby remembered how one time RuAnn had called Bobby her boyfriend, and she reasoned that it must have been Bobby who'd gotten RuAnn pregnant, and Mr. Tolliver had let it happen. Libby knew that if she went public with her story no one would believe her. But she couldn't stand the idea of Bobby getting away with what he'd done. That's why she stabbed him at the county commissioners' meeting. And that's why I came here today—to tell Mr. Tolliver that I knew what he and Bobby had done to his daughter, and that I wasn't going to stay quiet about it."

"And after you got here, what happened?" the sergeant said, maintaining his penetrating gaze.

"When I got here, Bobby was here too, with Mr. Tolliver in the den. I went in to talk to them and things got confrontational. Then Mrs. Tolliver walked in on us. She saw that something was amiss and wanted to know what was going on. When I tried to tell her, Mr. Tolliver attempted to shut me up. But Mrs. Tolliver insisted on hearing me out, so I told her what her husband and Bobby had done. That's when she went and got the shotgun and threatened Bobby with it, and he ultimately confessed to everything. Mrs. Tolliver was furious, and she pointed the gun at her husband. They argued. Mrs. Tolliver got very emotional and was screaming at her husband, and that's when the gun went off." I shook my head. "I don't think she really meant to pull the trigger. It just happened."

By the time I finished my narrative, my heart was in a full sprint. Sweat oozed from my armpits and snaked down my sides. A voice inside my head cried out, *He doesn't believe a word you said!*

Sergeant Wilkens sat there for a time without speaking, his silence swelling in my mind to an agonizing crescendo before finally being broken. "Tell me again," he said, and then had me repeat my story from the beginning. Only this time—taking notes—he interrupted me at every turn, asking questions, probing for more information, analyzing every detail of my account as if he were sifting through soil looking for fragments of bone.

When we were done, he rose and fixed me with feral eyes that presaged the threat he was about to issue. "You'd better be telling the truth," he said, "because if you're lying about any of this, I'll find out, and you will be in a world of hurt."

"It happened just as I said," I told him.

The sergeant kept me within eyeshot as he conferred in the

hallway with another officer—a state trooper who, as I was being quizzed by Wilkens, had been in the living room speaking with Mrs. Tolliver.

Wilkens returned to the dining room. "You're free to go. But don't leave town for the time being. You're a material witness to a homicide and we'll undoubtedly have more questions for you. And Coombs," he said, firing a double-barreled warning at me through the pupils of his eyes, "don't talk to anyone else about any of this. Do you understand?"

"Yessir."

"Good, because we'll be watching you."

"How is Mrs. Tolliver doing?"

"That's none of your concern."

"But I am concerned."

"Then get over it," the sergeant said, his shoulder muscles bunching. "Now make yourself scarce before I think of something to arrest you for. You may not have pulled the trigger on that shotgun, but if you hadn't come around here hurling accusations at Mr. Tolliver and Bobby Hobson, none of this would have happened."

"So, it's all my fault, is it?"

"Get the hell out of here."

He didn't have to tell me again.

29

I DROVE BACK to Grotin feeling deeply abstracted, my mind at once shrinking from visions of the bloodshed I had witnessed, while being pulled back to that moment by the tantalizing horror of it all. One thing I was sure of: As despicable as Cyrus Tolliver's actions had been, they did not warrant the death penalty. Yes, I had felt like throttling both him and Bobby to within an inch of their lives, but only to wring out of them an admission of their wrongdoing, which I believed was critical to Libby's defense. But things had gone sideways. Now Tolliver was dead, his wife was sure to be arrested, and Bobby—well, who knew how Bobby would respond?

And who knew how all this would impact Libby's case? I had promised her not to do anything crazy, but I'd broken that promise, and legal repercussions were sure to follow.

The forecasted rain had arrived. The roadway was glassy wet and the air carried with it the earthy smell of newly dampened fields. My windshield wipers weren't doing me any favors as their sweeping action did little more than create foggy rainbow-patterned streaks on the glass.

When I was about halfway back to town, something flickered in my rearview mirror. I peered at its reflection and saw red lights shimmering through a curtain of rain. Moments later, I heard the siren, faint at first, then louder and louder. A sheriff's cruiser was fast approaching from behind.

What was happening? Was the cruiser chasing me? Had the sergeant changed his mind and decided to arrest me after all?

With these questions and others swimming in my head, I pulled onto the shoulder of the road and stopped. Feeling battered on the inside as well as the outside, I slumped forward and braced my forehead against the steering wheel, while awaiting the inevitable knock on the driver's side window of my Explorer.

What was there about me and Grotin that, when conjoined, portended disaster? It had been a mistake for me to come here. But given the circumstances, it would have been a mistake for me to have stayed away. Damned if you do; damned if you don't. There it was—my life in a nutshell.

The sound of the siren peaked. Suddenly my car swayed side to side. I looked up, confused. The sheriff's cruiser whizzed past me in a wind-and-rain-whirling blur and continued up the highway. I took in a long pull of air and welcomed the sense of relief that washed over me as I watched the flashing lights disappear around a bend in the road ahead. Whatever that was all about, it wasn't about me, and I was thankful for that.

I pulled back onto the roadway. Where was that officer going in such a rush?

When I got back to town, I found out—and wished I hadn't.

Driving down Main Street on my approach to the Prairie Inn, I noticed an unusual amount of traffic—vehicular and pedestrian—a few blocks ahead, in the downtown area. My intent was to return to my motel room and crash after the ordeal I'd been through, but curiosity over what was going on up ahead prompted me to bypass the motel and continue down the street.

A couple of cars were in front of me, driving slowly. The rain was falling harder now, making it even more difficult for me to see out my windshield. The drivers ahead kept tapping their brakes and I guessed that they were looking for a place to park. But all the spaces in the block had been taken—recently, it appeared, because some people were just now getting out of their cars and walking, or in some cases jogging, up the sidewalk toward Center Street, unfolding umbrellas as they went. It was only then that I noticed the barricades blocking vehicular access to westbound Center.

In the next block a couple of spaces were open, and the cars ahead of me filled them. Two teenaged girls bailed out of one of the cars and began hustling back toward Center Street bareheaded and undeterred by the rain. I pulled to a stop and rolled down my window. "What's going on?" I hollered.

"Someone's climbed up on the water tower," one of the girls hollered back, "and is threatening to jump."

The city water tower is located on a fenced plot of land adjoining Center Street, four blocks west of Main. North of the water tower, across Center Street, is housing. Bordering the other three sides of the tower plot are shop buildings and an equipment lot used by county work crews. The threat of a tower jumper had obviously prompted the closure of streets leading to the area.

My curiosity satisfied, I did a U-turn at the first convenient intersection and headed back up Main. No way did I want to witness some nutcase commit suicide by jumping off the water tower. Truth was, I didn't care to go anywhere near that wretched fount of memory.

Back at my motel room, I shed my clothes, comprehending only then how widespread had been the splatter from the shotgun blast that had done in Cyrus Tolliver. The front of my trousers and shirt were speckled with dried blood and flecks of human flesh. Instead of adding them to the dirty clothes pile on the floor, I rolled them up and stuffed them in the trashcan.

I took a shower, scrubbing my body with excessive zeal in the hope of sloughing some of the accumulated emotional grime along with the physical. While towel-drying my hair in front of the bathroom mirror, I took stock of my split lip and the bruising on the side of my face that had taken the blow from Tolliver's big fist. My mouth would heal quickly, I reckoned, but the bruising would only deepen over the next several days.

I was pulling on some clean trousers when my cell phone rang. It was Libby. The inmate phone account I'd funded for her that morning before leaving the jail had apparently been activated.

"I can't talk long," she said, sounding out of breath (from excitement or anxiety?). "Other girls are waiting to use the phone."

"Then let me talk," I said. "There's something I need to tell you." I'd heard about prison grapevines. News from the outside made its way inside prison walls with uncanny swiftness, as if on wings of eagles. I wanted Libby to hear this from me. Briefly I recounted the salient facts about the events that had occurred earlier in the day at the Tollivers' house.

"Oh, my God," Libby said in a shrill voice. "Darryl, you could have been the one killed. Is RuAnn okay? What's going to happen to Mrs. Tolliver? Oh . . . oh . . . it's all my fault." She took a wheezy breath. "Oh, my God."

"Libby, listen to me," I said. "It's not your fault. It's just what happened. Things happen you can't foresee." I was saying this for my benefit as well as hers. If anyone was to blame for Cyrus's death, it was me. "Now, you hold yourself together. I'll come see you during visiting hours tomorrow."

"But what's going to happen now? Oh . . . this is so awful."

I couldn't lie. "Honestly, I don't know what's going to happen. But we'll deal with it as it comes. I'll visit you tomorrow, and I suspect Mr. Broward will want to see you too. So, try and get some rest and we'll talk again in the morning."

"Okay! Okay!" It took me a second to realize Libby wasn't speaking to me. "I have to go now," she said. "They're grabbing at the phone."

Before I had a chance to respond, the line went dead. One of her jailbird associates must have depressed the phone's plunger.

I flopped back onto the bed, barefoot and shirtless with my fingers laced behind my head, asking myself the same question Libby had just posed: *What's going to happen now?*

I didn't have to wait long for an answer.

When I heard the knock on my motel room door, I got up and drew back the curtain to see who was there. Suddenly that knot was back in my gut. It was Sergeant Wilkens.

"Coombs," he said as soon as I opened the door, "I need you to come with me."

"Why?" I said, feeling uncooperative. Had I not gone through enough for one day?

"Because we need your help."

I looked past him to where his cruiser was parked, the engine still running, the windshield wipers slapping back and forth metronomically. At least he had turned off his overheads.

"With what?" I said, unable to imagine a single circumstance that would have triggered such a need.

"Go for a ride with me and I'll show you."

I didn't like the sound of that. Anytime someone needs to *show* you rather than *tell* you what's going on, there's always a catch and rarely a desirable one. But, once again, I knew I didn't really have a choice; if he wanted to, the good sergeant could easily find an excuse to haul me off to jail.

"Let me finish getting dressed."

Neither of us spoke as Wilkens steered the cruiser onto Main Street, southbound. At the first side street, he turned west and drove through a residential neighborhood for several blocks before turning back south, at which point he had to veer off the pavement to maneuver around a cordon of barricades. Straight ahead of us now, its globular mass towering above the surrounding townscape, stood the city water tower. Viewed through a shroud of falling rain, against a backdrop of vaguely lit sky, it resembled a dark moon hanging over planet Grotin. I shivered at the sight of it—at the memories it aroused.

As we got closer to the tower, I took note of the cadre of police and fire vehicles parked helter-skelter around its perimeter fencing. A crowd of onlookers had gathered as well, braving the rain to watch the show. Everyone was looking up toward the giant tank. Some of them were pointing, but I couldn't tell at what. Two sheriff's cruisers' spotlights were aimed up at the tower, but their beams so bejeweled the raindrops that the result was more light show than illumination.

"Darryl," Sergeant Wilkens said as he brought the patrol car to a stop just outside the ring of onlookers, "I don't know what it is about you that attracts trouble, but it seems you're in the middle of it yet again."

"What do you mean?"

"We've located Bobby Hobson, and I'd very much like to have a chat with him." He gestured up toward the cloud-clogged sky. "Unfortunately, Bobby has climbed up on that goddamn water tower and is refusing to come down."

I shook my head in disbelief and uttered the first thought that entered my mind: "*Unreal.*" What a dumbass thing for Bobby to do. I didn't know whether to laugh or pity him for such an act of lunacy. Or was it desperation? Whatever it was, I wanted no part of it.

"A rescue team is prepared to go up and get him," Wilkens said. "But the fire captain has been talking to Bobby on his cell phone, and Bobby says that if they send anyone up after him, he'll jump. He said he'll only come down if you come up and get him."

"Me?"

"That's right."

"And what if I refuse?"

Wilkens shrugged. "Hell if I know."

I don't know if it's true that life always comes full circle, but in this instance anyway that's exactly what had happened. I gazed up at the tower looming above us, at the nearly straight-up ladder with its 130 rungs I'd have to mount to reach the catwalk, and had no more desire to climb it now than I had as a frightened fourteen-year-old boy. Yet here I was again being forced to choose between two potentially disastrous outcomes. And here again were the voyeurs, milling restlessly about, waiting to see what choice I made and what gory spectacle transpired.

"So, what do you say?" Sergeant Wilkens said. "Go up and get him or not? Your call. And no one's gonna blame you if you refuse. It could be dangerous. All depends on Bobby's state of mind, which, I'd say, is unsettled at best."

I tossed my head back and laughed at the irony of it all.

"I'll do it," I said. "But not for Bobby—for myself."

"You sure?"

"No. But I'll do it anyway."

I felt strangely detached from conscious thought as I got out of the cruiser and, with Sergeant Wilkens as my escort through the crowd of spectators, went to confer with the fire captain. He was easy to spot, his navy-blue military-style uniform a stark contrast to the yellow jumpsuits and fire hats of the would-be rescuers huddled around him near one of the red firetrucks.

"Thanks for coming, Darryl," the fire captain said. He looked to be in his mid- to late forties. He had a neatly trimmed mustache and close-cropped hair graying at the temples. He had a paternal air about him, which he immediately manifested by taking me aside and repeating what Sergeant Wilkens had just told me: *I didn't have to do this. It could be dangerous. They couldn't be sure of Bobby's state of mind.*

I restated my willingness to climb.

"All right, then." He opened a compartment on the side of the firetruck and retrieved a canvas bag that he unzipped. "Put this on," he said, holding out a harness that resembled something a zip-line participant would wear. It had a cable attached to it with a carabiner affixed to its end. He cradled the carabiner in his hand. "Fasten this to the highest rung you can reach as you climb. That way if you slip, you can't fall—not far anyway. Take your time, and don't take any chances."

I looked at the safety harness, and then I looked inside myself. "No offense, sir, but I'd prefer not to use the harness."

"Son," the fire captain said, "those rungs will be slick in this rain, and now the wind is picking up. Without the harness, you'd be taking your life in your own hands, and I can't allow that."

"Sorry, sir," I said. "I certainly don't have a death wish. Just the opposite. But I'm afraid it's *no harness or no go.*"

The captain's countenance hardened as he stuffed the harness back into the bag. "What is it with you, Coombs? I knew you were trouble, but this takes the cake." He got nose to nose with me, and whatever well of concern he'd been dipping from had dried up. "You don't recognize me, do you?"

"No, sir."

"I'm the man who saved your ass the last time you tried to climb this tower. A brave young boy died that day, and you're damn lucky you weren't killed too. This time—"

His cell phone rang. He glared at me as he answered it. He listened briefly, then said into the phone, "No, there's no problem here, Bobby. He'll be on his way up shortly. You stay put and don't do anything foolish." He jammed the phone back into its holster.

"I'll be careful, sir," I said, meeting his gaze. "And for your information, I don't need any reminders about what happened the last time I attempted to climb this tower." The door to that memory had already been kicked wide open. "No matter how hard you try, you can never fully put something like that out of your mind. And, by the way, that brave young boy's name was Lamar—Lamar Higgins."

My body pulsed with misgiving as I lumbered toward the water tower.

I didn't have to scale the security fence this time. Someone had opened the access gate. Not wanting to give myself time to rethink my decision, I stepped up to the base of the metal ladder and took a firm grip on the farthest rung I could reach. Someone in the crowd behind the fence said, "Who's that?" Another voice said, "That's Darryl Coombs. Didn't you know he was back in town? Because of what Libby done."

The rain came down in sheets now, but I paid it no mind as I commenced to climb—slowly, carefully, focusing on each body movement in turn. One hand up, one foot. One hand up, one foot. Below me someone yelled, "Go get 'em, Darryl! We're with you!" Another voice followed up with, "Yeah, but can he make it down without killing himself?" Surprisingly, only a smattering of laughter erupted.

Without stopping, or counting rungs, or looking down—I knew better—I ascended to the top of the ladder without falling. I was wet, winded, and wobbly legged when I arrived, but somehow my flailing heart had stayed inside my chest.

"Welcome to the club," Bobby said as I joined him on the catwalk.

I maintained a white-knuckled hold on the railing that circumscribed the metal framework under our feet, and I kept my face to the sky. "I'm not about to piss over the edge," I said.

"I didn't think you would. And I'm not about to jump, although I can't say I didn't entertain the notion."

We stood alongside each other as awkwardly as divorced spouses thrown together by happenstance after years of acrimonious separation. The rain pelted down and the wind swirled in gusts that required a wide-legged stance to stay upright. Bobby was drenched top to bottom. His hair was plastered against his head, and his sodden clothes clung to him like wrinkled skin. Water droplets dribbled from the end of his nose. And to him I must have looked equally as sad and bedraggled.

"So, what are we doing up here, Bobby?"

"Facing our fears," he said, his voice tremulous in the wind.

I closed my eyes and inhaled deeply in an effort to calm myself, all the while keeping a death grip on the handrail. This was no Mt. Everest moment of triumph for me. I had no flag to plant into the summit. No dramatic orchestral music played in the background. I had surmounted the water tower not because I'd conquered my fears, but because I had simply refused to give them credence, carrying them instead on my back as I climbed so as not to allow them to cast a shadow apart from my own.

"I know what I've been afraid of all my life, Bobby. What are you afraid of?"

He swept a hand in an outward arc. "Look out there and tell me what you see."

I had yet to look down and was reluctant to do so. My gut spasmed as I allowed my eyes to descend upon the scene below. From this high up, even with the dreariness that accompanied the weather, I could see out over the town and into the open countryside beyond its edges. "I see a smudge of civilization surrounded by a whole lot of . . . not much else." Feeling a queasiness akin to the advent of seasickness, I lifted my eyes to the clouds.

"Exactly," Bobby said. "And that's what I'm afraid of—the nothingness of it all. Because that's what my life is right now, has been for some time, and will continue to be unless something changes." He laughed mirthlessly. "You're lucky you got out of here when you did. This place sucks the life out of a person."

"But you've done well for yourself here. You married well. You're a county commissioner."

"Right. I'm a model of success—or so it would seem. Fact is, my marriage has been in a downward spiral for some time now. And being a politician is like being a pop-up target at a shooting gallery."

I didn't know what to say to that.

"How did you keep it together, Darryl, with all the bad things that happened to you growing up here?"

I repeated what I had said so many times before that it had become like a mantra to me. "The best thing about childhood is that you only have to go through it once."

"Yeah? And what's the best thing about adulthood?"

I shrugged. "Maybe that it's never too late to start over."

Bobby sighed, and in his eyes was the look of a man who is seeing himself in the mirror for the first time and is horrified by what he sees. "God, how do I start over from this?"

"Do your best to put the past behind you, I guess."

He combed his fingers through his waterlogged hair. "And how has that worked out for you?"

"Still a work in progress," I admitted.

He scuffed the soles of his shoes across the grating we were standing on. "Well, either you're right or you're full of crap."

He went silent then and I was happy to allow the silence to linger because there didn't seem to be a rational place for this conversation to go.

"Hell," Bobby finally said, "let's get down off this stupid thing before someone gets hurt."

"I'm all for that," I said.

"I go first," he said. "I don't want to have to climb over you if you freeze up."

I didn't freeze up.

30

ON THE MORNING of Libby's discharge from jail, one week to the day from my arrival in Grotin, I stood outside a gate in the razor wire–topped fencing around the jail compound—the so-called freedom gate—waiting like an expectant father for my sister's appearance. Harvey Broward waited with me. It was Broward's work behind the scenes that had made possible Libby's release on bail.

Over the course of the days following the tragic event that had taken place at the Tollivers' home, there had been a rising tide of public sympathy for Libby once her motive for assaulting Bobby Hobson had become known. The investigation into the death of Cyrus Tolliver at his wife's hands was ongoing, but the salient facts had already come to light and the local newspaper had spared no ink in covering the story. Young Roger Stokes was in his element.

Not surprisingly, Bobby's illicit affair with RuAnn (COUNTY COMMISSIONER CAUGHT IN UNHOLY TRYST!) received the most press. It also generated the biggest reaction from the townsfolk, many of whom expressed the opinion that Cyrus had gotten what he deserved for allowing such an appalling thing to happen, and that Mrs. Tolliver would have been well within her rights to have emptied the other barrel of her gun into Bobby.

And there had been political fallout as well. Commissioner Bacchus had called on Bobby to resign from the board. A special election should be held to fill his seat, she said. Then the new board should meet to revisit the issue of zoning for land use. It was a sentiment that seemed to be gaining traction.

For his part, Harvey Broward had been quick to use the public support for Libby as leverage in convincing the county attorney to reduce the charge against her from attempted murder to aggravated assault. Based on the lesser charge, the judge in the case lowered Libby's bail to $20,000, which meant a bond fee of $2,000. It had taken me less than an hour to arrange a wire transfer of that amount to the bail bondsman, who allowed me to sign a promissory note as collateral against forfeiture.

There was still the possibility of a trial, and if convicted, Libby could face a year or more in jail. But it was Broward's assessment that the county attorney had little resolve to go down that road. "A trial would only generate more bad publicity for the county," he said. "My sense is that the county attorney will be amenable to a minimal sentence and a period of probation."

I hoped he was right.

When Libby appeared on the other side of the freedom gate, she was a sight to behold. Gone were her pumpkin costume and floppy sandals, replaced by black skinny jeans, a white blouse with ruffles down the front, and red running shoes. Her hair was neatly brushed and her face radiated relief.

Deputy Rawlins was her escort. He unlocked the gate and swung it open. "Good luck," he said as she passed through, and he seemed to mean it. He glanced at me and nodded. I nodded in return.

The next moment Libby was in my arms. We were both crying. It's odd how elation can bring about the same biological response as despair.

"Thank you, thank you," Libby kept repeating as she wetted my shoulder with her happy tears. She reached out and clutched Broward's hand. "And thank *you*," she said. "You two are my heroes."

Broward beamed.

When we were all hugged out, Libby and I said goodbye to her attorney, and I loaded her into my car for the short ride home.

I STAYED IN TOWN three more days, spending most of that time with Libby, who, despite her initial euphoria upon being freed from jail, was an emotional powder keg because of her continuing concern for RuAnn and the yet unextinguished threat of being sent back to jail. I assured her that she was strong enough to face whatever came her way. She had already proven that.

By now the summer sun had reasserted its dominance as overseer of the plains. The storm had passed through, leaving behind a sky scrubbed to a renewed brilliance. Libby and I spent much of our time outside, walking hand in hand around town, bearing the sun's warmth like a heating pad on our backs. We took occasional respites from the heat, lounging on a shaded bench in Gristmill Park accompanied by the shouts of children at play on a nearby jungle gym, or sitting at the counter in Waldrop's Drugs (whose air conditioner had been repaired) relishing the ambrosial taste of a chocolate malt. The townspeople we encountered nodded in greeting. If they spoke at all, it was generally a kind word or two directed at Libby: "Good for you." "Poor girl, what they put you through." "You have nothing to be ashamed of, you know." Libby, of course, was of a different opinion.

During this time, I tiptoed around my mother as best I could. Mother's reaction to Libby's homecoming was sadly predictable. "I thought I was going to die of worry," she said as she smothered Libby with kisses. But in the next breath, the relief she expressed morphed into criticism of Libby's behavior. "Well, I hope you learned your lesson, young lady. You should know that you can't right a wrong with another wrong. What got into you?"

"Mother, can't you just be happy I'm home and not still stuck in that awful jail?"

"I am, dear. But I hope the next time you get it into your head to do something foolish you'll stop and think about the consequences of your actions."

A lesson apt for all of us, I wanted to say, but held my peace.

Mother resented the time Libby and I spent by ourselves. She had always been quick to interpret our brother–sister time as an act of conspiracy against her. More than once while I was growing up she had said to me, "I know you love your sister more than you love me. That's all right. But do you have to make it so obvious?" I had no comeback for such a remark, because I had never learned to play the shell game with the truth.

The day before I left town, Libby and I took a drive out into the countryside. There were things we wanted to say to each other in private.

"Where would you like to go?" I asked her as we headed west on a rural road that soon had us surrounded by crop fields inlaid with an occasional wood or pond. Here and there stood a farmhouse with attendant barn and silo. Cattle grazed in a sun-splashed meadow. Horses lazed in the shade of a lean-to, swishing flies with their tails. And posted at seemingly every dip and bend in the road was a WATCH OUT FOR SLOW-MOVING VEHICLES sign.

"Turn left at the next junction," Libby said. "I want to show you something."

It was the road to Thomasville, I noted as I negotiated the turn.

When we had gone about five miles, Libby had me pull to the side of the road. There was hardly enough shoulder to allow me to stop without impeding traffic, although there hadn't been much traffic on the road this day.

Libby pointed up ahead to a depression just off the pavement on the opposite side of the road. "That's where the car ended up when that drunk ran me and RuAnn off the road. The guy came right at us. There was nowhere to go except into the ditch."

In my mind's eye I saw the impending head-on collision and Libby's counter-maneuver on this tight, two-lane road. The ditch looked unforgiving. "The car turned over?"

"Yes, onto its side—the passenger's side, RuAnn's side. Then it plowed up the ground before coming to a stop."

I observed the long scar in the earth that the upended vehicle had made.

"We were both wearing seat belts," Libby said, "but RuAnn's head got slammed over and over against the doorframe." Tears pooled in her eyes as she spoke. "You saw her. She's not herself anymore and probably never will be."

I reached over and clasped my sister's hand and repeated what I'd told her before, hoping this time she would take it to heart. "Sis, it wasn't your fault."

Her lips tried to form a smile but failed. "I know. But think about it. If the accident hadn't happened, none of the rest of this would have happened—RuAnn getting pregnant, me stabbing Bobby, Mrs. Tolliver shooting her husband. I can't help but think—" She looked away, unable to finish.

I completed the thought for her. "You can't help but think you've taken up where I left off—that you've become the new Coombs family lightning rod for tragedy."

"You're right," she said. "But there's more to it than that." She looked at me with profound sadness in her eyes. "I love RuAnn."

"I know, Sis. The two of you have been friends for such a long time. It has to be devastating."

"No. You don't understand. We were in love."

I fell silent as I considered how much speculative light to shine on her remark. The comment by David Pierce echoed in my mind: *Let's just say, I don't think I'm her type.*

"Are you telling me you're gay?"

"No," she said, studying my face as if to judge my reaction to her words. "RuAnn's gay. I'm bi. But once RuAnn and I became intimate, I swore off men forever." She issued a mournful sigh. "So you see, in that accident, I lost more than just a friend. I . . . I . . ." Her lips quivered and her face contorted. "I lost the love of my life." She tilted her head back and squeezed her eyes shut, causing tears to leak at their corners. She took big breaths through her mouth, and I could tell she was struggling to keep her emotions in check. "And then," she said, "what that creep Bobby did to RuAnn." She shuddered. "Unforgiveable."

I leaned across the center console of my Explorer and held her in an awkward embrace. "Libby, why didn't you tell me any of this before?"

She drew back and looked at me with the sweet innocence of that little girl I'd known and loved and done my best to protect all those years ago. "I was afraid."

"Afraid of what?"

"Afraid of what would happen," she said, her face etched with lingering concern. "I knew that if you found out why I stabbed Bobby you'd feel compelled to do something about it. And I knew that whatever you did would put you in danger. Cyrus Tolliver is—*was*—a scary man, always shooting guns and killing things for sport. I was afraid you'd become his next target. I was also afraid for RuAnn—what Cyrus might do to her. He'd already threatened to send her away to a home for the mentally disabled. And—" She pressed the back of her hand against her mouth. "To be honest," she said in a timid voice, "I was afraid of what you would think—of what *everyone* would think—of me, of RuAnn, of the two of us together, you know, as lovers. That's why I didn't want to talk to you, or anyone, about any of this."

"Oh, Libby—sweet Libby," I said, reaching out and caressing her cheek. "I'll tell you what I think of you. I think you're the best sister a guy could ever have, and I love you now more than ever."

We were quiet for a time, neither of us ready to let go of the moment. Then, her voice barely rising to the level of a whisper, Libby said, "You were right to leave here. And now I need to leave here too."

The remark surprised me. It was the first time I'd heard her say such a thing. Always before, it was *I have to stay here and take care of Mom.*

"Come to Texas with me," I said, excited at the prospect.

"No," she said. "I don't think that would be good for either of us. And Mother would feel mercilessly abandoned. I have another plan."

"What plan?"

"I'm thinking about applying to some colleges. It's too late for fall term. But I could apply for winter term. K-State maybe. It's far enough away, but not so far I couldn't come home weekends. Besides, I can't stay here. Even if I don't end up going back to jail, I can't return to my job at the Farm Bureau. They don't employ criminals. And RuAnn and I . . . we can never have—" Her voice clotted.

"I think college is a great idea."

"It's a selfish plan," she said, "but it's the best one I can come up with."

"It's not as selfish as my running out on you ten years ago."

She shook her head. "I'm not so sure about that. If I didn't understand before this why you left, I understand now."

"That's good," I said, "because I plan on going back to San Antonio tomorrow. That's what I wanted to tell you. I need to get back to work before I get fired from *my* job."

"Then tonight let's go to Thomasville and celebrate our last night together."

And we did.

EARLY THE FOLLOWING morning, I went to the house to say my final goodbyes. Libby met me at the door and gave me a rib-crushing hug. "Mom's in the kitchen," she said. "I'll wait for you outside."

Mother was sitting at the kitchen table in her housecoat, drinking coffee. Her hair had yet to greet a brush. Her hollow-cheeked face befitted more the dead than the living. I retrieved a cup from an overhead cabinet, poured myself some coffee, and sat down at the table.

"You're killing me," Mom said when I told her I was leaving town.

"No, Mom, I'm not."

We sipped from our cups in beleaguered silence.

Mom clunked hers down on the tabletop. "What about Libby? She needs you, too, you know."

Not wanting the conversation to fall off a cliff and onto the jagged rocks of acrimony, I got up and poured the remainder of my coffee in the sink. "I have a feeling Libby is going to do just fine on her own," I said. "She's got more courage than I'll ever have." I put my hand on my mother's shoulder. "I'll call more often, Mom, I promise."

She surprised me by covering my hand with hers. She gazed up at me, her eyes conveying an agony that could only have come from deep inside her. "I didn't know what he was going to do to you," she said. "He seemed like such a sincere young man."

I knew exactly what she was talking about.

"Mom," I said, "we don't have to talk about that." The fact is, we never *had* talked about it.

"I'm just so sorry," she said, her voice breaking pitifully. Tears filled her eyes to overflowing. Silent sobs racked her chest.

I kneeled down beside her, slipped my arms around her, and held her close. "Mom, you didn't do anything wrong. You didn't know. And I didn't even understand at the time that anything bad had happened."

"Do you forgive me?" she said.

"There's nothing to forgive."

She looked at me with the eyes of a supplicant, as if I possessed the priestly power to absolve. "But do you forgive me anyway?"

"Yes, Mom," I said, my vision blurred by my own tears, "I forgive you."

31

IT HAS ALWAYS fascinated me how one seemingly isolated event can change the course of so many lives. Libby's stabbing of Bobby Hobson wasn't exactly on par with the 1914 assassination of Archduke Franz Ferdinand for its far-reaching consequences, but it had set in motion a series of events that ripped apart the fabric of a community, and the extent of the damage had yet to be determined.

I had been in Grotin ten days and it felt like years. Time is not always measured in ticks of a clock, but in body blows. I had taken a barrage of punches to the gut recently and, to my surprise, had survived.

I drove home to Texas with a sense of hopefulness bubbling up inside me. For so long I had hidden from my past, and the only thing I had accomplished was the abdication of my future. But during my sojourn back in Grotin, I'd learned that the past was not something to shovel dirt on and then live in fear of because it might rise up zombie-like and attack you. Rather, the past is a living, breathing memorial to the infinite possibilities residing within each of us. We fear it or we cherish it, as the case may be, because it is what guides us with savage truth into the next phase of our existence. How then do we best cope with the inglorious aspects of our personal history? Fearlessly, with the knowledge that hope resides in the nobility of coming face to face with life in all its dubious permutations.

I did my best to communicate these feelings to Charlotte after I got back to San Antonio. We made love in her apartment and I felt a passion for her and for life I had not known before. But our reunion was bittersweet, because I poured out my heart to her in word and deed and she didn't know how to respond.

As we lay in bed, our sweat-slickened bodies intertwined, she stared at me with narrow-eyed intensity, as if probing my essence. "Who are you?" she said.

"What do you mean?"

"You're not the same person you were when you left, and I'm not talking about the bruise on your face."

"Maybe I'm not the same person," I said, returning her gaze. "Or maybe I'm the me you never knew because I've kept this part of myself hidden from you all this time. All I know is that I feel lighter and freer than I ever have in my life—and less afraid."

"Less afraid of what?"

"Of life. Of my future—of *our* future together."

Charlotte went silent then and I didn't know why. Was this new me not to her liking? Had I exposed so much of myself that the status quo of our relationship had been disrupted? And was there a potentially greater disruption quivering beneath the surface? I didn't know. All I knew was that I was no longer willing to hold back my feelings. I was done with being a captive of my ill-starred past.

I pulled her close and kissed her with an outflowing of pent-up emotion. I had never told her I loved her. I told her now.

She drew back from me, turning her head away, but not before I saw the glimmer of tears in her eyes. "Don't say that," she said.

"I love you," I repeated with fierce affection. "Charlotte Robinson, *I love you.*"

"No," she said in a wrecked voice, covering her face with her hands. "You don't even know me."

I pried her hands away from her face and pressed them flat against my chest. "I may not know who you once were," I said, "but I know who you are now. And that's all that matters."

"No . . . no," Charlotte cried, jerking her hands away. She rolled over and curled up in bed, facing away from me. She was sobbing now. For some reason, the force of my proclamation of love for her had caused her great distress.

Shaken by her response, but determined to allow the moment to play out as it would, I decided to let her be. So I settled in bed beside her and tried to bridle my newborn exuberance for life.

I stayed with her all night and was awakened several times by her crying. The power of her sobs shook the bed. Each time she cried out, I enveloped her in my arms and held her until she hushed.

When I awoke to a crush of morning light permeating the bedroom window sheers, Charlotte was not in the bed with me. I squinted at the digital clock on the nightstand: 8:16. Rolling over, I glanced toward the master bath but detected no movement. I sniffed the air for the aroma of freshly brewed coffee but scented none. I cocked my head and listened for signs of life elsewhere in the apartment but heard not a one. "Harrumph," I said, and tugged myself out of bed. I stumbled into the bathroom and relieved myself.

"Hello-o. Good morrr-ning," I said as I ventured unclothed into the living room. It was dim and deserted. The floor-to-ceiling drapes covering the slider onto the balcony were drawn closed. The adjoining kitchen area was vacant and unlit.

Standing there in the dusky silence of the living room, I experienced a still-life moment of confusion. Had I miscalculated what day of the week it was? Was this a workday? Had Charlotte gone into the office, kindly allowing me to slumber away the freight of my fatigue? In my mind, I ran through the timeline of the last twenty-four hours. I had left Grotin approximately eight o'clock in the morning on a Saturday. I'd driven back to San Antonio, straight through, nearly fourteen hours. After a brief stop at my apartment, I arrived at Charlotte's place a little after 10 p.m. the same day—Saturday. I stayed with Charlotte overnight. This had to be Sunday morning.

Okay then, Charlotte had probably just gone out on some errand and would soon return with a bag of bagels or breakfast burritos. Or maybe she'd gone for a walk to clear her head, or for a jog in Brackenridge Park, which she sometimes did on weekends.

Thusly convinced she would soon return, I put water in the coffeemaker's reservoir and grounds in its basket, and while it was *drip-drip-dripping*, I took a shower and dressed in clothes from a bureau drawer Charlotte, a year into our relationship, had reserved for me.

It was shortly after nine o'clock when I sat down at the glass top table on the balcony to drink my coffee and read the Sunday paper, which I had retrieved from outside the apartment's front door. Now and then, I peered through the wrought-iron railing down into the courtyard below on the chance I might glimpse Charlotte returning from her outing. I would wave at her and she would smile and return my wave.

By a quarter to ten I was glutted with news and Charlotte had yet to appear. I am slow-witted at times when it comes to diagnosing the needs of the women in my life, but I finally came to the conclusion that Charlotte's prolonged absence this morning signaled her desire for space. Space was something we had freely given each other over the course of our time together. It was part and parcel of this loose-leaf liaison we had entered into, and if space was what Charlotte needed at the moment, I was willing to give it to her.

I would go back to my apartment, I decided, and connect with her later in the day. Upon returning to the Alamo City, I had stopped at my place only long enough to confirm that it hadn't burned down or been inhabited by aliens. Awaiting me yet were the joyous tasks of sorting through a pyramid-high stack of mail, paying bills, and restocking my refrigerator after ridding it of all the contents growing fuzzy green stuff.

Thinking it best to leave Charlotte a note, I went to her antique writing desk in the living room where I knew she kept a notepad. The pad lay in plain sight on the desktop. As I picked it up, I noticed writing in Charlotte's hand on the top sheet. It was a message for me. I read it three times without gaining an ounce of understanding of its contents: "Dearest Darryl, don't wait for me. I am a part of your past." The note was unsigned, but it was unmistakably Charlotte's handwriting.

I continued staring at the words, trying to decipher their meaning, because surely there was some subtext I wasn't absorbing. Where could Charlotte have gone that I would find myself in a position of waiting for her, or not? And what did she mean in saying that she was a part of my past? Had I not made it clear to her last night that I wished for us to have a future together?

At a loss to understand Charlotte's note, I began a search of her apartment to ascertain what she had taken with her when she'd left, thinking that would give me some insight into where she had gone and how long it might be before she returned.

The first telling thing I discovered suggested that she hadn't planned on being away for long. Sitting on a shelf in her walk-in closet, where she normally kept it, was her everyday purse. Inside the purse, among other miscellaneous items, were her cell phone, wallet, key ring, and checkbook. That she hadn't taken her cell phone was puzzling, but if she'd merely gone for a walk or a jog, and especially if she was looking for solitude, she easily could have opted to leave it behind. I also knew that she wouldn't have needed her full set of keys, because she kept a spare house key on a separate key ring, along with a mailbox key. This was what she usually took with her on walks.

Other details I noted as I continued my perusal of her apartment confirmed that Charlotte's absence was meant to be short term. There was no array of empty hangers in her closet indicating that she'd taken numerous articles of clothing with her. She had two suitcases that I knew of; both were tucked away in her hall closet. Her medicine cabinet looked untouched. Nothing seemed to be missing or out of place in the bedroom, living room, or kitchen. Except for the clothes she'd been wearing when she left, it appeared that the only thing gone from Charlotte's apartment was Charlotte.

Belatedly, I went down to the apartment building's basement parking garage. Charlotte's car was in its assigned space, the hood cool to the touch.

Back in her apartment, I slumped down on the sofa to think. What was going on here? It made sense that Charlotte might have gone for a walk or a jog in the park. But if that were the case, she should have been back by now. Also, the walk/jog explanation didn't jibe with the note she had left me: "... don't wait for me ..."

I imagined another possibility. What if Charlotte, prior to my informing her of my anticipated day and time of arrival back in town, had made plans to spend the morning with a friend? The friend could have picked her up and they could have gone ... wherever. When girlfriends get together they often lose track of time.

Be patient, I told myself.

I waited another half hour or so for Charlotte to return, or to call and kindly put a stop to the mental pacing that was wearing out the carpet in my brain. When she still hadn't shown, I decided to further investigate her absence. I retrieved her cell phone from her purse and, using my own phone, began dialing the numbers stored in her contacts list, which were surprisingly few. I recognized most of the names—acquaintances of Charlotte. A few of them I had met, but none of them I knew more than casually.

I asked each person I was able to reach if they'd seen Charlotte that morning or heard from her. Did they know where she might be? I had just returned from an out-of-town trip, I explained. I didn't tell them that I'd spent the night with Charlotte at her apartment and that she had disappeared earlier this morning.

No one I talked to had seen her or heard from her that day. I got a few suggestions as to her whereabouts. "Sometimes on weekends she goes for long drives," her friend Annette told me. "I went with her once and we ended up in Louisiana. I had some explaining to do to my husband." A woman I didn't know named Carla said, "I haven't seen or spoken to her in months. She was a much better friend before you came into the picture."

Pricked by this last remark and, at this point, disinclined to duct-tape together the shattered remains of my patience when it came to playing this waiting game, I went back to the writing desk and took up the notepad. I tore off the sheet with Charlotte's message on it and wrote a note of my own on the pad. "Call me when you get home. I'm sorry if I frightened you with my—" I scratched out "with my" and signed my name.

I returned to my apartment and busied myself unpacking my suitcase, wading through mail, and engaging in some halfhearted housekeeping chores while awaiting Charlotte's call. By midday it hadn't come and I had already lost interest in raising the livability index of my lodging. I thought again about the wording of Charlotte's note. What had I done with it? Had I thrown it away? I didn't think so. I checked my pants pocket and found it wadded up there. I smoothed it out and read it again, hoping I'd missed something—some subtlety in the note's language that affected its meaning. But its language was very precise (". . . don't wait for me. I am a part of your past"), even if its implications were unclear.

I was more confused than ever now and had become afflicted with dark thoughts I didn't like. Had something happened to Charlotte? A mugging? An accident? A kidnapping? I considered calling the police but quickly realized how silly it would sound, reporting that my girlfriend had been missing for a whole four hours. I took some aggressive breaths as I struggled to purge the negative notions from my thinking. Stay calm and wait, I told myself, and immediately sensed the irony in that advice, because *wait* is exactly what Charlotte's note told me not to do.

A hunger pang intruded on my thoughts, issuing a stern reminder that I hadn't eaten anything all morning. I apologized to my stomach as I opened a can of Chunky Sirloin Burger soup and heated it up in a pan. There wasn't much else in the apartment to eat. All the perishables in the place had long since perished, and it had been a while since I'd stocked the shelves with my favorite prepacked goods. I turned on the TV for distraction and sat down at the dining nook table to eat.

The local one o'clock news was coming up, a voice-over announcer said. He continued with a teaser about the arrest of an alleged member of an eco-terrorist group who had evaded capture for more than a decade. I spoon-fed myself while ignoring the intervening commercial.

When the news came on, the in-studio anchorwoman introduced the teaser story and then turned the telling of it over to an on-the-spot reporter who, microphone in hand, stood outside the San Antonio Police Headquarters building. "At eight o'clock this morning," the reporter said as he gazed into the camera, "Susan Bollinger walked into police headquarters and turned herself in. Ms. Bollinger was identified ten years ago by authorities as a member of the eco-terrorist group known as ELF, which was responsible for a series of destructive acts, including arson, over a period of years. Despite a nationwide effort by the FBI to find her, Susan Bollinger has until today eluded capture. Just minutes ago, she was transferred from police headquarters to the Bexar County Adult Detention Center."

News footage ran of the transfer. Amid a crush of reporters, the camera captured only a glimpse of Susan Bollinger's face as she was loaded into a police van. It was enough of a glimpse for me to know where Charlotte had gone.

I sat there stunned beyond thought, unable to swallow a mouthful of masticated meat and vegetables while around me the world shrank to a single point of light awaiting extinction.

"Susan Bollinger's motive for turning herself in at this time is unclear," the reporter said.

32

AS IT TURNED OUT, I hadn't known Charlotte Robinson, a.k.a. Susan Bollinger, well at all. In the days following her arrest, I thought back on our relationship, on all the things about Charlotte I didn't know: where she came from, what her upbringing was like, what her dreams were for the future. We'd kept hidden from each other all these things and more, confidences most couples share as casually as sips from the same wine glass. But in our coming together, we had sponged out of our communion the impurities of our respective personal histories in order to soak up the unsullied pleasure of the present moments of our lives.

I had known my motives for keeping my past to myself. I hadn't bothered to question hers—had simply chalked it up to some prior hurt, the memory of which she had long since buried in the nether region of her mind, not to be exhumed. In the end, it turned out to be a much darker past that she had secreted.

But was I to condemn her for this? Was her silence about her former life any more of a betrayal of trust than was mine? After all, don't we all live our lives wearing masks, exposing as little of our true selves as needed to carry on the business of living?

The more we reveal of ourselves, the more we open ourselves to scrutiny. So we draw down the window shades on our inner being and show the world a breezy fashion-show façade of self. Our hopes and fears and the fetid soil from which they sprang we keep bottled up like corrosive acid.

Within days of her arrest, Susan Bollinger pleaded guilty to one charge of conspiracy to commit arson and one count of destruction of federal property. According to news reports, federal investigators were convinced she had participated in other criminal acts, mostly in Oregon, which I learned from the media accounts was Charlotte/Susan's home state. But the evidence against her was reportedly insufficient to prosecute her for those other alleged crimes, so the government settled for a plea agreement on the charges for which their case was strongest. The following week, a judge sentenced Susan Bollinger to five years in federal prison. The likelihood was that, with time off for good behavior, she would serve no more than thirty-six months.

Like many people, I had heard of the Earth Liberation Front, or ELF as the organization was dubbed by the media, but was ignorant about the makeup of its membership and their motivation for engaging in the criminal acts they committed. According to the various news stories I heard and read following Charlotte's arrest, the Earth Liberation Front was a loosely organized, leaderless network of individuals who, beginning in the 1990s, participated in destructive acts—mostly arson—in order to further certain environmental causes. What those causes were was unclear, but they came under the banner of "putting a stop to the exploitation of the environment." The targets of ELF's wrath were such industries as logging, mining, trapping, and land development.

Beginning in 2005, as a result of an FBI initiative known as Operation Backfire, a number of ELF members were caught and sent to prison. Several suspected members of the group, however, avoided capture. Susan Bollinger, who was a teenager when she fell in with ELF because of her romantic involvement with a male member of the group, was one of them.

The second evening after Charlotte's arrest, two FBI agents visited me at my apartment. They were waiting outside my front door when I got home from work. Based on their dark suits, narrow ties, and buttoned-down demeanors, I knew they weren't party planners who'd mistakenly come to the wrong address. They invited me to the local FBI office "for a little chat."

I had suspected such an interrogation was forthcoming, even though Charlotte, upon turning herself in to the police, had identified herself only as Susan Bollinger. That apparently was why, when she'd left her apartment the morning she'd *gone missing*, she hadn't taken her purse or anything else that connected her to her life as Charlotte Robinson. I think she was looking to do me and her friends and co-workers the favor of disassociating herself from us. But I was certain it wouldn't take long for the authorities—through fingerprints or face recognition or a tip from someone who'd seen Charlotte/Susan's photo in the newspaper or on TV—to link the identities of Charlotte Robinson and Susan Bollinger. I'd been Charlotte's intimate acquaintance for almost three years now, which meant the authorities would come knocking at my door sooner rather than later.

The FBI agents took me to a back room at their offices, where they began asking me questions about Susan Bollinger. I told them I didn't know anyone named Susan Bollinger, but if they wanted to talk about Charlotte Robinson, I'd be happy to do so. Whenever one of the agents used the name Susan in a question, I responded with, "I'm sorry, but I don't know who you're talking about." They got the message, and from then on we talked about Charlotte. How long had I known her? How and when had we met? What was the state of our relationship? What did I know about Charlotte's life before we met? Did I know that Charlotte Robinson was an alias? How much did I know about the Earth Liberation Front? Did I have any knowledge of any criminal acts Charlotte had committed before I met her? What about her activities during our relationship? And, by the way, was it okay if they sent some agents to "take a look around" my apartment? It was useless to say no.

The FBI agents found nothing in my apartment or in Charlotte's to tie me to ELF or to lead them to believe I had any knowledge of Charlotte's past as Susan Bollinger. I knew what they were after. It's a criminal offense to knowingly harbor, aid, or abet a federal fugitive. But the only person I had aided and abetted was a young woman in search of some inner peace.

I tried to visit Charlotte at the county detention center before she was transported to the federal prison in Beaumont, but was denied access. I don't know if that was Charlotte's decision or a no-visitors restriction put in place by the federal prosecutor's office.

For the first few weeks after Charlotte's arrest, I brooded about how much responsibility I bore for her decision to turn herself in to the police. Had I, in my zeal to express my new-found sense of self, made it impossible for her to continue in her life as Charlotte Robinson? I had told her that I loved her. I didn't regret that. How could I regret expressing how much I cared for her? I had finally felt free to do so.

Time and again, I thought about Charlotte's note. "Dearest Darryl," she'd said, "don't wait for me. I am a part of your past."

I had to admit that her assertion was true: she *was* a part of my past. The Charlotte Robinson I'd known was gone. Susan Bollinger had taken her place.

So, would I wait for Susan Bollinger? I didn't know. I had only recently unshackled myself from my own dark past and rushed into the sunlight of infinite possibilities. The radiance was both exhilarating and terrifying.

Acknowledgments

I want to thank Greg and Marilyn Jenkins, who once again did me the favor of serving as first readers on this novel; their feedback and encouragement over the years means a lot to me.

Thank you to Lieutenant Mike Root of the Corrections Division of the Douglas County Sheriff's Office for taking the time to answer my questions regarding jail procedures pertaining to the processing of inmates from booking through assignment to general population, including the jail visitation policy. And a nod of appreciation to Andrea Zielinski, the sheriff's department's Community Outreach Coordinator, for being the conduit for this very helpful information.

High praise and thanks go to my editors extraordinaire, Elizabeth Lyon (story editor) and Arlene Prunkl (copy editor). Their editorial marks may have been red, but their guidance was golden.

Finally, abundant thanks to my wife, Karen, for enduring the revolving task of reading and commenting on this novel as it progressed through its various stages of development, and for her unwavering support of me as a writer.

About the Author

B K Mayo's short fiction has appeared in literary journals and story collections. His novel *Tamara's Child* won the 2011 Eric Hoffer Book Award for Young Adult book and was a finalist in the Popular Fiction category of the 2010 National Indie Excellence Book Awards. Although he writes mostly fiction, his newspaper column "Now That I Think About It," which appeared in Roseburg, Oregon's *The News-Review*, was widely applauded. Mayo and his wife, Karen, live in an area of southwestern Oregon known as "the hundred valleys of the Umpqua."

Author's Note to the Reader

I've always said that only through the reader does a story truly come to life.

Thank you for spending time with the characters in this book. I hope it was a rewarding reading experience.

I welcome all comments about *The Water Tower Club* or any of my other works. Feel free to email me at bkmayo.comment@gmail.com with your thoughts.

CPSIA information can be obtained
at www.ICGtesting.com
Printed in the USA
LVHW042249040323
740953LV00004B/154

9 780981 588445